AN AJ DOCKE

LAST PATIENT OF THE NIGHT

GARY GERLACHER

Black Rose Writing | Texas

The author grants the final approval for this literary material.

First printing

This is a work of fiction. Names, characters, businesses, places, events, and incidents are either the products of the author's imagination or used in a fictitious manner. Any resemblance to actual persons, living or dead, or actual events is purely coincidental.

ISBN: 978-1-68513-329-0
PUBLISHED BY BLACK ROSE WRITING
www.blackrosewriting.com

Printed in the United States of America
Suggested Retail Price (SRP) $21.95

Last Patient of the Night is printed in Minion Pro

*As a planet-friendly publisher, Black Rose Writing does its best to eliminate unnecessary waste to reduce paper usage and energy costs, while never compromising the reading experience. As a result, the final word count vs. page count may not meet common expectations.

For Chris, whose formidable work ethic motivated me to write.

For Tammy, whose love and discerning eye
improved my story in every way.

For Hannah and Jessica, whose courage inspired me
to share my story.

LAST PATIENT OF THE NIGHT

CHAPTER ONE

I stood alone in the morning silence, looking down on 4,000 vertical feet of pristine powder, and picked out my line for the first run of the day. It was a black diamond trail, but no match for my six foot, one inch frame, latest ski equipment, and twenty years of experience on tough terrain. I stood still for another moment to savor the calm solitude of the snow packed mountain. Nothing can ruin the peaceful joy of a ski slope recently covered in six inches of fresh powder.

Except for a tourist from Oklahoma. Another skier approached at speed and shattered my serenity. He went for a late stop and caught an edge, resulting in a fall at my feet. Gear, snow and clattering noise sped off in every direction.

He looked up at me with a silly grin. "Howdy, partner. Beautiful morning. Fancy meeting you here. The name is Sam, by the way," as he tried to get up and collect his gear. I took in his expensive coat, cheap equipment and lack of ability with growing concern about his choice of this advanced slope. I would have been happy to leave him there to enjoy my run, but mountain etiquette required me to help him get up and get his gear together.

It took only a minute to collect his gear and help him get clicked back into his skis. "Yes, siree," he said, as he finally stood up and wiped the snot and snow off his face. "Look at that trail. Fresh powder waiting for first tracks. Looks pretty steep. Hey, you mind if I go down first? I've never had first tracks on a trail like this."

The truth was that I did mind, but right now, I wanted Sam to leave so I could get on with my day. "Sam, the honor is all yours. Enjoy the fresh powder, but take it slow. This trail is pretty steep and those trees can come at you fast."

"Well, then, thanks. I'm going to make this a run to remember."

He had no idea how memorable it would be. He started out okay and made the first turns back and forth with no trouble. About forty feet down, he caught an edge and stood up straight to catch his balance, pointing his skis straight downhill and gaining speed rapidly. I expected Sam to initiate a turn to slow himself down, but instead, he rapidly accelerated out of control toward the trees. I was already calling ski patrol when he entered the tree line, and an aspen tree that had been waiting fifty years for that moment abruptly halted his momentum. Sam took a four-inch branch directly to the head and neck area, went down hard, and wasn't moving.

Ski patrol answered as I launched down the hill. Unlike Sam, my skiing had purposeful control and no wasted motion as I sped toward him.

"Ski patrol. How can I help you?"

"I need a medical team and evacuation to the top of Devil's Bend trail. A gentleman skied into the trees and is going to need to be evacuated. Tell them to follow our tracks down the center of the trail to the first line of trees."

"I've alerted a team. What are the nature of his injuries?" Ski patrol asked.

"Hold on, I am pulling up to him now." With one glance, I knew it was bad. A barely conscious Sam gasped for air. "Listen, you need to get a medical chopper to land as close as possible to us." I clicked out of my skis, wiggled out of my backpack, and hustled over to Sam as best I could in ski boots. Bad, definitely bad.

"Sir, I cannot authorize a chopper until one of our medical teams has requested it. What are his injuries?" Ski patrol was still on the open line.

I ignored the ski patrol, but left him on speaker as I began my initial exam. Every major trauma exam begins the same way by checking for airway, breathing and circulation, or ABC for short. The first thing is to make sure the patient has an airway. I would not have to worry about anything else, because Sam had no airway.

Sam had taken a tree branch directly on his throat and already had significant swelling in the neck. Worse, he was not moving any air at all. His panicked eyes pleaded with me, as he reached for his throat in the universal sign of choking. Sam was not choking on anything, though. His larynx was crushed, and Sam was suffocating.

I ripped off my ski gloves, opened my backpack, and pulled out equipment as I spoke to Sam in a reassuring voice. "Sam, look at me. You have crushed your throat and lost your airway. You can't breathe now. In a minute, you're going to pass out, and when you do, I am going to put an airway in for you and fix you up." I thought my tone was re-assuring, but Sam's eyes grew even wider as I spoke.

I laid out my scalpel, gauze, tape, and an endotracheal tube. Most folks do not carry supplies like this on the mountain, but as an emergency room doctor and an adrenaline junkie, I like to be prepared for all situations. That preparation was about to pay off big time for Sam. "How far out is the medical team?"

"Four minutes." The dispatcher's voice was shaky as well.

"Okay, then, I am doing this without them. Did you order a chopper yet?"

"Yes, sir, they are about twenty minutes out."

Sam's attempts to breathe became more feeble. I held his hand with my hands and said encouraging words until his efforts stopped alto-gether. Before brain damage started, I had about sixty seconds to restore oxygenation. Time slowed as I went into full doctor mode. First a quick swipe of an alcohol pad. This was hardly a sterile procedure, but old habits die hard. Next, a one inch vertical incision over the Adam's apple with a scalpel, much larger than I would normally like, but I had only one shot at this and no help. I held the scalpel steady and made a firm cut through the superficial and deep layers of the skin. Skin is a lot tougher than most people realize, and even a scalpel needs significant pressure to penetrate deep. There was some bleeding, but luckily no major vessels were hit. Pure luck determines whether a small artery is nicked and blood spreads everywhere, obscuring the area and making the procedure more difficult. I ignored the small amount of bleeding and continued.

I spread the skin and tissue, revealing the pearly gray surface of the cricothyroid membrane that covers the airway. The rest of the trachea is thick cartilage, which is difficult to penetrate, but the fragile cricothyroid membrane is about the size of the top of a pinky, and I easily punched a hole in it with my scalpel. There was an immediate rush of air from the lungs, which was a good sign, meaning the blockage was above where I had cut. Next, I threaded a breathing tube into the hole and down his airway toward the lungs. Normally, a breathing tube goes through the mouth or nose and down the trachea and into the lungs. Entering through the cricothyroid membrane is a shortcut to the lungs. The open end of the tube is normally connected to a bag to blow air into the lungs, but even I did not have an airway bag on the mountain. So, I went old school, taking a deep breath and blowing into the tube. Sam's lungs expanded, and then I heard the air whoosh out of the tube as his lungs deflated.

I could do this for a while, but I really wanted Sam to take breaths on his own through the tube. The body's desire to breathe is not based on a lack of oxygen but on a buildup of carbon dioxide in the bloodstream. Sam had already had plenty of time to build up carbon dioxide in his bloodstream in the last few minutes, and his body would be screaming for him to breathe. Sam eventually took hesitant breaths, then deeper breaths, as he cleared the carbon dioxide from his body and added oxygen to his bloodstream with each breath, which meant he was about to wake up.

Sam sputtered and spontaneously took a deep breath in through the tube. His eyes opened in panic, and he predictably reached for the tube, but I was ready for him and pinned his hands down.

"Sam, listen to me. You're going to be alright. You're breathing through a tube, and I need you to slow your breathing down. Breathe with me, in and out. You won't be able to talk with that tube in place, so focus on deep, even breaths." I took a few deep breaths, and Sam slowed down his breathing to match mine until he got into a comfortable rhythm.

Members of the Ski Patrol arrived, and soon we had six people working to stabilize Sam. I held his hand as they got him immobilized in a neck brace, transferred to a sled, and Ski Patrol began the process of getting him down the mountain to a place where the helicopter could safely land. In the distance, we heard the thump of its imminent arrival.

After Sam started down the mountain, I packed up all of my supplies, and an older Ski Patrol member came over. "I assume this is not the first time you have done one of these, correct?"

"Well, it is the first time I've done one of these on a mountain, but I have done a few." We took a measure of each other. He was a solid man who looked like he had lived on this mountain his whole life, and probably the only one up here besides me with a pulse under 100.

"Sir, I have been on this mountain for 43 years and that is the first time I've seen a tourist cut an airway into another tourist. I'm gonna need you to come down and fill out some paperwork and buy us both a drink."

"I'm happy to oblige, but there's one thing. You see, there are still 4,199 acres of pristine snow that I haven't had a chance to see yet. Last lift goes up at four o'clock. I'll make you a deal. You tell me where I can find a warm fire and a warm drink, and I'll be there by 4:30 to give as long a statement as you would like. In the meantime, I would like to get some skiing in today."

"Unfortunately, I am off at noon today. Hey, Michelle, can you get his statement after work today?"

As Michelle approached, her eyes lit up as she focused on me. She was a gorgeous five foot ten brunette with brown eyes that threatened to melt the snow. Time for a change of plans.

"You know, on second thought, my statement could take a while. How about we do it over dinner? Say, seven o'clock at the steakhouse?"

Michelle held my gaze and nodded. "Happy to help. I'll be there. The resort makes it a priority to meet all the needs of its customers," she stated, while staring straight through me with those killer eyes.

"Then I'll make sure to compile a list of all my needs before dinner."

Her boss looked back and forth between the two of us and shook his head. "Enjoy your evening. And don't forget to give a statement." He wandered away muttering something about "Damn kids these days."

I clicked into my skis and prepared to head down the mountain. "Wait, I at least need your name," Michelle called out.

"AJ Docker, but everyone calls me Doc."

CHAPTER TWO

Clearly, I had left the peace of Wyoming's mountains for the aggressive chaos of Houston's traffic as I made my way into work. There are no good places to drive in Houston at rush hour, but The Texas Medical Center may be the worst of all. The Center is a two square mile area south of downtown that contains thirteen teaching hospitals, eight specialty hospitals, two medical schools, and a host of other medical services. Over 100,000 employees work there, treating over ten million patients each year. It is the largest medical center in the world, and second place is not even close.

My destination was Ben Taub Hospital, the crown jewel of trauma care in Houston. People who were shot, stabbed, crushed, beaten, mangled or drowned needed Ben Taub. Given that all of those tragedies occurred frequently in Houston, it was a popular place with over 100,000 emergency room cases per year. There was no such thing as a quiet day at Ben Taub.

I made my way to the garage and fought for a parking spot on the fourth floor. Any lingering thoughts of Wyoming evaporated as I walked through the front door of the hospital, greeted by a mass of humanity speaking in a cacophony of voices dominated by English and

Spanish, but if you listened carefully, you could hear languages from around the world.

The one thing that could never be found elsewhere was that hospital smell. A heavy dose of antiseptic cleansing fluids mixed with a hint of sweat, fear, frustration, blood and guts so strong you didn't just smell it, you could taste it. Eau d' hospital was never gonna make it as a cologne or candle scent, but it was home to me.

After a quick trip through the metal detector, not even doctors get to carry a gun in a Texas hospital, I walked into the ER.

Everyone thinks of doctors and nurses when they think of an ER, but the large, dysfunctional family includes respiratory therapists, registration clerks, transport assistants, housekeeping, phlebotomists, radiology techs, medical assistants, child life, and many more people from different backgrounds, genders, races, and ages, with different levels of training and experience. The ER is a mixed bag of wildly different patients and staff.

No one intelligent would design an ER staffing model the way it has evolved. The delineation of duties and interactions between individuals doesn't make much sense on paper, but they work in the real world. Everyone knows their responsibilities and nowhere is that seen more clearly than when a trauma patient arrives. To an outsider, it looks like chaos, but to me it looked like a well-choreographed ballet.

As for many others, the ER really was my family. We worked closely together, and we also hung out together outside of work, probably because our stories were unsuitable for "normal" people to hear. Our humor was definitely not appreciated by people who had not been there.

Humor was the number one coping mechanism in the ER. If we could find a way to smile and laugh after witnessing so much pain and suffering, we knew we could handle the stress and trauma that confronted us every day. When one lost the ability to laugh, it was time to leave the ER.

Every ER ran on sugar, caffeine, and adrenaline, and this one was no different, which is why I arrived on my first day back carrying two dozen Krispy Kreme donuts. Jean, the Charge Nurse for the ER, confronted me as I walked in the door. Don't make the mistake of focusing on the Nurse part of her title, focus on the Charge portion. Because Jean was in charge. Nothing happened in the ER without her knowledge and approval. Many a young doctor had learned that the hard way.

Jean was about five foot three and solid, not heavy, not muscular, but solid. She grew up in west Texas and had learned to ride on a ranch at an early age. She was roping cattle by the time she was ten, although she probably yelled at them to lie down, and they did. Jean had a commanding voice and presence that would make any Sergeant Major proud. She had climbed the nursing ranks to become the top dog in the ER. The staff loved and feared her, while the administration only feared her.

"Well, if it isn't the world-famous Doc gracing us with his presence again at the Tub," she greeted me. "And I see you've brought food into my ER in violation of JCAHO rules. What did I tell you about bringing donuts into my ER?" she asked sternly.

I thought for a moment. "I believe you said I had to make sure you got two of them before everyone ate them," I smiled genuinely, glad to see her.

"You're damn right. Give me a hug and my two donuts. Good to have you back." She hugged me as she swiped one donut in a well-practiced maneuver. I grabbed a donut as well, and we both bit into them. "Still warm. You're a good man, Doc. I don't care what everyone else says. How was Utah?"

"Wyoming." I corrected her. "Fresh snow, peace, and quiet. Good for the soul."

"Uh, huh? And I suppose you had nothing to do with a tracheotomy on the mountain?"

I winced. "I was kind of hoping that news didn't make it down here."

"Well, it did, and I figured it was you. Not sure how many other people on the mountain carry a scalpel."

"Just me and a few serial killers."

"Ain't that the truth. And I assume you left some broken hearts in Utah."

I looked offended. "Jean, a gentleman never discusses his possible relationship with a beautiful ski patrol medic. And it was in Wyoming."

Jean laughed. "You're not a fucking gentleman."

"Ah, but you Jean are most definitely a lady. Now take your other donut, m'lady," I said with a bow. "Some of us have actual work to do."

• • •

I made my way back to the nurses' station, the heart and soul of the ER, and command central for ER operations. It was chaotic and orderly, with staff moving in and out for phone calls, charting, and patient visits. Despite being a paperless hospital, papers blanketed every surface.

"Listen up, people. We all know there is no food allowed at the nurse's station, so I want all of these donuts gone in the next ten minutes. And wash it down with coffee. We got a long day ahead of us. Make me proud, team." A positive attitude and warm donuts took care of my leadership duties for the morning.

The team converged on the donuts like a pack of starving piranhas. This process was Darwinian and only the strongest got a donut. In under a minute, the only evidence the donuts ever existed was a bunch of sticky fingers and a happy staff.

I plopped down in a chair next to Deb, the Co-Director of the ER alongside yours truly and a good counter to me. She had trained alongside me and knew her medicine. She was tough as nails, but where I was the loud and usually politically incorrect one, Deb was a quiet leader and more considered in her approach. Her brown eyes missed nothing and her youthful appearance and petite figure led many patients to underestimate her at first. She quickly gained their trust. Deb was a perfect partner to oversee this chaos.

"I see you survived without me for five days," I said.

Deb rolled her eyes. "The struggle was real, but we managed somehow. It is almost like this place runs fine without you. I heard you were busy on the mountain."

"Just a quick case to keep my skills up."

"And I assume that besides the repaired airway, you also left at least one broken heart up on that mountain?" Deb asked with a raised eyebrow and a smirk.

"Why does everyone assume I met a beautiful lady on the mountain?"

Deb continued to stare straight at me with that raised eyebrow that demanded truth, barely stifling a laugh.

"Michelle, ski patrol, memorable."

Deb let the laugh escape and held out her hand. "I believe that will cost you a dollar, Finn."

Finn had also trained with us and made me look serious and focused. A product of a Southern California hippie and free love family, Finn enjoyed life to the fullest. His lanky six foot tall frame carried a constant smile. He was also one of the best athletes I knew, good at every sport, not just the common ones like football, basketball, and baseball, but every sport. Finn could win at aquatics, bowling, badminton, and Frisbee golf. He was pretty much unbeatable at sports, but betting was another thing altogether. I looked at him in disbelief. "You bet against me? Five days in Jackson Hole, and you bet against me?"

We always had standard one dollar bets going in the ER. We could bet on anything. Finn bet on everything and lost more than he won. I am sure he had a stack of dollar bills in his locker to hand out to people. About ten percent of his salary must have gone to supporting others in the ER through lost bets.

Finn shook his head. "You have to strike out, eventually."

"Not before you run out of money."

CHAPTER THREE

Two hours later, Deb sat up straight in her chair, a sure sign that danger approached. "Watch out. Incoming."

"It's not the Loser, is it? Please tell me it is not the Loser," I murmured, hopefully. I was not in the mood to deal with that idiot.

"It's him, and he has a stack of papers and a smug look on his face. Good luck. I think I'm gonna go find a patient who needs my help," she said as she slid away.

I took a deep breath, put on my politician's smile, and turned to face my antagonist. Lou Gallagher was one of a growing number of thirty-something Vice Presidents in the hospital. They all had degrees in Healthcare Management, as well as MBAs, and spent their days in meetings and conference calls, deciding how to run things. Armed with excel spreadsheets and PowerPoint presentations, they didn't know a damn thing about how medicine actually got delivered in a hospital, and most of their great ideas rated somewhere between ignorant and downright dangerous. Their numbers had grown over the last two decades, and now herds of VPs wandered the administrative floors looking for someone to join their newest committee.

Lou was among the worst, because he was convinced that he was always the smartest guy in the room. That may have been true when he sat in his office alone, but out here in the real world, he was another smug asshole in a suit with bad ideas, no empathy, and a limited personality. Hired about a year ago, he was a pain in the ass from day one.

He approached with purpose. "Good morning, Doctor Docker." As usual, Lou was in a suit with a dapper vest, a big, gaudy watch, and really shiny black dress shoes. With his close cut dark hair and beady eyes, he looked like an undertaker about to sell me a casket. For some reason, he always wore brightly colored socks in contrast to his dark suits. I am sure there was a reason for it, but I had never bothered to ask.

"Good morning and HUHA to you, Lou. Please have a seat. Always nice to see our administrative leaders on the front lines, and please, how many times do I have to tell you? Call me Doc."

"Okay… Doc, but I must tell you, I prefer to be addressed as Vice President Gallagher."

"That seems a bit formal for the ER. How about we compromise, and I call you VP Lou? Now, how can I help you this morning?" I asked as I leaned back and grabbed another donut, thankful someone else had brought donuts this morning. Great minds think alike.

"I thought it was illegal to have food at the doctor's stations."

"This is actually a nurses' station, and you are correct that this donut is illegal. That is why I am trying to hide the evidence before anyone notices. Want to help, VP Lou?" I asked as I passed him the box.

"No, thank you. I am here to talk to you about the ER census."

I interrupted him. "Before we get into that, I have to ask about the socks. What is with all the color?"

Lou smiled proudly. He had probably been waiting a year for someone to ask that question. He pulled up his pant leg and raised his foot for me to see a pattern of brightly colored ducks dancing in the rain. "I have an entire set of child-friendly socks that I wear every day to remind me of the importance of our pediatric patients at the hospital."

I stared at him blankly and waited for further explanation, but none was forthcoming. He stared back at me, and the silence became awkward. I decided to let him off the hook. "Well, a good pair of socks is important. Did you know your feet can sweat up to a half a liter per day? Good socks are important for foot hygiene. Do you have a matching set of boxers for each pair of socks?"

Lou was flustered. "Uh, no. I do not."

"Sorry, inappropriate question. You are probably a briefs kind of guy, anyway, or maybe you go commando. A discussion for another day. You were mentioning the census?"

His face relaxed in clear relief to get back to the ER census. "Your numbers are down 2.7% for the week and 3.1% for the month below projections. What do you have to say about that?"

"That is great news! Hey, everybody, listen up! Fewer people got sick and injured last month! Houston is healthier! Let's hear it for the people of this city!" I cried, eliciting a small cheer and a smattering of applause from the staff nearby.

Lou, however, was not smiling. "This is not good news at all. When volumes are down, revenues are down. I cannot show a profit for this department with these numbers," a clearly stressed Lou fumed.

"I forgot that you are the money person and that I am just a people person. This seems to be a problem for you. How can a lowly ER doctor such as myself help you in your time of need?"

"We need more volume in the ER. We need more patients to meet projections."

I pretended to think hard and then snapped my fingers. "I got an idea. Jean, come here a second." Jean was walking by and detoured over to us. "Tell all the interns and residents that when they are driving home tonight, I need them to hit a minimum of two pedestrians with their cars. Not hard enough to kill anybody, but preferably hard enough to break some bones. And tell them to focus on folks with insurance for VP Lou here."

"Consider it done, Doc," Jean said as she sauntered away.

Agape, Lou could barely speak. "You're not really going to do that, are you? That's illegal."

"It's only illegal if we get caught, and it gets the job done. Last time we did this, we got thirty-two trauma cases in six hours. Great idea, Lou. Thanks for suggesting it. I will make sure everyone knows it's your idea."

"No. No. Stop her. This was not my idea. I don't want to hit people with cars. You have to stop her."

I looked around, but Jean was out of sight. "She's busy now, but I'll tell her to hold off talking to the residents before the end of shift. Let me write myself a note to remind her." I painstakingly wrote, "Don't hit people with cars!!" on a sticky note and pasted it on my computer. "Now, what else can I help with today?"

"One other thing," as he regained his composure. "You are using too much AC down here. This is Mike from maintenance." He pointed to a man in coveralls standing nervously nearby. "He is going to install a lockbox on the thermostat, and I have the only key," Lou said, holding up a key. "From now on, the temp stays at seventy-four in the ER. We can save 5.3% on electricity costs with this change."

"VP Lou, I'm going to lose 5.3% of my body weight in sweat each shift and probably lose 5.3% of my staff if you do that. We gotta get gowned and masked up down here and work under the hot lights. We need to keep it cooler for the staff."

"My decision is final. The needs of the hospital come before the needs of the employees. Seventy-four degrees from now on. Now, it appears you have patients to see, and I have meetings to attend. Goodbye... Doc," he said with a smirk.

"HUHA to you, VP Lou," I said with a matching smirk.

"HUHA? What does that mean? I've been meaning to ask."

"Just a way we say hello and goodbye to each other in the ER, kind of a team bonding thing, and since you are part of the team, HUHA."

"I see," Lou said with a smile spreading across his face. He probably wasn't used to getting picked for any teams. "Well, then, HUHA to you, Doc. Have a good day," he turned on his heels and left.

He made it around the corner before I burst out laughing and held out my hand. Finn laughed as he put a dollar in my outstretched hand.

"Figured it would take longer than one day to get him to say it. You had four days to go before you lost the bet. HUHA, HUHA, HUHA," he chanted as he walked away.

Mike from maintenance asked, "What the hell was that all about? And what the hell is HUHA?"

"I bet Finn a buck I could get Lou to use HUHA as a greeting within five days, and I did it in one. Easy money."

"So, what does HUHA mean?"

"Head up his ass. We use it to describe hospital administrators who pretty much fuck up everything they touch around here. Lou is a major HUHA." Mike laughed.

I put my arm around his shoulder and headed for the thermostat. "Mike, are you a football fan? I have two tickets to the Texans–Chargers game this Sunday, forty yard line, and they are all yours, if you can do one little favor for me. I need a slight adjustment to Lou's thermostat plan."

CHAPTER FOUR

"Well, if it isn't Officer No Clue and his much better looking partner. Come here, Banshee. Give me a kiss." Officer Banshee is a police dog, a Belgian malinois, and sixty pounds of solid muscle and brains. He sprints at about forty mph, jumps eight feet into the air, and bites at about two hundred pounds per square inch. This means he can run people down and hold on to them until the other officers catch up. Put him in a custom Kevlar vest that can hold cameras, microphones and other equipment, and he becomes one badass war machine.

The most amazing thing about Banshee is how smart he is. He knows over four hundred verbal commands and one hundred visual commands. He can wear an earpiece and camera to receive commands from afar. He knows how to attack, retreat, find, crawl, search, listen, or scan all on command. With subtle hand commands, he can sit, lay, or, my personal favorite, growl. Two fingers tapping on his handler's arm twice, and Banshee will go from a cheerful dog to a growling monster with teeth bared. All in all, he is better trained than the average orthopedic surgeon.

Banshee hopped up onto my lap to give me kisses. I had known Banshee since he was a puppy from my work with the local swat teams, and he made frequent trips to the ER with his partner for ongoing training. Occasionally, he stayed at my house when his partner was out of town, so Banshee and I were best friends.

"Stop kissing my dog. I have no idea where your mouth has been, but I'm sure it was someplace fucking nasty." Officer Tom Nocal, or No Clue, as I liked to call him, was a regular in the ER and Banshee's partner. Tom came from a family of cops, and he looked like one, even out of uniform. He was proud of his mustache for reasons that were not particularly clear to me. He had been growing it for twenty years, but it had never completely filled in. He was a good man in a fight, a good man to smoke cigars and exchange stories with, and he was the closest thing I had to a friend outside of the medical community.

Tom and Banshee were called to the scenes of many arrests, and Banshee had sent many criminals to the ER with large bite wounds on their calves. It reduced even the toughest guys to quivering masses of compliance when Banshee sat next to them in the ER.

"You're jealous because he likes me better than he likes you. But everyone likes me better. I assume since you are here, the food court at the mall is all secure." It was a standing joke that he was nothing but a mall cop riding a scooter all day.

"Yeah, some folks littered by the pizza place, but I fired some shots over their heads, so it probably won't happen again for a while. How was your ski trip?"

"Relaxing. Three days of perfect snow and two nights of perfect bliss."

"I swear, you would get laid at a convention of nuns. At least you got away from the doctor stuff for a while."

Deb butted into the conversation. "Guess again. Our doctor hero trached a guy on the mountain."

"Are you fucking kidding me? How do you end up in situations like that?"

"Lucky, I guess."

"I assume you were able to prevent a visit by the reaper once again."

"In this instance, yes, but I lost a patient on the plane home because of a medical emergency."

Deb dropped what she was doing and turned towards me. "You lost a patient on a plane? And you didn't feel the need to share this information before now?"

"In my defense, you didn't ask."

"Well, I am asking now." Deb and Tom leaned forward to hear the story.

"So, I was minding my business, and I heard the dreaded call overhead for medical help on board. Being an upstanding member of the medical community, I leapt into action. The patient was in the back of the plane and had become unresponsive, with no pulse and some bleeding from the nose. Both pupils were blown. Most likely a stroke, but clearly deceased. Not much I could do."

Deb was incredulous. "You didn't do anything?"

"Well, I explained the situation to the family. He was old, so not entirely unexpected."

"How old was he?" Tom asked.

"I think they said seventeen or eighteen, definitely near the end of life."

"What the hell are you talking about? Eighteen isn't old. You sat there and watched an eighteen-year-old die? What is wrong with you?"

I looked at them with feigned confusion. "I was told that eighteen is old for a cat."

Tom threw a punch at my arm. "A fucking cat. You killed a fucking cat on that plane?"

I rubbed my arm where Tom hit me. "No. I pronounced a cat dead on the plane. The cat died without help from me."

Deb burst out into laughter. "I hope the airline appreciated your expertise."

"They actually gave me a $200 voucher for helping the family."

"This is what's wrong with medicine," Tom griped. "Doctors getting paid two hundred bucks to say a cat is dead. Are there any actual doctors here today or just your cat-killing dumbass self? We need to pick up one of your customers to transfer downtown. Some piece of shit who hit his wife and got a bottle to the head for his troubles."

"Ah, yes, the distinguished gentleman in room eight. They should be done sewing him up. Glad you brought Banshee. That dude could kick your out of shape ass up and down this hallway. He could play defensive lineman for a good college team or even for your Steelers. Probably wouldn't make it on a real NFL team, though." Banshee smiled when he heard his name, or perhaps he smiled at the prospect of some action.

"Be careful talking shit about my Steelers, or I'll sic Banshee on you."

"This little cutie?" I said, as I got more kisses. "C'mon, let's go meet your new best friend."

•   •   •

The distinguished gentleman in room eight was indeed a large man at about six foot two, 220 pounds of muscle, an IQ of a hundred, and a personality score of zero. I had seen this story play out many times, but it was always fun to watch. "Good morning, sir. I am Officer Nocal, and this is Officer Banshee. We're here to take you downtown. I am going to need you to stand up, turn around, and put your hands behind your back.

He stood up, but instead of turning around, he flexed his arms and shoulders with a threatening grimace. "Get that fucking dog away from me."

Tom subtly tapped his forearm twice with two fingers. Immediately, Banshee lowered his body, raised his hackles, bared his teeth, and let out a growl from some place deep where demons roam. "Officer Banshee does not appreciate foul language. Here is the way this is gonna work. You are going to turn around and put your hands behind your back. If you do anything threatening, Banshee is gonna bite you and hold you down. Now, he can attack your leg. LEG BANSHEE!" Banshee immediately crouched and stared at the lower leg while continuing to growl.

"He can also attack your arm. ARM, BANSHEE!" Banshee stood up and stared at his arms. Banshee now had the full attention of the man, but the best was yet to come.

Tom shook his head. "Every now and then we get some idiot who doesn't believe in Banshee, and so I have to give my last command. BALLS, BANSHEE!" Banshee leaned forward and focused all his attention on the man's groin, all the while growling and baring his teeth. I had seen this many times, but I still subconsciously crossed my own legs every time.

No one ever made it past the "BALLS, BANSHEE" command. Their shoulders slumped, eyes downcast, and inevitably, they turned to put their hands behind their backs, as this patient did. Handcuffs clicked into place, and Tom escorted our latest customer out of the building with Banshee at his side. Officers Tom and Banshee would turn him over to a squad car and get back to making rounds in the ER until they were needed again. Another five star review from a happy customer was clearly in our future.

CHAPTER FIVE

"So, how can I help you today, Ms. Palmer?" I asked my next patient.

"I hurt my wrist, and please, call me Tracy." She was a 22-year-old female with a petite, athletic build. Her beautiful brown eyes, marred by recent crying, exuded an unexpected deeper sadness.

"Sorry to hear that, Tracy. Tell me how this happened."

"I was clumsy and fell. Not much to say about it." Her eyes were downcast, and she refused eye contact. Her foot thumped a mile a minute on the footrest of the bed, and tension radiated from her.

Warning bells blared. Anyone, but particularly a young female, who showed such nervousness with a vague history of an injury clearly indicated abuse. I went through the rest of the history, but couldn't get any details from her.

"Let's take a look." She pulled up her sleeve and exposed her left wrist.

"Wow, that is an impressive tattoo." In the ER, we see a lot of tattoos and impressive is not a word I use often. Most are low dollar, inferior quality work, and lots of people get them in places that should never be tattooed. This one was clearly fresh and a high quality artistic rendering of a sorceress about to cast a spell with light shooting out of her wand

and with a bubble above her head that held a jumble of numbers and letters. "I've never seen a tattoo like this. What's the story behind it?"

She brightened and even smiled a little. "She represents all the power I want to have to fix things. That spell is the answer to her problems. All she has to do is untangle the letters to get the spell right, and everything will be perfect. Silly, but I enjoy knowing that the answer is right there." Sadness overtook her again.

"Not silly at all. Where did you get that done? It is really high quality."

"Finnegan's Tattoo in uptown. They do a lot of work for me and my friends." I knew the place. Not the highest quality parlor, but a decent shop with some talented artists.

"I will keep that in mind. Now, let's get to business." A quick exam revealed some swelling and point tenderness, suggesting a mild fracture. I explained everything and told her we would get an X-ray to confirm if it was broken. "Tracy, I want to make sure you are safe. Are you sure no one hurt you on purpose? We can get you help if needed."

Through the long pause, I hoped she would tell me what really happened, but it was not to be. "I'm fine. Nothing but a clumsy fall." Lack of eye contact suggested this wasn't necessarily the truth, but I can't force adults to tell me the truth. "Okay, wait here, and we'll get that X-ray."

I left the room, ordered the X-ray, and then tracked down Officer Nocal, who diligently guarded the remaining donuts. "You're gonna get fat eating those things."

"I'm not eating these. Some nurse set them down and asked me to watch over them."

"Well, wipe that chocolate off your lip, Officer No Donut. I got some work for you."

I explained Tracy's situation and asked him to go speak with her. Sometimes victims will open up to the police.

He knocked on the door and entered the room with Banshee at his side. Tracy's eyes lit up when she saw Banshee. "Good morning, ma'am. I am Officer Nocal, and this is Officer Banshee. Your doctor asked us to come speak with you for a moment just to make sure everything is alright."

"Is it alright if I say hello to the dog?" She asked as she reached out her hand.

"Officer Banshee loves to be spoiled. FRIEND."

Banshee walked over and sat down next to Tracy. She rubbed his ears, and he rewarded her with a few kisses on the arm. "He is a sweet dog."

"He is sweet when he wants to be, but he can be pretty tough when he is on duty."

"Maybe I can borrow him for a few days," she said wistfully.

"I would like to let you do that, but the Chief would have me on parking duty for a month. Any particular reason you need a guard dog?" He knew the drill and hoped this would open up a truthful conversation.

She thought a moment before answering. "I could have used him in the past, but I think everything will be okay from now on."

"Are you sure there is nothing we can do to help?" Tom asked one last time.

"Thanks, but no. I got things figured out for once. Everything will be okay."

"If something changes, call 911. Banshee and I can solve a lot of problems."

She cast a small smile. "I will keep that in mind. I may call so I can have this sweet dog come visit me." She gave Banshee a hug and a kiss. "Goodbye, Officer Banshee."

Shaking his head, Tom returned to the nurses' station. "Someone hurt her, but she ain't saying a thing. I gave her my card to call me if she changes her mind, but nothing I can do right now without her asking for help. Sweet girl. Hope everything works out for her."

Her X-ray showed a hairline fracture of the radius near her wrist, and we put her in a splint and arranged a follow-up visit with an orthopedist. I went over discharge instructions, and once again, asked her if

I could help her. She smiled, pointed to her tattoo, and said, "My sorceress is gonna cast her spell today, and everything will be fine. Thanks for your help, Doc."

I sighed as I watched her leave. We got a lot of patients like her, most of whom we never saw again, a story left untold.

CHAPTER SIX

Tracy Palmer left the ER and climbed into her truck, a reliable vehicle, but well worn, having passed through 100,000 miles many trips ago. Like many things in her life, she would upgrade soon.

She planned to head home, grab a small bag of personal items, and hit the road. She didn't need to take much with her, and didn't want to remember anything about her time in Houston. New things awaited at her dream destination.

Once again, she fantasized about her new life. She would get a cute little house on the beach. She had always wanted to live near the ocean. It would have palm trees in front and an enormous deck with a hammock in back, where she could relax in the afternoon sun and read romance novels. It would have a small gym where she could work out and do yoga, and a hot tub in back to relax in afterward.

The new car would definitely be a red convertible. She had never driven a convertible, but she knew she would love it. The thought of driving with the sun beaming down on her and the wind blowing through her hair exhilarated her and brought a rare smile.

And she would get a dog. A nice, loyal companion to keep her company and to keep her safe, like that police dog in the ER, who would protect her at all times. No one would ever hurt her again.

Her fantasies continued as she drove to the apartment. A new king-sized bed, new pots and pans for the kitchen, all new clothes. She was planning a whole new life.

By the time she reached her apartment, she felt almost happy. She looked upon the decrepit building for the last time. Faded paint and rusted balconies accented a square building of dubious integrity. She would not miss this depressing place.

She climbed to the second floor, unlocked her door, and pushed into the living room. She never even saw the fist that smashed into the side of her face and knocked her out.

CHAPTER SEVEN

When we're not too busy, we squeeze in quick teaching sessions with the residents, lasting ten to thirty minutes, and usually ending abruptly when something more interesting happens.

"Trauma alert, pediatric. Trauma alert, pediatric," the overhead speakers announced, setting off a flurry of controlled chaos as everyone responded to their assigned duties. "Deb, you have the lead on this, and Julie and I are going to take the airway." Deb gave a thumbs up as she headed off to get set up.

Julie, a second-year resident who wanted to be a pediatric emergency medicine doctor, had started her first rotation in the emergency room, and she looked wide-eyed and petrified. "Come with me," I said. "Let's get everything set up for the airway."

She followed along and said, "I'm excited to watch you manage a pediatric airway."

Without breaking stride, I replied, "Sorry to disappoint you, but I'm the one who's gonna be watching today, and you're the one who's going to be managing the airway."

By the time we arrived at the head of the bed, Julie visibly trembled. Time to do some teaching. "Okay, Julie, I know you're nervous, but you can do this. The first thing you have to do in any code situation is calm yourself. The crazier the situation, the calmer you need to be. Let's take a look." I grabbed the pulse oximeter off the bed and put it on her index finger. Her pulse showed up on the monitor running at 118 bpm. Then I took the monitor off and put it on my finger and it was running at 62 bpm. "You need to take some deep breaths, okay? Right, let's get everything ready. What size equipment do we need for a seven-year-old?"

"It's age divided by 4 plus 4. That would make it between a 5 1/2 and a six. Let's use a 5 1/2 cuffed tube." She answered automatically, a good sign.

"All right, see how easy this is? Now remember, this is a trauma victim, so we cannot extend the neck at all. You're gonna have to use a jaw thrust to visualize the vocal cords. Don't worry about anything else going on in the room. Your job is to secure the airway. Get ready, they're coming in the door."

The paramedics arrived, giving a report as they transferred the child from the stretcher to the bed. "This is a seven-year-old female who was hit at approximately 35 to 40 mph while crossing the street in front of a school bus. She has been unconscious since we arrived at the scene, obvious lower extremity injuries, no spontaneous breaths, but bags easily." A paramedic blew air into her lungs with a bag and mask.

The team went to work with the time-tested prioritization of ABC, airway, breathing, circulation. To resuscitate a patient, you need a way to get oxygen to the lungs, a way for the lungs to exchange that oxygen for carbon dioxide in the blood, and a way for that blood to circulate throughout the body. Without circulating oxygen, cells died, and death could occur in minutes.

A bag and mask can blow air into the lungs temporarily, but that process blows air into the stomach, too. Eventually, the stomach distends, the patient vomits into the lungs, which leads to pneumonia and potential death. So we needed to get an endotracheal tube into the trachea to blow air only into the lungs. This was going to be a challenge, as the girl had some facial trauma and blood in her mouth. "Julie, it's go time. Get that tube in there."

Julie reached down to slide the jaw forward and then slid the laryngoscope blade down her throat. With so much blood, she called for suction. "I can't visualize the cords through the blood."

I pushed on the patient's chest. "Do you see bubbles coming out anywhere when I push on her chest?"

"Yes," Julie replied.

"Then get ready, because I'm gonna push on her chest again and you're going to push that ET tube right at the bubbles. Ready, one, two, three, now," and I gave a push.

Julie advanced the ET tube forward. "I think I'm in, but I can't see for sure."

"Let's give her some breaths," I said to the respiratory therapist as he hooked up the bag. I put my stethoscope on the chest and heard good bilateral breath sounds with strong chest movement. "ET tube is in place, and patient is ventilating well." Deb nodded acknowledgement without taking her eyes off everything else happening in the room.

The respiratory therapist taped the tube in place and ventilated the patient, and Julie stepped back to watch the rest of the team in action. While we had focused on the airway, they had placed two large bore IVs to run fluid into her body. Blood samples had been obtained and sent to the lab for baseline labs and for the blood bank to match it with four units of blood. Nurses cleaned and applied dressings to the wounds on her legs. The radiology tech prepared to shoot an X-ray of the chest to confirm the placement of our tube. Jean had already notified the ICU that we would need a trauma bed. Residents had contacted orthopedic and neurosurgical teams to get them up to speed on her injuries. Radiology prepared to perform CT scans of her head, neck, abdomen and pelvis and X-rays of the extremities.

In less than ten minutes, over thirty people had coordinated to stabilize this young girl. The leg injuries would require surgery and rehab, but would heal well, given her youth. As long as her head injury wasn't too bad, she would recover most, if not all, of her normal functions. One thing was for sure, she would not die in my ER today.

I turned to Julie, still shaking from the adrenaline of her first pediatric trauma intubation. I shook her hand and announced to the room, "Attention everyone. We got ourselves a new BAFERD." A small cheer went up as the team continued to work on the child.

Julie looked at me, puzzled. "BAFERD?"

Without missing a beat, Deb said, "Stands for Bad Ass Fucking ER Doctor. You earn the title when you do cool ER stuff."

"Come on BAFERD, we need to talk to the family and let them know we're going to get their little girl fixed up. Deb will finish up here."

CHAPTER EIGHT

With only about an hour left of my shift, I thought it had been a pretty good day, so my disappointment was partly my fault when a minute later, "Trauma CPR coming in the door. Trauma CPR room one," called overhead.

I ran to room one to see what happened. Usually, we get a few minutes' warning from emergency medical services before patients arrive. The paramedic had just started a report. "And then a car pulled up to the ambulance dock, and a guy yelled for help and said his wife had been injured. We ran over, found no pulse and brought her inside. No history available."

The woman was in her mid-twenties and had been beaten badly. No pulse and no respirations. I turned to the paramedic. "Go find the driver of that car and get him in here. We need some history. Someone find me No Clue as well."

Deb and I began our assessment. While it helps to have some history and context on the patient, the protocol was always the same. ABC. I took the airway and intubated her easily with a 7.0 endotracheal tube. I hooked up the bag and gave her a few breaths. Deb confirmed good air movement as her chest rose and fell. We bagged her at twenty breaths per minute.

With no pulses present, one paramedic performed forceful compressions at 120 beats per minute, pushing her chest wall down two to three inches with each beat. It was exhausting work, and the staff took turns every two to three minutes. Other staff members had established two 16 gauge IVs and pushed normal saline as fast as it would go in.

Deb ran the code and already had the first one milligram dose of epinephrine drawn up and ready to push through the IV. I turned the endotracheal tube over to the respiratory therapist and began a secondary survey of the patient. Pupils were fixed and dilated with no response to any of our painful stimuli. She showed significant trauma to the head, torso, and hands. Whatever had happened had not been accidental. I glanced at Deb and quietly shook my head back and forth, and she nodded once in agreement.

We knew it was beyond our ability to save her, but we went through the protocols for fifteen minutes, anyway. Compressions and respirations continued. Three more doses of epinephrine were not effective. CPR halted every two minutes to check for a pulse. No change.

Finally, Deb called for a halt to CPR. "I am calling this code. Does anyone else have anything they want to try?" Silence enveloped the room. "Time of death is 9:58 p.m. Bag up her belongings and bags on her hands. Thanks, everyone."

It seemed like such an impersonal way for a life to end. A doctor tells everyone to stop, calls out a time, and another person is officially dead. She was alone in the ER with no one to grieve for her. Everyone had tasks to complete and new patients to see. One minute there were twelve people working intensely to save her, and the next minute they had all moved on to the next task. Death in the ER was stark and lonely.

Although we could do nothing more for her in life, we could do something for her in death. Her belongings would be handed to the medical examiner for review and put into a collection of evidence. The bags on her hands would protect any DNA that might be under her fingernails if she had fought with her attacker. A certain homicide, we would do our part to help find her killer.

Jean called out, "Hey Doc, check this out!" and held up the patient's left hand. Someone had amputated the last knuckles on the fourth and fifth fingers and burned the skin.

"Fucking monsters. Bag her hands, and we will let the detectives know."

Officer Tom Nocal came into the room. "I saw the film. Guy who dropped her off never showed his face to the camera and took off as soon as they grabbed her out of the car, a late model silver Accord with plates conveniently covered with mud. Only about a million of them on the road in Houston right now. We got any ID on the girl?"

Jean responded. "No ID, putting her in as a Jane Doe."

"She is not a Jane Doe. I know exactly who this is." Everyone stopped and looked at me.

"How the hell do you know who this is?" asked Nocal.

"I put that splint on her arm a couple of hours ago."

CHAPTER NINE

We gathered around a computer at the nurse's station and pulled her chart from earlier in the day: Tracy Palmer. Tom noted all the information and called it into police headquarters. Ten minutes later, he had his answer. "No Tracy Palmer with that birthday, and her address is fake. Gonna take some time to ID her. Maybe the prints will be on file."

"Well, we only have eight prints to check on her." Which got me thinking. "Why did that dude drop her off at the ER?"

"What do you mean? Where else you gonna drop someone with no pulse?"

"We're thinking about this wrong. The ER makes perfect sense if you want her to live, but why would he beat her almost to death, cut off her fingers, and then drop her off at the ER to be saved? He's obviously not concerned about her well-being after doing that to her. And if by some miracle she survived, he would go to jail for a long time. So why not dump her body anywhere else but at an ER? Makes no sense."

"Nothing about this makes sense. Maybe the dude is crazy."

"Probably, but something else is going on. We see crazy all the time in here, but this was a methodical beating and torture. The only reason to do that is to get information, but they went too far, and she died on them, so they brought her to us, hoping we could save her. Because they never got the information from her. That's the only thing that makes sense."

"You may be on to something, Doc. I'll make sure to let the detectives know your theory."

I paused a minute, then looked at Nocal. "We are gonna get the motherfuckers that did this to her."

'No, no, no, no, no. We are not getting involved. Detectives are on their way, and this is their case now. Leave it alone, Doc. Not your case anymore."

"It is my case. This was my patient, my last patient of the night. I let her go, and someone tortured her to death, and she died alone in my ER. I can't let that happen. So, we are gonna get those motherfuckers. And you are helping me."

"What the fuck are you thinking? We don't even know her name or where to start without her ID. We got nothing."

I walked over to the body, rolled back the sheet, and took off her splint. "What the fuck are you doing now, Doc?" Tom asked.

I took out my phone and got a picture of the tattoo on her arm. "Tomorrow night we are going to see a man about a tattoo."

CHAPTER TEN

"Looks like Skinny Jeans caught the case," Jean said, as a couple of detectives approached the desk.

Detectives Lenny Newsome and Jane Ormund were an odd pairing affectionately known as Skinny Jeans. Lenny was six feet six inches tall and probably weighed about 140 pounds fully dressed and soaking wet. He looked fragile and gangly, but as a superior triathlete in his free time, he enjoyed an advantage when his competitors had to take two steps for every one of his.

His partner, Jane, contrasted as his direct opposite at five feet two inches in heels. Jane hailed from east Texas, but her family originated in the French Cajun area of Louisiana, and she could speak with an accent so thick no one in Texas could understand her. Into fashion and rarely seen in the same outfit twice, her favorite item of clothing was the black belt she earned in Krav Maga, one of the most efficient self-defense fighting techniques created for the Israeli Defense Force. Quite a few criminals had learned this the hard way and been restrained by her as she said, "Y'all are under arrest." If she were to arrest more than one person, "All y'all are under arrest." They had worked in sync together for years.

"I hear y'all got a bad one, Doc." Jane did most of the talking while Lenny observed and documented everything in his ever-present notebook. Probably easier to be a lookout from way up there.

"It's a bad one even by Houston standards, and this one is personal, so I'm glad Skinny Jeans is on the case. She is over here in room four." We had left her exactly as she was when we had called the code. Her clothing and belongings rested in a bag carefully placed on the end of the bed. A sheet covered her to preserve some dignity, but all the tubes and IVs remained in place.

With no nonsense, and after pulling on some gloves, Jane walked to the body and pulled back the sheet. "Talk to me, Doc. Tell me something useful." Her eyes paused on each injury as she scanned the body from head to toe.

I explained how I had seen her earlier in the day and had discharged her, and how she was dropped off back at the ER. That raised some eyebrows. "Don't get your hopes up. The guy kept his face hidden from the cameras; plates are covered in mud; and the car is nondescript. Nocal is getting a copy of the video for you."

"No Clue to the rescue," Lenny muttered as he continued to document everything in his notebook.

"What in fuck all heaven is this about?" Jane asked as she took the bag off the left hand and lifted it for closer inspection. Lenny leaned over to get a closer look.

"Our best guess is that someone was trying to get some info out of her. Too methodical to be a crime of passion. Whoever did this was focused," I offered.

Lenny and Jane shared a momentary look, and then Lenny scribbled again in his notebook. I am pretty sure those two had telepathy skills.

"You said the info from her earlier visit to the ER was fake and no ID on her. And you're sure this is the same girl?"

"X-rays will confirm it, but I recognize the tattoo." I held up her arm. The sorceress stared at us, ready to cast her spell.

"Nice work. Recent. Wonder who did it," Lenny muttered as he made another note.

At the chance to tell them who did the tattoo, I held off for the moment. I soothed my guilt by quietly assuring myself that I would tell them right after I visited that tattoo artist myself.

"We'll post her Wednesday. Make sure her belongings stay with her. We need a cause of death and ID to start tracking this motherfucker down." Jane looked at me. "I can see why it's personal. We'll get him."

·   ·   ·

Jane spoke before Lenny could say a word. "Run the prints and check with missing persons for any reports that might match. We need a copy of that security video to see if anything was missed. You interview the paramedics who talked to the guy and see if anything useful turns up. I'll check the files for any other cases with missing fingertips, but it doesn't ring a bell. Am I missing anything?"

"Nope, but it's not much to go on."

"True. But we've started with less and solved them. Autopsy will at least give us a cause of death, and if we can get an ID on her, we can hunt this asshole down. All we need is a starting point."

Lenny put his notebook away and matched his partner's stare. "Let's go hunting."

CHAPTER ELEVEN

I finished my charting and made my way home to West University, only about eight minutes away at night, but over a half hour during rush hour. I owned a small, older brick house with stone accents, like most in the neighborhood. Mine was a single story with three bedrooms, big enough to be comfortable and small enough to be cozy.

In an affluent area where most of the residents were well-educated, my next-door neighbor, Carl, stood out as an exception. Carl always seemed to be outside whenever I arrived or left the house. A typical busy body, nosy neighbor who always spoke even though he had nothing to say, he wandered outside when I returned home at 10:30 p.m. that night.

"Evening Doc, just getting home from work?" Carl always asked obvious questions to confirm obvious information that he then proceeded not to use. Usually I messed with him, but today I only wanted to go home.

I grabbed the mail from the box on the curb. "Yes, sir, Carl. Been a long day, and I am looking forward to getting a good night's sleep." I trudged toward the door, hoping he would take the hint.

Not Carl. "Cool, see anything interesting today?"

I stopped in my tracks and debated letting loose on him. People are always asking ER docs to describe the worst things they have seen, but none are prepared for the brutality of the answer. Emergency room personnel, along with paramedics, police and military, see things that no one should ever have to see. We all have at least one worst case that haunts us, but it's not something we share with others. No reason for two people to have nightmares instead of only one.

"Nope, nothing interesting. Just another day in the ER. Goodnight, Carl. Get some sleep."

"Good night, Doc. I'm gonna stay out here a little while longer. I enjoy the quiet of the night. See you in the morning."

I knew I would see him in the morning. I unlocked the door, threw the mail on the counter, grabbed a cold water and headed for the living room, my favorite room in the house with a large leather sofa, fireplace, and pictures from all the places I had traveled. Action shots from river rafting in Idaho, skiing in Utah, hiking in California, and racing in New York reminded me of happier times. I lit a fire and sat back on the couch. One click from the remote, and the sounds of Cat Stevens singing Wild World, a suitably somber song and one of my favorites, reverberated through my house. It was indeed a wild world out there.

I lived alone, but I appreciated the solitude after the chaos of the ER. I sat there in the dark, staring at the fire, and thought about my last patient of the night.

I ran through everything that had happened during the first visit. Could I have done anything differently? Could I have said something differently? What happened after she left the ER, and how could I have prevented it? And most importantly, who was she?

Perhaps surprisingly, her second visit was not as troublesome to accept. We have protocols to identify and reverse common causes of death, but they work only with reversible causes. Sometimes dead is dead, and no amount of therapy can possibly change it. She had come in dead and not even a battalion of BAFERDs could make a difference.

Death is not uncommon in the ER, but almost always, the patient's family is present at the time or can be immediately notified. This girl had died alone without family or even a name. And she had died horribly.

I knew this one was going to sting for a long while. Every time I tried to sleep, her hauntingly sad eyes stared through me. She had been such a vibrant young soul with so much life ahead of her, now violently gone. Her brief smile and laugh had lit up the room, but those eyes carried a sadness too deep for one so young. Determined to work with No Clue and Skinny Jeans to find her killer, I had to do everything I could to help her now after I had somehow failed her earlier.

•   •   •

After a late start the next morning, I locked my door and stepped over to my car. Carl apparently knew my schedule better than I did. He loitered in my driveway as he paced along the sidewalk.

"Morning, Doc. Get a good night's sleep?"

Maybe I didn't appear as bedraggled and tired as I felt. "Wonderful, Carl, freaking wonderful."

"Are you headed off to work?" the ever-observant Carl asked.

I looked down at my scrubs. "No Carl, some friends are having an all-day pajama party, and I am headed over there."

Carl' face scrunched in confusion, an expression I had seen before. "Oh, okay. Well, I am going to trim up my trees today."

That stopped me in my tracks, and I looked at the collection of red oaks, live oaks, and magnolias in his front yard. "I don't think they need trimming, Carl. Mother Nature is doing a great job growing them all by herself."

"True, true. But I read up on how to make them look even better."

I doubted that was true. I doubted Carl could read, but felt certain he would fuck up the trees. "Okay, but please don't take too much off them. And be careful. I don't want to see you in the ER today."

"I thought you were going to a pajama party today."

"Have a good day, Carl." He makes me smile sometimes.

CHAPTER TWELVE

By ER standards, my shift bordered on mundane, thankfully. A brief rush in the afternoon included two Asian gangs who had gotten into a knife fight. These fairly regular conflicts led to lacerations, of course, but not any serious injuries. They challenged each other one on one and fought until someone opened a big cut on his opponent. They never stabbed or went for the neck, and the fight ended when blood was drawn. They put pressure on the wound, came in for stitches, and the next two squared up for their knife fight.

Unfailingly polite in the ER, members from opposing gangs often received stitches at the same time without trouble. Occasionally, round two erupted in the parking lot outside the ER, and a patient immediately returned for a new set of stitches. No one ever pressed charges, so the police looked the other way. Barbaric by civilized standards, the knife fights settled differences fairly reasonably by gang standards. If nothing else, it helped teach new generations of doctors how to repair large lacerations.

Tom showed up wearing jeans, a flannel button down shirt, and a pissed off look on his face as I finished my last chart.

"For the record, this is a bad fucking idea. Any chance I can talk you out of this?"

"You know better than that. And for the record, we have had much worse ideas than this. Remember when you wanted to double date those twins from Dallas? How did that turn out?"

"All right, all right. Definitely not our worst idea. But still..."

"Your brave behavior is noted for the record. Let me get changed, and then we're out of here."

As usual, we argued as we walked to the garage. Tom wanted to take his truck because he could drive. It was high up, and in Houston, it blended in. I wanted to take my Mercedes, because I could drive. It had more horsepower and was a lot more fun.

"We take that car to uptown, and we are gonna get shot for it," Tom noted.

"Wrong. We might get shot at, but both of us are armed, and as an officer of the law, you should protect me, stand in front, and take the bullet. So, it is unlikely I will get shot. Let's take the Mercedes. Besides, I got some anger to work out."

"Shit, I didn't even update my will this week. Let's go," as Tom climbed into the passenger seat.

I hopped in the driver's side and fired up the engine. The E63 S is the pinnacle of luxury and power. A four-door that can seat four adults comfortably, it has 603 HP, two turbos, and a traction control system to keep it on the road. I reached down and turned it to race mode, which turned off the traction control.

Tom shook his head and looked at me. "Gonna be like that, huh?"

I smiled, punched the gas and let the acceleration throw me back in the seat. Time to release some frustration.

• • •

We arrived in uptown sixteen minutes later in one piece, with a little less traction on the tires and with a lot less gas in the tank. Two minutes later, we entered Finnegan's Tattoo. Designs covered the walls, and a few people wandered around, trying to decide which permanent mark to needle onto their bodies. A couple of artists worked on customers in the back. The distinct aroma of marijuana permeated the air and smoke hovered under the ceiling, making a contact high a distinct possibility. A reggae beat pulsated in the background. Tom and I spontaneously bobbed our heads to the beat as we approached a smiling young woman with a bunch of face piercings at the desk. "Ask her how she gets through airport security," Tom muttered as we approached.

"Welcome to Finnegan's. How can I help you boys today? You looking for matching tattoos?" Her eyes glinted mischievously.

"Well, now that you mention it, that might be a great idea. Tom, I can get one on my arm that says clue, and you can get a matching one that says no clue."

Tom rolled his eyes and muttered, "Fuck off," as he wandered over to go look at some designs on the wall.

"Don't mind him, he gets grouchy after 7 p.m." I pulled out my phone. "I met a lady who says she got this tattoo here recently. I really like the work and wanted to see if I could talk to the artist who did this to get something similar," I said with my friendliest smile and brightest eyes.

The woman took one look at the photo and said, "That's Anne's work. She was proud of that one. More interesting than the Chinese characters everyone wants these days. Half the city is walking around with Chinese food menu items tattooed on their arms, thinking it says something profound. She should be finished in a moment. Hang out and I will get you when she's free."

I moved beside Tom, who scanned the designs on the walls. "Planning a classy tramp stamp for yourself? Maybe a couple of handprints on your lower back? My treat."

"What the fuck is wrong with people? Who needs a tattoo of the Pillsbury Doughboy playing baseball with a duck on their calf?"

I wasn't sure if that was rhetorical, so I waited a moment before replying, "You're right. That would make more sense on an arm."

We continued our curious observation of tattoos until the pierced woman called to us. "C'mon back. Anne is available to talk now."

She led us back to Anne's work area, where she carefully sterilized her equipment. In her twenties, Anne sported bright red and purple streaks in her hair. Her sleeveless shirt showed off well-muscled arms covered in high-quality ink. Her eyes locked onto mine with a genuine smile. "How can I help you fellas today?"

I introduced myself and held out my phone. "We are looking for whoever did this tattoo, and the woman up front thought it might be yours. Did you do this tattoo in the last couple of weeks?"

Anne only glanced at the phone before looking back at us more appraisingly. "Let's start over. Who exactly are you guys, and what is your interest in this tattoo?"

"I'm an ER doctor downtown, and she was a patient of mine. Tom is a police officer who works with me. She gave some false information at registration, and we are trying to identify her."

"Hmmm. Why was she at the ER, and why are you fellas looking for her? Sounds kind of serious."

"Pretty damn serious. She came in yesterday morning with a small crack in her wrist. We fixed her up and discharged her. Later the same day, someone dropped her off outside the ER, beaten to death. We tried to resuscitate her, but unfortunately, she passed away."

Anne fell into her chair and cried. Tom looked at me, rolled his eyes, and motioned for me to handle it. Did I mention Tom does not have a high empathy score?

"I'm sorry to spring this on you, but we're trying to figure out what happened. During her first visit, we sensed she was in some trouble, but she wouldn't confide in us, and a few hours later, she was dead. We don't even know who she is. The only clue we have is that she mentioned getting this tattoo here recently. So, anything you can tell us about her would be appreciated."

Anne dried her eyes and straightened herself. "I only met her that one time, but the ink took about three hours, so we had some time to talk. Something about getting a tattoo makes people open up to you like a lifelong friend." She caught her breath. "She said her name was Jennifer, but she went by Jen. May have been fake, but I think it was her real name. No reason for an alias in here. We don't do any paperwork or keep records."

Tom asked hopefully. "Did she pay with a credit card?"

Anne laughed. "Girls like Jen don't use credit cards. They pay with cash."

"Girls like Jen?" I asked.

She looked at us like we were idiots, and she may not have been incorrect. "Jen was a dancer. Lots of cash in her purse, but no cards."

We looked at each other and shrugged. Dancing is big business in Houston. Girls at high-end clubs made $5,000 to $10,000 a night, although most made significantly less and suffered a high rate of drug addiction, violence and prostitution.

"Any idea which club she worked?" Tom asked.

"She never said the name of the club, but she mentioned a bunch of crazy Ukrainians were in charge of the place. She was terrified of those guys."

Tom piped in, "Smart to be scared of those guys. A small group of Ukrainians out in East Houston runs guns, girls, and drugs. Not nice people at all. Definitely capable of this. Their primary place is called The U. Rough place."

We didn't get any more meaningful information from Anne. We thanked her, and she walked us back to the front. "By the way, nice artwork on her arm. Her idea or yours?"

"A combination. She was really particular about the sorceress. She wanted her powerful and vibrant and casting a spell, but she left the spell up to me. Told me to pick a random combination of numbers and letters. She said that when the sorceress unscrambled the letters, the spell would be cast, and everything would be okay. Seemed to mean a lot to her."

I nodded. "Thanks for your help. Call me if you think of anything else." We made for the door.

"Will do. I hope you find the guys. And call me if you ever need some ink. I'd be happy to look over your body and find a perfect place for a tattoo."

"Might be interesting. I don't have any tattoos yet, but I might be talked into one. Maybe we could get together and discuss my options sometime."

"I am off this weekend. Maybe I could give you some suggestions over dinner?"

Tom grabbed my arm. "Let's go Casanova. We got work to do." Did I mention Tom is a really shitty wingman?

We headed out to the car. "You know, Tom, I think you should go back and ask out that woman at the front desk. I think she might like you."

Tom paused in mid-stride. "You really think so?"

"I think there is a pretty good chance. She obviously likes needles, so she would probably be thrilled with your dick."

Tom shook his head and kept walking to the car.

"Why you gotta do me like that? I was moments away from my first date with a tattoo artist. Who knows, she may even have had a friend who would go out with you," I complained.

Tom rolled his eyes. "I don't need any help to get a date, and you do not need to be dating a tattoo artist."

"It could have worked. Did you know tattoos go back at least 5,000 years? They found a dude covered in tattoos buried under a glacier in Europe."

Tom looked at me sideways. "How do you know stupid shit like that? You always got some random fact shooting out of your mouth."

I smiled back at him. "I know them because I read, Tom. Authors fill books with information, and when you read them, you get smarter. You wouldn't know that because you think books are for coloring. Anyway, what do you know about The U? We heading over there tonight?" I asked as we arrived at my car.

"Enough to know that we are not showing up in this car. Let's call it a night. I'll get some info on the place, and we can head over there this weekend when it's busier."

"We gonna let Skinny Jeans know about The U?"

Tom thought for a moment before answering. "Let's hold off. They will have to go official over there. Below the radar may be more effective. Will probably get me in trouble, but that's nothing new when I listen to you."

CHAPTER THIRTEEN

I wasn't ready to head home after I took Tom to his truck, and I needed some nutrition before going to bed. IHOP is the only choice after 10 p.m.

The bell rang as I walked in, and the cook looked up, "Good evening, Doc. The usual?"

"Sounds like a plan to me, Little D," as I slid into the nearest booth. Little D was anything but little. About 6 feet 4 inches and a solid 230, he was a former defensive lineman from the University of Houston. Little D cooked and kept the peace on the overnight shifts.

The server glided over with a large orange juice as I sat down. "Good morning, Doc, I assume you have bypassed me and ordered directly with our executive chef, as usual."

"Good assumption, Gladys. And I will give you a hint. With taxes, my bill should come out to $9.63"

"Big surprise. A normal person would get bored with the same meal all the time."

"I have been accused of being many things, but normal is not on the list. Do you know how much time and money I save every week by not thinking about food? How are the kids doing?"

A single mom with three kids at home, her oldest was 17, and the youngest was 14, and she was only 31. She worked nights so that she could be home to get the kids to school in the morning and to help them with their homework in the evening. Life had not been easy for Gladys, but she made the best of it.

"Good and bad. Tina is a finalist for a scholarship at the University of Houston, and her teachers think she has an excellent shot at it. That's the good news. The bad news is Brandon keeps getting into trouble at school. Boy has a mouth on him that does not know when to shut up."

"He'll be fine. Used to know a young man with that problem, and he turned out fine. Maybe he will become a doctor, too," I said with a wink.

Gladys genuinely laughed, a musical sound that could make your entire night. "More likely, he will become a crazy IHOP stalker in the wee hours of the morning. I'll go check on that order."

The relaxing IHOP visit helped me to wind down and load up on carbs after a long day. Little D could whip up my breakfast in four minutes, and I could eat it in five. Some days, I was in and out in under ten minutes. Other days, I took my time shooting the shit with Gladys and Little D, but I am a firm believer that friendship is based on quality of time, not quantity.

"Here you are, sweetie, a grilled cheese sandwich, french fries, ketchup, two buttermilk pancakes with butter on the side, and a large orange juice. Here is the check. Came out to $9.63. What a surprise. Enjoy."

One thing I liked about Gladys was that she understood that breakfast is better hot, so she always left me to wolf it down as quickly as possible. Eating for me was not for pleasure, but only for refilling my energy stores. Five minutes later, I finished the last of the pancakes, polished off the orange juice, and stood up to leave. On the way out, I gave Gladys a hug and handed her the check back with a $100 bill inside. "Thanks for the service, and you and Little D keep the change."

"Thanks, Doc," Little D called from behind the grill. "You be safe out there."

"Don't worry about me. Houston is one of the safest places in America," I chuckled as I pushed out the door and turned to find three teenagers lounging on my car. They looked me over as I approached. "Is this your car, gringo? It's a nice car," said the first.

"Yeah, it must be fun to drive around in a car like that," the second chimed in.

Then the third guy joined in, the largest and the actual leader of the three, the only one who really mattered. He stepped forward and held out his hand. "Why don't you hand over those keys and let us take it for a test drive?"

This sticky situation wasn't out of control yet. "Evening gentlemen. It is indeed a fine car. A Mercedes E63S, with 603 HP, two turbo systems, and enough torque to move a wall. Runs zero to sixty in about three seconds and still gets good mileage on the highway. If you are interested in a test drive, I can get you the name and number of an excellent agent at the Mercedes dealership."

"What the fuck is wrong with you, man? I want to drive this car right now. Give me the fucking keys," the center guy yelled. He took another step forward and pulled out a four-inch switchblade, technically an illegal weapon, but now was not the time to discuss that issue.

One last chance for de-escalation. "Son, it has been a long day. I just had a delightful meal and want to get home to bed. Put the knife back in your pocket and walk away. I don't want anyone to get hurt." While talking, I had subtly shifted my left foot in front and had my weight on my back foot and now had both hands up in front of me.

He took another step closer. "Give me the fucking keys, maricon." It occurred to me that these guys had no imagination of insults, but now I had to turn my attention to the fight, and it was a fight, even though no punches had been thrown yet. I did not have any weapons on me, and none were within reach. There was a gun in my car, but no way to reach it before getting stabbed by this idiot. I still had the option to run, but was in no mood for that.

Mind made up, I faced the fight. I needed him one step closer. The danger in a knife fight is letting the other guy stay too far away. He could just slice at me with little I could do about it, but if I could draw him in close, I could even the odds. I could get inside of the arc of the knife and cause some damage of my own. So, I needed him closer, preferably angry and charging. "If you want to impress your boyfriend, then come take my keys," I challenged him.

That did it. After a moment to process what I had said, his face bunched up, his body tensed, the knife came up, and he charged. Fortunately, he held the knife low with his palm up, like they do in the movies, which meant he knew more about watching movies than about knife fighting. He probably expected me to retreat, but I launched off my back foot, which meant the knife was in range before he was ready and exactly when I was ready. A quick strike to the nerves on the inside of the wrist with my right hand and a counter strike with my left, and his hand went numb and unable to hold the knife, which was not an issue since the knife was already in my left hand.

The fight wasn't over, though. Most people with knives tend to forget that other weapons may be in play. He was still coming toward me, and I was still closing in. While he focused on the knife, I reared my head back and aimed at his nose. The timing was perfect as the crown of my forehead struck him right in the center of his face. An audible crack meant his nose broke, and probably one of his cheekbones, too. Now the fight was over. He fell backward to the ground with blood gushing from his face and with his buddies looking on in stunned silence.

I walked over and helped him up, still holding the knife casually. "Gentlemen, we have a decision to make. Obviously, you are not driving my car tonight. Do you want to ride in a police car or go home? Take your knives out, drop them on the ground, and you can take your buddy with you. Any more shit and I call the cops." I really did not want to call the police and have to deal with reports and interviews. I knew I would not get in trouble, but I also knew I would not be in bed for another two hours if I called.

The other two looked at each other, and then slowly dropped their knives on the ground. I pushed their injured buddy at them. "Get out of here, and I don't want to see you around here again." The three moved away with their friend draped between them.

"Strong work, Doc." I spun around to find Little D with a smile on his face and a baseball bat in his hands. The bat looked like a toothpick in his grasp.

"I thought you played football."

"I like all sports. A little baseball now and then is good for the arms," he said, flexing his massive biceps.

"Thanks for the backup," I said, as I walked over to pick up the other two knives. I handed all three to Little D. "Throw these in the trash for me, please. Have a good night."

"You, too, Doc. You, too."

CHAPTER FOURTEEN

With the autopsy scheduled for 10 a.m. the next morning, I left the
house at 9:30 a.m., stopped in my tracks by an unbelievable sight. When
I imagined Carl was going to fuck up his trees, I had seriously underestimated him. He had topped off and squared a 15-year-old oak, now
literally the stupidest looking tree in Texas. Amazingly, Carl's absence
prevented his bragging about his work, but I was sure to get an earful
at some point.

My day did not improve at the medical examiner's office. Autopsies
are always horrific, and even the building itself induced foreboding. A
square eyesore with all the charm of a 1970's Russian tenement building, the drab yellow and green walls clashed with the mismatched
furniture. The fluorescent lights failed to banish the gloom of the autopsy room crouched in the basement, as if to get as far away from
sunlight and cheer as possible. A heaviness pervaded the air, a constant
reminder of the solemnity of questioned death.

The pungent odor of formaldehyde permeates the air and clings,
especially in your hair and clothing, to haunt everyone for the rest of
the day. Rightfully associated with the smell of death, the only worse
odor emanates from the actual bodies in the autopsy room.

I arrived a few minutes early to find Skinny Jeans already gowned and ready to go. No one wants to bring real clothes into the autopsy room. "Showing some nice ankle there, Lenny." Lenny could rarely find a pair of scrubs long enough for his legs.

"Morning, Doc. I'm prepared for any surprise flooding in Houston today," he said, showing off his lower leg. "What brings you here this morning?"

"This one still bothers me, so I thought I would peek at the autopsy, if that's okay with you guys."

"Fine by me," replied Jane.

"Who's on the schedule today?" I asked.

They both turned to me and spoke in unison, "Morquist."

In a profession of odd characters, Morquist Levy is uniquely eccentric. Undeniably brilliant, his social skills unapologetically suffered. If he were alone in a room with a corpse, Morquist could be the second most social person in the room. He had about one hundred different eccentricities and peculiarities, but was also a very detail-oriented thinker. Nothing escaped his notice in an autopsy, while social cues routinely escaped him.

In his sixties, Morquist had been with the pathology department for over forty years. His frail looking five-foot nine-inch frame carried about 140 pounds, about one percent of which seemed muscle. His eyes appeared perpetually surprised, magnified by the thickest glasses I had ever seen, like a scientist from a poorly financed science fiction film who had way too much caffeine for breakfast.

But over his career, Morquist had seen everything. After thousands of autopsies, no secret of death eluded him. Meticulous perhaps to a fault, no lawyer had ever successfully challenged his findings in court.

We walked together to the room in silence to find Morquist already at work. Laid out on a metal table, naked, with eyes staring at the ceiling, this corpse incredibly had been a vibrant young lady only hours before.

Morquist had no time nor need for greetings and went straight into his report. "I have already cataloged the belongings. Clothes with no markings and no other personal effects. Nothing of interest. Fingernail scrapings collected and sent, only eight, because two are missing. No materials of interest noted. X-ray of the body completed. Here you see the results."

Morquist spoke in short sentences at a speed that would make most auctioneers stare in wonder, without a pause between sentences. Most people briefly hesitate while speaking to inhale, but Morquist seemed unburdened by such human limitations, as if he could absorb oxygen directly through his skin. He could probably read an entire book aloud in one breath. Lenny furiously took notes.

I gave Lenny a chance to catch up. "Good morning, Morquist. What number autopsy is this for you?"

Morquist paused and looked at me. "Good morning, AJ. This is autopsy number 16,237 for me. It's the 8,329th I have performed on a female, which represents 51.3% of my cases." He looked at me expectantly, prepared to give his best answers.

"But how many had blue eyes?"

"I have had 1,120 autopsies where the patient had at least one blue eye. This is 6.9% of my cases, which is lower than the national average of blue-eyed people. I attribute this to the large Hispanic population in Houston, where blue eyes are less common."

He could go on like this all day. He remembered every autopsy in detail. If asked to describe a fracture he saw in 1983, he could give a detailed response without hesitation.

Lenny was ready to move on. "Anything on X-rays?"

We walked over to the computers. "X-rays show a known fracture of the left forearm. This matches the X-ray from yesterday in the ER, so it is the same person. Also, three new rib fractures. Likely around time of death from blunt trauma. Painful, but not life threatening. No obvious injuries to cause death on X-ray."

He moved back to the table to start a detailed skin exam, scanning every inch of her skin with a magnifying glass, beginning at the scalp and working his way down to her feet, all the while dictating his findings into the attached microphone. He did not pause at the severed fingers. When he got to the feet, he spoke. "Roll her." Assistants turned her body over, and he resumed his exam of the skin. Ten minutes later, he announced, "No unusual lesions or punctures. Cause of death is not clear from external exam."

After his assistants turned the body back over, next came a vaginal exam that included multiple swabs. "No evidence of trauma or sexual assault." He made a long y-shaped incision from both shoulders to the mid-chest and down to the pelvis. He started in the abdomen and pelvis, removing organs and weighing them, dictating his findings along the way, all normal. Then he moved to the chest to remove the heart and lungs. A brief exam revealed them to be healthy and normal. Neck exam showed no evidence of trauma.

Lenny was getting impatient. "So, what killed her, Dr. Levy?"

Without looking up, he replied. "I cannot yet say what killed her. I can only say what did not kill her," and went back to work.

I smiled at Lenny under my mask. "You should include that in your report, all the things that did not kill her."

Lenny rolled his eyes and kept taking notes.

Morquist started on the head, the most gruesome part of an autopsy. He made an incision across the top of the scalp and pulled it forward over the face to expose the skull, not for the faint of heart or for those who prefer a hearty breakfast. Next came the bone saw cutting a cap off the skull.

Morquist removed the top of the skull, and for the first time, paused. He looked back at the X-rays of the skull in careful detail, then returned to the table. He looked up at us. "Too much blood."

Skinny Jeans looked at me in unison and I shrugged.

Morquist removed the brain, set it on a side metal table, and dissected it, tedious work, but Morquist moved quickly and precisely. After five minutes of work in silence, he looked up to announce "AVM," and resumed his silent task.

I explained to Skinny Jeans, "An AVM is an arterial venous malformation. Some people are born with it. The arterial and venous blood systems are connected directly to each other. Since arteries are high pressure, and veins are low pressure, this puts too much pressure on the venous side. Over time, that can lead to rupture and massive bleeding in the head. Like a stroke, it can kill quickly."

Morquist added, "There is more work to do, but she died of a ruptured AVM in her brain."

Jane asked, "Is that common? I've never heard of an AVM."

"It occurs in about 1 in 100,000 people. No symptoms until it pops and causes death. This is the thirteenth I have seen at autopsy. The last one was March 8, three years ago."

"Did it rupture because of trauma to her head?" Lenny inquired.

Morquist shook his head. "No evidence of significant trauma to the brain. Likely ruptured due to increased blood pressure from stress. She died of fear. She was literally scared to death."

Lenny closed his notebook with sad compassion in his eyes. "Thanks, Morquist. Appreciate the help." He muttered to Jane, "Gonna get these motherfuckers," as he walked out.

I couldn't agree more.

Outside the room, we changed into our regular clothes, but we still reeked of formaldehyde, our grim companion for the rest of the day.

"What's Morquist's story?" Lenny asked as we walked along the drab corridor. "He is one seriously weird dude."

"Morquist is one of the smartest people I have ever met. He has a genius level IQ and remembers everything. He is a totally different guy outside of work: has a wife and two kids, a suburban home, a dog. Lives a pretty normal life, but at work he becomes this super intense creature with no time for inefficiency, like an eccentric artist who will not talk to anyone while painting or composing music."

"He may be a good man for that job, but he freaks me the fuck out. Having said that, make sure he does my autopsy if I get killed in the line of duty. Only the best for me."

"Strange request, but I will make sure it happens. You guys making any progress?" I asked hopefully, as I pushed through a set of double doors.

"Not a single fucking thing so far. Prints are not in the system; no one has reported her missing; and nothing in the files shows any similar cases. All we know is the poor girl's brain exploded from fear," Jane said.

"How about the car video?" I asked.

"We watched the tape repeatedly frame by frame and got nothing. Nothing unique about the car or driver. Descriptions could fit about 300,000 people in Houston."

"So, where do you go from here?" I asked.

"We keep working the case. We need an ID on her, and then we can start tracing her last few days. But without an ID, we ain't got shit. We will start hitting up the tattoo parlors to see if anyone recognizes her ink. Was hoping to avoid that since there are about 1,000 parlors in town and half the artists are too stoned to remember what they did yesterday." Jane grumbled.

I came close to telling them what Tom and I had discovered, but held off at the last moment. Jane would be furious, and Tom would be demoted back to an actual mall cop. I rationalized we were going to The U that night to see if we could learn anything. So, in twelve hours, they would know everything we knew. Hopefully, we would have something so useful they would not be too mad.

"Do you think you will get an ID on her?"

Lenny replied, "We always get the ID. Not sure how, but the ID will turn up, eventually. Have a good one, Doc."

"You, too."

CHAPTER FIFTEEN

Dot's arrival brightened my next shift. Every ER has regulars, and Dot was the queen of ours. She checked herself in at least three times a week. You might think that Dot was chronically ill for so many visits, but she was actually in pretty darn good physical health, other than her schizophrenia.

"Good morning, Doctor," she said as she blew me a kiss. "Excited to see you again. I missed you last week. Where were you?"

"Dot, I've missed you as well. I had to go do some work in Wyoming. How have you been?" This question to Dot always led to a long, animated summary of her activities over the last few days. It was always the same on every visit.

"So what seems to be the problem today, Dot?" I asked as she finally ran out of stories.

She stared at me with a pensive look on her face, thinking real hard. "I think it was back pain today, Doctor."

"It says here on the chart you have left shoulder pain."

"Well then, that's why I am here. My left shoulder hurts."

I looked at her with a smile. "Dot, does your left shoulder really hurt, or are you just visiting us today?"

She looked around conspiratorially. "My shoulder is fine. I just wanted to say hi."

Her visits always comprised minor complaints, never chest pain, weakness or dizziness, followed by, "Is there a box lunch I could have today?"

"Of course, dear. Chicken or turkey?"

She put on her thinking face.

"How about one of each?" Her delight lit up the room.

"And when you're done, how about a cab voucher to get home?"

"Thank you, Doctor. Thank you."

"No problem, Dot. Take your time. We aren't too busy right now, and some other folks will want to say hello."

Social workers stayed in touch with her, but she liked to visit us in the ER, an important part of her routine. She had visited us over five hundred times in the last three years and knew most of us by name. She had become part of the ER ecosystem; her visits helped to keep her life in balance as well as ours. Dot was family.

. . .

Another regular, Delgado, rolled in at 6 p.m. passed out on the stretcher pushed by EMS. "Where did you find him today?"

"In the park. Again."

Delgado was an alcoholic and terminally drunk. A layer of empties covered his apartment because Delgado drank all day, every day. He probably hadn't been sober once in the last ten years. When he went outside and passed out, which happened frequently, people thought he was dead and called 911. Paramedics in the area knew him and brought him in to sober up.

"Room seven. Y'all know the drill." He would get an EKG, screening labs, and a blood alcohol level to make sure nothing else was going on. Everyone knew the Delgado protocol.

I went back to the nurses' station and pulled a specimen cup out. "The Delgado pool is open. You can only enter once. Closest guess to blood alcohol level without going over wins bragging rights. Price is Right rules!"

Everyone wrote their guesses and put them in the jar. Our latest medical student looked horrified. "Is this legal?"

"To be honest, I haven't run this by the administration's legal department, but it's good for morale, and bragging rights are important in the ER. You should enter."

The medical student looked doubtful, but the promise of transitory fame was too much to pass up. She wrote her answer and reached for the jar.

"0.23? He would probably start seizing if he got that low."

"But that's three times the legal limit. Anything above that can be fatal."

"True, unless you are a chronic alcoholic. They reset their baseline much higher. My man here has an ER record of 0.548. Enough to kill three normal humans."

"Oh, my god. How do you even know when to discharge someone like that?"

Deb did not look up from her chart. "Eventually, he will stop pissing on himself in the bed, and he will stand up to pee on the floor next to his bed. That is when we get him clean clothes and discharged home."

The glamorous life of the emergency room staff.

CHAPTER SIXTEEN

That night, Tom picked me up at my house around ten.

"You ready for this?" I asked.

"I got a Glock on my hip, a .38 on my ankle, and a knife on my belt in back. All set. What are you carrying?"

"Just a Glock on my hip and a bazooka in my pants. Let's go."

We were definitely taking Tom's truck for this trip. The U was not in the worst part of town, but it may have been the second worst, an industrial area with every other building burned out or abandoned and every building covered in trash and gang graffiti.

"Where do you suppose they get all the paint for the graffiti? You never see a paint store in this neighborhood. Nearest Sherwin Williams has got to be fifteen miles away."

Tom just looked at me like I was the village idiot. "For a doctor, you are pretty fucking stupid."

"Maybe, but I think I'm gonna find some property down here real cheap and open a paint store. Bet I would make a fortune. Maybe call it 'Village Idiot Paint Store,' and use a picture of you for my logo."

Tom replied with a single finger and kept driving.

Unsure what I expected, my first view of The U underwhelmed me. An old warehouse had been converted into a bar, a square monstrosity with no personality other than a garish neon sign that differentiated it from the surrounding abandoned buildings.

"How do you even get a permit to run a bar in an industrial area?" I wondered.

Tom snorted. "I doubt there is a permit for this place. I doubt a building inspector has been within ten miles of this place in the last twenty years."

We found a pot-holed parking space with faded paint lines near the back, and Tom backed in. "Well, at least it's well lit," Tom noted as he looked around the parking lot at young toughs drinking and smoking beside pickups and muscle cars.

"Probably makes it easier to count the bodies at the end of the night. Let's go. Time for a new vehicle, anyway." We left his truck under the watchful eyes of some seething gang members and walked inside.

Whatever the outside lacked in class and sophistication, it surpassed the inside. Electronic techno music blared; a haze of smoke clouded the air; and an overall stench pervaded, suggesting that cleaning occurred monthly at best. A sweaty crowd, high humidity, and poor lighting completed the ambience. Stained, mismatched furniture skirted debris littered all over the floor. Large Ukrainian bouncers wandered among the guests to keep the peace with their bulk. Not sure what they ate to get that big, but raw meat would be a good guess.

On stage, three disengaged girls danced lackadaisically. Other girls ambled among patrons looking for business.

Tom poked me and shouted in my ear, "Looks like private dances are upstairs," he pointed to a staircase. "I'll hang at the bar, and you go see what you can find out."

"Sounds like a plan. You should order some food. I hear the seafood is flown in fresh, and the chef was trained in France. Maybe get the crab cakes and grilled salmon?" I joked.

"Fuck you. I ain't eating anything that comes out of this kitchen. Probably make me so sick I would be a patient in your ER tomorrow."

"You show up as a patient in the ER for anything, I can guarantee you there will be an order on your chart to check your prostate hourly for any changes."

"Banshee would attack the first gloved finger that came near me. Now, shut the fuck up and get to work so we can get out of this place. I'm gonna sit here and have a beer. Try not to cause any trouble tonight. We're significantly outnumbered."

Our plan was to get one girl alone and ask her if they knew Jennifer or recognized the tattoo. That meant a private dance in the VIP area, although I doubted there was very much VIP about the area. Maybe the furniture was less sticky up there, and hopefully, the music was quieter. I wandered off and left Tom at the bar.

I wasn't looking for any particular girl, just one that didn't look incoherently stoned, which proved difficult. Eventually, I approached a promising young girl with clear eyes.

"Hey, how much for a private dance in a quieter area?" I yelled at her. She held up two fingers. I pulled three $100 bills from my pocket. She took the money, grabbed my hand and led me upstairs, away from the pounding music. We passed another massive thug on the way up. Apparently, ginormous Ukrainians could be purchased in bulk. She led me into a red upholstered cubby, closed the curtain, unbuttoned her top and asked what I would like.

I held up my hands."Hold on. I only want to talk."

"You want to talk for $300? That's a new one. Okay, let's talk." She eyed me suspiciously as she stood over me.

"I'm looking for a girl."

"You came to the right place. Lots of girls here."

I held up my phone. "I'm looking for this girl. Her name may be Jenny and she had this tattoo on her arm." I could tell instantly that she recognized the tattoo.

She stood up straighter and became more business-like. "Who are you, and why are you looking for her?"

"I'm a doctor in the ER, and I'm trying to figure out what happened to her."

"What happened? Is she okay? Tell me she's okay," her eyes pleaded.

"I am sorry to say she is not okay. Someone dumped her at the ER after beating her up. She had some bleeding in her brain and she died. I am sorry to tell you she's gone."

She broke down in tears, as she sat beside me, a normal reaction to a friend's death, but I wasn't sure how to handle it. Normally, I would hold her hand and offer comfort, but I wasn't normally on a sticky couch with a half-dressed too young stranger in a strip club.

"I'm sorry. I don't even know your name. I go by Doc."

"I'm Linda and Jenny was my friend. They told us she left to see her family. I can't believe she's gone." Tears streamed through her makeup as I patiently waited.

"We're trying to figure out what happened to her. What can you tell me about her?"

"Jenny had been here about a year. She came from a small town in Arkansas. Mom died when she was in high school from breast cancer, and she never knew her dad. She had no family left, so she stayed with friends to finish high school, and then left for the big city. Like a lot of us, she had dreams of a better life here."

"How did she end up here?"

Linda sighed. "Same way most of us end up in this hellhole. You need a job to pay rent. Dancing is pretty easy money, although not the most rewarding work, but once these assholes get a hold of you, there is no quitting or leaving. The only way out of here is in a body bag. Oh, my, I'm sorry," as she realized what she had said. Another round of tears ensued. Finally, Linda composed herself enough to ask, "What else do you know about what happened to her?"

"She came into our ER earlier in the day with a fractured wrist. Jenny appeared upset about something, but refused our offers to help. She was discharged, and several hours later, some unknown man dropped her off at our ER door. She had been beaten up pretty bad, but she died from some bleeding in the brain, and there was nothing we could do to save her. Her death would have been instant and painless once the brain bleed occurred." I spared her the details of Jenny's torture. "Any idea who might have done this?"

Her eyes blazed. "I know exactly who did it. These fucking animals who run the place. They're all crazy and enjoy punishing women. The rules are clear. If you piss them off, there is a severe beating for you. If you try to leave, they will beat you and a member of your family. Crazy fucking Ukrainians; and each one is worse than the last."

"Who's in charge here?"

"That giant asshole in the office down the hall leads these fucking goons. And before you ask, I don't know his name. No one knows his name. Everyone calls him Dyyavola. He is the one responsible for Jenny's death. No one would dare do anything without his permission."

"Dyyavola? What the hell kind of name is that?"

"Apparently it means 'devil' in Ukrainian. The devil could take lessons from this animal on how to be evil." She visibly trembled as she spoke about him.

"I'm sorry to spring this news on you, and I'm sorry you are in this situation. Do you want to leave with us?"

She wept again. "No, the rules are clear. If I leave, he will hurt the others."

"Anything I can do for you?"

"Please don't let them know I talked to you. If they find out I talked, it will be bad. Really bad."

"Okay, here's my card. Call if I can do anything to help. Anything at all."

She took the card and slid it into her bra.

I had run out of questions and time with Linda. "Thank you for your help. Last thing I need is Jenny's last name and address. That will help us get to the bottom of this."

"Her last name was Smithton, and she lived alone in an apartment near here." Linda gave me the address. "Do you promise you will get these guys?"

"I promise we will get every one of these motherfuckers. Now, I need to get out of here and share this info with the police," I said as I rose. "Call that number on the card if you or the other girls think of anything I can do. We can get anyone out of here that wants out."

I got up to leave, and she grabbed my hand. "Wait a minute. I need to go downstairs with you. They will rough up any guy who walks down alone. They want to make sure the girl is in good enough shape to keep working. Give me a minute."

She quickly dried her eyes and pulled herself together, but it was still obvious she had been crying. "Okay, let's go." She grabbed my arm and led me downstairs.

Two sets of eyes bored into me as I descended the stairs. Tom nursed a drink at the bar and surreptitiously watched me closely. I gave a subtle nod toward the door, and he threw cash on the counter and slid off his barstool.

The other set of eyes belonged to a very large and angry Ukrainian bouncer. Low intelligence struggled to flicker behind those eyes, but he could probably bench press a small bus with little effort. He looked from me to Linda and approached like a focused bull. Linda kissed me on the cheek and whispered, "Get out of here. Now. Bohdan is coming this way."

I had never met a Bohdan before and wanted to keep it that way. I turned toward the exit as Bohdan approached Linda, speaking briefly to her. She shook her head 'no,' but he immediately let her go and came for me. Time to leave. Tom was already out the door, and I pushed through the final crowd with the exit in sight. A roar behind me warned of Bohdan before a large hand gripped my shoulder and spun me around. Ready for it, I used the momentum to continue the spin and to deliver a World Cup worthy kick to his groin. Bohdan's eyes widened and rolled back into his head before he collapsed to the floor in agony. Really, time to leave.

I turned back around to race through the exit. The bouncer at the door grabbed for me but missed. I slipped away and sprinted for the truck with the bouncer and a limping Bohdan chasing me. Tom had the engine fired up and had already pulled his pickup truck out and turned toward the street. The crowd in the parking lot froze to watch the chase unfold, hoping for a fight. Happy to disappoint them, I sprinted at full speed to the truck and launched over the tailgate. Airborne, I wondered if Tom left any sharp tools in his truck bed, but it was too late to worry about that. I thumped onto the empty metal platform and Tom floored it, spraying the Ukrainians with gravel as we made our escape.

Two blocks later, he stopped, and I climbed into the cab. "Did you enjoy your leisurely drink at the bar?"

"Did you enjoy your lap dance?"

"No lap dance, but I was able to get her name and address. She cried about her friend's death, and Bohdan probably thought I had damaged his merchandise. We have to get all these girls out of there."

"Which one was Bohdan?"

"The big ugly one with two swollen testicles."

Tom laughed. "Well, at least they don't know who you are."

I wasn't laughing. "I am not so sure about that."

• • •

Still limping, Bohdan pulled Linda into the office. He collapsed into a chair and placed a bag of ice on his groin. She had been in the office before and had hoped never to set foot in there again. She knew Dyyavola. All the girls knew Dyyavola, unfortunately. He made it a point to introduce himself to the new girls. No one knew his real name, but he was in charge and definitely crazy. He gestured for Linda to sit in a chair in front of his worn wooden desk and fixed his cold eyes on her.

Dyyavola approached slowly until his massive frame towered over her, easily six feet six inches tall and over 330 pounds of muscle. His dirty, matted beard contrasted with his bald head, crisscrossed with scars. Massive arms protruded from a stained, sleeveless t-shirt that had been white many years ago. Tufts of thick dark hair protruded from the neck and armholes of the stretched shirt. As he approached, his misshapen nose and dark eyes filled Linda's entire world, as his fetid breath oozed over her face.

"Who was this man who upset you? Did he hurt you?"

"No, no, he didn't hurt me."

"Then why upset?"

Linda paused, and he picked up a seven-inch knife from his desk. "You tell me what this man does to you, or I peel skin off your feet."

Linda pulled Doc's business card out of her bra and passed it to him with a trembling hand. "He's an ER doctor, and he asked about Jenny."

Dyyavola snatched the card and glanced at it. "What else are you hiding from me?"

"Nothing. I swear, that is all he gave me."

"Stand up," Dyyavola ordered.

Terrified, Linda rose, keeping her eyes focused on the floor.

"Take clothes off. Now." Linda sobbed as she slid out of her bra and stepped out of her panties. Bohdan watched the show with interest as she stood naked in front of them.

Dyyavola circled her slowly, like a predator. "Very important to check everywhere. Make sure nothing else is hidden." From behind, he reached around her and gave each breast a painful squeeze and each nipple a painful twist that brought fresh tears to her eyes.

He continued circling her until he was once again in front of her. "Look at me," he commanded in a voice all the more terrifying with its calmness. "Open mouth. Wide."

She knew what was coming, but was powerless to stop him. She opened her mouth, and he leaned down until his repulsive breath overwhelmed her senses. He made a show of looking in her mouth, and then he shoved two of his massive fingers into her open mouth. She gagged at the stench of onions and dirt. She gagged further as he pushed them deeper into her mouth and moved them around.

Finally, he removed his fingers from her mouth, but the ordeal was not over yet. He leaned over until he could whisper into her ear. "Need to check one more place where whores like to hide things."

His hand made its way down between her legs and forced them apart. He sighed as he forced the two massive fingers inside her. Linda sobbed now, helpless to fight him.

After what seemed like an eternity, Dyyavola turned from rapist to business executive. "Get clothes on and get back to work. I have business to discuss with Bohdan."

Linda did not waste a second throwing her bra and underwear back on and scampering out the door. Outside, two other girls waited for her. They had all suffered such a visit before, and they all knew what kind of horrible things happened in there. Linda cried again as she told them what had happened, and the other girls wept with her when they learned what had happened to Jenny. Linda wondered for the thousandth time whether this life was worth living at all as she went back to work.

Back in the office, Dyyavola studied the card Linda had given him, finally handing it to Bohdan. "This Doctor asks too many questions about Jenny. When your balls are better, make sure Doctor does not ask any more questions."

Bohdan nodded and left.

CHAPTER SEVENTEEN

"Always an interesting night with you, Doc."

"Almost too exciting. Not sure I want to meet Bohdan again."

"Afraid of a little Bohdan beat down?"

"I'm pretty sure a Bohdan beat down would take an entire team of orthopedists to correct. At least we got a name and address," I said.

"You know we need to give that information to Skinny Jeans."

"I know, and they're gonna be pissed, and I don't want a Skinny Jeans beat down, either. I got an idea. Pull into that gas station."

Tom pulled in, and I ran inside. Forty dollars and two minutes later, I had a cheap phone with fifty minutes of call time on it and two Lotto tickets.

Tom looked at the phone. "Let me guess. Skinny Jeans is about to get an anonymous tip."

"Wrong. Skinny Jeans is about to get an anonymous tip from a female friend of the victim. Stop by the ER. Let's see if Jean is there."

"Jean is always there. Jean lives there. Place would fall apart if she ever left the building. Why the fuck do you waste your money on lottery tickets?"

"First of all, I have enough money to waste. Second, the money goes toward education and veterans, two things I like to support. And finally, I did a detailed analysis of every lottery winner in Texas and found they had only one thing in common."

"What would that be?"

"They all bought a ticket."

Tom shook his head. "For a smart guy, you are a fucking idiot sometimes."

• • •

Twenty minutes later, we walked into the ER, where Jean yelled at a drunk. "I told you the gown has to open in the back. If I see your junk hanging out again, I am gonna snip it off and staple it to the wall. Now put a second gown on, cover yourself, and get your ass back in your room."

"I see you're utilizing your skills from the latest customer service workshop."

"You know me, I like to act mean. Although it's easy when he runs around with his wrinkly junk hanging out. I've never had a penis, but if I had one like that, I would cover it."

"Good advice for Tom and his wrinkly junk. Come to the office here. I need a quick favor."

"Why the hell should I do a favor for you two clowns?"

"Because I am charming and worship the very ground you walk on?"

"Charming, maybe. But the rest of that is BS. What do you need?"

"We found out some information about that girl that died the other day, and we want you to call it into the police as an anonymous tip."

Jean looked back and forth between us. "Any reason you boys can't tell them yourselves? Last I checked, one of you actually works for the damn police."

Tom fidgeted a bit before answering. "Our intervention in this case was not entirely authorized and may lead to some consternation from the lead detectives."

Jean actually laughed. "So, you dumbasses went and played detective and actually learned something, but are afraid to tell Jane, because she will pull out your short hairs and shove them down your throat?"

"That's a pretty accurate description of one of the likely outcomes if our involvement became known."

"All right, give me the phone. I'm only doing this to help the girl. And you owe me a fancy dinner if I ever get a night off from this place."

I let out my held breath. "Agreed, and thank you."

A few minutes later we walked out, after the duty sergeant on call had taken notes on an anonymous tip giving the name, address, and place of work of a recent Jane Doe. Information that would be passed on to the Detectives in the morning.

Tom drove me home. "You off tomorrow?"

"Yes, sir. Two whole days off. Time for some rest and relaxation."

"You mind watching Banshee for a couple of days? I have some extended training, and I hate to leave him alone."

"Love to. That dog is a chick magnet. Bring him by in the morning. In case you get lost, remember that I live in the house next to the square oak trees.

Tom looked out the window at Carl's trees. "Fucking Carl landscaping again?"

"Fucking Carl being Carl. Goodnight, Tom."

CHAPTER EIGHTEEN

Jane found Lenny smiling from his desk and holding up a piece of paper. "We got a break last night. Anonymous female caller said our recent Jane Doe is a Jennifer Smithton, and she lives down in South Houston. We got a name, address, and place of work."

"Well, the case is almost solved, then. I assume the call was from a burner phone?"

"Correct, but I already have the papers filed, and we should have a warrant any time now for the apartment."

"A good start to the day. Hopefully, we find something useful in there."

An hour later, they knocked on the door of a rundown apartment in a decrepit building in a broken down part of town. Jane looked out over the property. "I like what they've done with the place. If they get the sewage out of the pool and clean up the needles in the lot, this could be a really nice place."

Predictably, no one answered the door. A flash of a badge and warrant got the manager out of his office with a set of keys. Concerned he'd have a heart attack as he huffed up the rickety stairs, Skinny Jeans felt a glimmer of relief as he unlocked the door.

Guarded curiosity snuffed out relief as they scanned the tiny apartment that looked devastated by a tornado. The place was literally torn to pieces with every piece of furniture smashed apart, drawers emptied, holes in the walls, and carpets torn up. Determined and angry people had spent some time in there.

"Looks like somebody is going to lose their security deposit," Lenny observed.

"Let's get a team over here and lock this place down." Jane turned to the manager. "This is now a murder crime scene. Please wait for me in your office. I have some questions for you. Lenny, secure this until the team arrives and then knock on doors. I want everyone in this building interviewed. You know the drill."

• • •

Four hours later, Lenny and Jane compared notes. "We have confirmation on her ID. Multiple neighbors recognized her photo, and we found some pictures in here that match our victim. We collected DNA samples from the bathroom, but for now, we are confident the victim is Jennifer Smithton, age twenty."

Lenny reviewed his ever-present notebook. "Not much interesting from the neighbors. She was quiet and polite, never any trouble. Worked late hours. Consensus was that she was a dancer, but no one was sure where she worked. Caller said it was The U, but unable to confirm that. No regular visitors. No boyfriend. A couple of girls visited infrequently, but no names. All in all, a quiet tenant."

Jane added, "She had been here for eight months, paid rent on time. Apartment shows no evidence of blood, so wherever she was killed, it wasn't here. Place was torn apart, obviously looking for something. Either they didn't find it, or they found it in the last place they looked. Our guys checked a few places they missed, but found nothing interesting. I have a list of tenants from the manager. We can run them for priors and see if a link turns up."

Lenny closed his book. "Hope your shots are up to date. Next stop is The U."

· · ·

Lenny and Jane arrived at The U at about 4:00 pm, and Jane marched right up to the front door, whipped out her baton, and banged three times.

Lenny looked on disinterestedly. "I assume this means we're taking an aggressive approach here."

Jane smiled back at him. "You bet your ass we are." She put on her serious face as someone more aggressively yanked open the door.

"Who the fuck is banging on my door?" A large man gripped a large baseball bat. A foot taller and a hundred pounds heavier than Jane, his torn jeans and dingy sleeveless shirt painted a sharp contrast to Jane in her pinstripe blazer and slacks. His scraggly beard still had pieces of his last meal hanging from it.

If he thought his appearance would intimidate Jane, he was mistaken. She took a step forward and raised her badge to his face. "Police, asshole. Put that bat down before I take it from you and shove it up your ass."

Lenny stood two steps back with his hand on his weapon. He half hoped the guy would take a swing. Despite the size difference, he was confident Jane would have the bat in her hands in under three seconds and would crack his kneecap in the next two seconds. He had seen her do it before.

The guy must have sensed something as well. Some primal instinct of his must have recognized danger in front of him. He begrudgingly threw the bat down behind him.

"What the fuck do you want?"

"I want to speak to whatever asshole is in charge here," Jane responded.

"I am Bohdan. I am in charge here."

"Okay, Mr. Asshole-in-Charge, we need some information." She held up a picture. "Do you recognize this girl? Her name is Jenny Smithton, and we think she was a dancer here.

Bohdan replied, "Many girls dance here. Why this one is special?"

"Because earlier this week this girl was murdered," Jane challenged, hoping to get a response.

Bohdan shrugged, "I guess she no dance here anymore. We get new girl."

Jane looked at Lenny in their silent communication. Bohdan obviously knew her and obviously knew she was dead already. "We are going to look around and talk to your employees," Lenny said.

"You have warrant? If no warrant then get the fuck out and no talk to anyone."

The problem with true crime documentaries was that it had taught even the dumbest criminals to ask for a warrant, and while Bohdan was obviously dumb and clearly a criminal, he was right that Lenny and Jane could not proceed without a warrant.

Lenny closed his notebook. "We'll be back with a warrant, and then we will go where we want and talk to everyone."

Bohdan stared at them. "You leave now. Bohdan has work to do."

"Exactly what sort of work do you do here?" Jane asked.

"Bohdan in charge of girls here. Maybe you come work here and Bohdan be in charge of you as well. Maybe you like to have Bohdan in charge." Bohdan sported a lascivious grin.

Lots of folks would back down. Jane leaned forward, grabbed Bohdan's beard and pulled it down until he was face to face with her. "Let me be clear about something, you little prick. I am about two seconds away from ripping off your tiny testicles and shoving them down your throat. I will get a warrant, and I will come back. When I do, I am in charge, and you are nothing but my little bitch. Any questions?" She let go of the beard without breaking her hard stare.

Bohdan stepped back and peered down at her with a derisive sneer. His eyes shifted to Lenny with his hand still on his weapon. "Get the fuck out of here and take that crazy cunt with you." He slammed the door shut.

Lenny made it back to the car before he burst out laughing. "Well, that went well."

Jane smiled back. "Always good for a five-foot-tall woman to put the fear of God in an asshole like that. He definitely knew her and already knew she was dead. The answers to what happened to her and why are inside that building."

"You know we don't have enough evidence to get a comprehensive warrant on that place?"

"Yeah, we need something definitive to justify a thorough search. I'm not sure how, but I'm gonna get a warrant and get that son of a bitch. And I'm gonna rip his balls off if he calls me a cunt again."

Lenny had no doubt that Bohdan and his balls were in big trouble.

An angry Bohdan watched them on a security camera as they got into their cars and left. He would hunt down that girl cop after he got that doctor. He imagined many evil things to do to her when he had her alone. A phone call from Dyyavola, who had been watching everything on screens from his office, interrupted his tortuous fantasies.

Bohdan listened for a moment. "Okay, I will take care of it tomorrow."

CHAPTER NINETEEN

The next morning, Lenny handed Jane two files. "Something interesting popped up when we ran the tenants. Twin brothers live a few doors down. They weren't home yesterday, or at least, had the sense not to answer when we knocked. They both have a history of assault and drug use, mainly meth."

"Not meth heads. You know I hate tweakers."

"That's not even the good part," he said as he laid the files in front of her. "Let me introduce you to JT and JL Hobbins. In case you were wondering, JT is short for Jethro Thunder. Want to take a stab at what JL stands for?"

"If it is anything but Jethro Lightning, I will be both disappointed and furious."

"We have a winner."

Jane compared the files until she shook her head. "What sort of redneck, inbred, country shit is this? Twin Jethros? Thunder and Lightning? How the fuck do you even tell them apart?"

"It looks like JT has one more tooth in front than JL," Lenny added.

"That's not a tooth. It's a blackened nub."

"I agree it will not scare any apples, but it's a tooth to him."

"All right. Let's go find these idiots. It's not yet noon, so they should still be asleep."

Twenty minutes later, they approached the apartment, with Jane still complaining. "I am not in any mood to fight today. I have a brand new blouse on, and I hate that those meth heads like to bite for some reason."

"So you're saying shoot first before they get uppity?"

"Exactly what I'm saying." She proceeded to the door and tapped it with her baton. This time, she kept it in her hand. Movement rumbled from inside, but no one opened the door, so Jane banged louder.

Eventually, a sad-looking creature slowly opened the door. His gaunt shirtless frame was covered in scabs and grime. His unfocused eyes darted around in random circles and his hands trembled.

Jane held up her badge. "Police, are you JT or JL?"

He held out his arm, which had Thunder tattooed on it. "At least we won't have to look at his tooth," Lenny muttered under his breath. Jane elbowed him in the ribs.

"We have some questions. Mind if we come in?" Jane asked, as she nudged through the door.

"Sure, okay," JT slurred as they passed him into the apartment, depressingly similar to other hovels of drug addicts they had been in before. Food, trash, empty beer cans, and dirty laundry competed for space on the floor along with the body of JL. At least they presumed it was JL, as he looked like JT and had a lightning bolt tattooed on his arm.

"Is JL dead?" Jane inquired.

JT laughed. "Nah, man. He's taking a snooze." He picked up a half full beer can and threw it at his brother, hitting him squarely on top of the head. JL sat up with beer dripping off his hair. "Da fuck you do dat for?"

JT laughed too hard to respond. Jane lost patience. "Listen up you two idiots. Jenny Smithton, who lives down the hall, was murdered a few days ago. You guys know anything about that?" She showed them a picture.

JT and JL looked at the picture and then at each other. "Never seen her before," JT claimed.

"You sure about that? She lived five doors down. You never saw her?"

"We don't exactly get out much to meet people," JL offered.

Jane and Lenny questioned them for another ten minutes, but nothing useful emerged. Clearly, JT and JL did not have the ability to pull off a murder without witnesses and without leaving obvious evidence. They barely had the ability to pull off staying alive each day.

"You want to clear them?" Lenny asked.

"They're not clear, but move them to the back burner. We can circle back if nothing else pans out, but I can't see how they could be organized enough to do it."

"Back to the drawing board?"

"Back to The U. As soon as I find an excuse for a warrant, back to The U."

CHAPTER TWENTY

While Jane and Lenny explored the intricacies of meth head interior design, I spent the day relaxing with Banshee at the neighborhood pool and catching up on emails and reading. Banshee put on a good show with his various activities throughout the day. One woman complained about a dog at the pool, and I explained that as a police dog, he was exempt from homeowner's association rules. Technically, not true, but it sounded good, and it sent her off to review her records to see if police dogs were truly exempt from HOA pool rules. I hoped to be long gone before her return.

With evening came cooler temperatures and an opportunity for a run. By 7:00 pm, the temperature dipped below eighty degrees, and more importantly, in Houston, the humidity was less than thirty percent. I collected the gear needed for the run and turned to Banshee, wagging his tail to let me know he would happily join me.

"All right, good boy. You can come, but you have to wear your vest or a leash." Banshee turned his head sideways, trying to understand what I had said, but I decided for him. "Let's go with the vest. Easier for me and it makes you look like a badass, which makes me look like a badass." Banshee eagerly wiggled into his vest.

• • •

Parked on the street four houses down, a white van, the kind normally used by workers, attracted no attention in the neighborhood, but no workers waited inside.

"Maybe we break in tonight and cut him into little pieces," Bohdan suggested to his partner in the passenger seat, who seemed capable of only grunting or farting to communicate, and fortunately, grunted in reply. Bohdan still fumed over his being kicked in the groin and hassled by the cops. He would resolve one of these issues tonight. Like all of his ideas, he harbored a simple plan. Wait until dark, then break in and kill the doctor. But not before cutting off his balls and shoving them down his throat.

An even simpler plan came along fifteen minutes later when Doc and Banshee left the house for a run and started down the street at a matching pace. Master criminal Bohdan revised his plan. "When he comes back, we get out of van and shoot him, then leave." His partner farted in agreement.

• • •

I hustled out with Banshee, anticipating the run, and found Carl outside admiring his trees. "Evening, Doc. Trees came out great, don't you think?"

"Fantastic, Carl. We will refer to this time as your cubism period."

"Uh, okay. You going for a run?"

"Now that you mention it, I find myself out here in running gear. Maybe I will go for a run."

"Is the dog going with you?"

"Great idea, Carl. Wish I had thought of it."

"Dogs are supposed to be on a leash."

"Banshee is kind of special. He doesn't need a leash. He has immunity from the leash laws, as he's a police dog."

Carl thought about this for a moment. "But you're not a police officer," Carl observed proudly.

"Correct, Carl, but Banshee is a police dog, no matter who he's with. Let's go, boy." And we took off down the street.

Banshee stayed exactly one pace to my left and kept up the whole way. He ignored other pedestrians, dogs, and a few squirrels to stay right at my side. A comfortable four miles in 29 minutes, not too shabby. I felt refreshed, but a little winded, and Banshee seemed ready to go another four miles.

We slowed to a walk to cool down as we turned the corner to my street. A couple of car doors slammed and two large men rushed out of a white van. They looked vaguely familiar, and as I tried to remember them, they purposefully zeroed in on us from fifty yards away. I couldn't be sure, but better to be safe than sorry.

"ALERT, BANSHEE." Banshee immediately perked up his ears, pulled in closer to me and scanned for threats. With the alert command, he is trained to seek threats and to attack without further commands. Every muscle tensed up as he noted the two men's approach. I felt I had a loaded weapon at my side who would attack immediately if he detected any hostile movements.

I casually stretched and rubbed my back, and at the same time, reached for the Glock 26 secured in the small of my back. A perfect concealed carry weapon, light and compact, it sends ten 9 mm rounds down range, and it has no safety. Simply aim and shoot. I had spent quite a few hours at the range with this weapon.

I rarely jog with a gun, but I do if I have recently pissed off some mobster types, and it had seemed like a good idea. I now had a loaded weapon in my right hand, in addition to the one at my side.

The men continued to approach with their heads down, talking to each other. I still wasn't sure it was Bohdan, but these two large guys were not my neighbors. Banshee remained on alert.

When they got about twenty yards away, they stopped, pulled guns out of their pockets, and time slowed down as all hell broke loose.

CHAPTER TWENTY-ONE

I immediately dropped to one knee to make myself a smaller target, while I brought my gun up to acquire the sight picture in a well-rehearsed move that I had practiced thousands of times at the range. Muscle memory served me well.

As the sights came up, I put them on the center mass of the man on the right. He now had his weapon pointing at me, and we fired in quick succession. He had a short automatic pistol he held out with one hand. His automatic fire started high and sprayed higher as he held the trigger down. His bullets whizzed overhead. I fired four controlled shots down range, and I was pretty sure all four of them hit. The right-hand shooter went down. I rotated left to turn my attention to the other guy.

By now, adrenaline rushed through me. I fought to keep my hands steady as my pulse and breathing quickened. Sweat slicked my hands as I gripped the pistol more tightly. The air reeked of cordite, and all my senses burned with focus as I turned to the second shooter.

As soon as their hands had come up, Banshee had launched at the man on the left, aiming for the hand holding the gun. His entire world was intent on grabbing that wrist and not letting go. When he hit the wrist at speed, it usually ripped the gun out of the hand, and it always threw the shooter off balance.

Twenty yards may sound like a long way, but Banshee closed quickly. The remaining shooter had another automatic rifle pointed at me and was already depressing the trigger, as I was dealing with his buddy. He had me dead in his sights and would have shot me before I even had time to turn toward him, but Banshee drew his attention instead, as a black mass hurtling at him with teeth bared. Primal instincts took precedence over his mission, and the shooter angled the gun at Banshee as he pulled the trigger.

Banshee had launched at him from five feet away, and the rounds struck him in midair. He fell to the ground in a heap. Banshee was out of the fight; he was not moving.

Only minimally aware of all this, I turned toward the gunman, who now had his weapon pointed straight at me. I knew I had no chance of getting shots off before he hosed me down with his weapon. I braced for the impact of bullets, and suddenly the shooter jerked forward and fell to the ground, dropping his gun. He started to get up and reach for his gun when another shot rang out, hitting him in the head and leaving him prone on the sidewalk.

I swiveled my gun to find the other shooter and discovered Carl standing across the street with a pistol pointed at the downed man. I didn't have time to process Carl's perfect shot. All I knew for sure was that both shooters were down, and so was Banshee.

The whole altercation had taken less than six seconds, and then time sped up again. I quickly scanned for other threats and saw none. I rushed over to the shooters and kicked their guns away. Both of them had multiple wounds and showed no sign of life. My phone was already in my hand, calling 911.

"911, what's your location?"

"Southeast corner of Morningstar and Third, shots fired, shots fired, officer down, officer down." I repeated the message once more, then focused my attention on Banshee.

If you were paying attention from a helicopter in the area, you would note that every police car in a five-mile radius suddenly turned on their lights and sirens and headed my way. Any call of Officer Down initiates a general alert to all vehicles to respond immediately. Watch commander and headquarters would be notified in the next thirty seconds. Paramedics would be dispatched, and trauma units would be put on alert.

Banshee had taken at least three shots to the vest at close range, and while it had slowed the rounds, it had not stopped them. He bled from at least two of the wounds and struggled to breathe. I gently loosened his vest to get a look at the wounds. Two of the wounds actively bled, and I put pressure on them to staunch the blood flow.

I looked up to see Carl staring at me. He had already holstered his weapon and looked unusually calm. "Carl, go to my front closet and grab the red medical bag in there. Run!" I yelled in my commanding voice. Carl took off for my front door. Scenes of violence paralyze most people, but if you give them a simple command, they can follow it, relieved to have something to do. Carl was no different.

The 911 operator was still on speaker. "Scene is secure, repeat, scene is secure. Perpetrators are down. Tell all units to come in weapons cold." I didn't feel like getting shot by some high-strung rookie after all this. I dropped my magazine and emptied the chamber, then laid my gun on the ground beside me.

"Officer down is K-9 unit Banshee. Three gunshots to the chest through his vest. Alive, but critical. Going to need emergency vet trauma activated. Get Officer Tom Nocal and Detectives Skinny Jeans to the scene ASAP." By now, we were being broadcast openly to all responding officers. Word would quickly spread to the right people. I could already hear sirens approaching from multiple directions.

Carl returned with my trauma bag and handed it to me without a word. "Empty your gun and put it on the ground. Gonna be a lot of trigger-happy cops here in a moment." I ripped the pack open and reassessed Banshee, as Carl complied. Banshee was worse. A lot worse.

He was unconscious and unresponsive to any stimuli. His breathing had become ineffective. He was hardly moving any air at all.

I am not a vet, but I had seen plenty of gunshot wounds to the chest in humans. How would I handle a human patient acting like this? ABC. A quick assessment showed his airway was fine, but his breathing was labored and ineffective. Penetrating gunshot wound to the chest and ineffective breathing equaled a pneumothorax in humans. I hoped it meant the same thing in dogs.

A pneumothorax is when air escapes the lung but is still trapped in the chest cavity. The air volume outside the lung grows and compresses the lungs and heart. A compressed lung is useless because lungs need to expand to exchange air. As this condition progressed, it would also compress the heart. My best guess was that Banshee had a tension pneumothorax, and if I did not do something immediately, he would suffocate.

In humans, the solution is simple: put in a chest tube which releases the air and allows the lungs to expand. There are several locations to do this which are easy to locate using landmarks on the body, but I did not know the correct landmarks on a dog.

I grabbed a 14-gauge IV needle from my pack. This is a very large IV or a very small tube, depending on perspective. I was going to use it as a small tube. Several tiny air bubbles formed in the bleeding, which was a good sign. I pushed the needle into the existing wound and advanced it until air whooshed out of the needle. No sweeter sound for a BAFERD. It means that the excess air is draining. In this case, it meant the sound of life breathing back into Banshee. I realized at that moment how much Banshee meant to me, and I was determined not to lose him.

"Come on, Banshee," I pleaded as I willed him to improve.

Instantly, Banshee's breathing improved as he took a deep breath, and his chest expanded properly. I took the needle out of the IV, but left the catheter in the chest. Once all the air was out, I put a syringe on the tip of the catheter to seal it. Air would begin to slowly collect in the chest again, but as long as I removed the syringe intermittently to allow the new air to escape, he should be fine. I was taping everything in place as the first units arrived.

They immediately confirmed that the two shooters were dead and secured the area. Officers pushed back onlookers and put up a mile of yellow tape. Carl pointed out the white van they had exited and more tape was put up.

My attention remained on Banshee. His breathing was much better, but his pulse was rising and getting weaker from the effects of the blood loss. He needed surgery immediately.

An EMS team arrived, and the rookie balked at taking care of a dog. His partner turned to him. "That is not a dog. That is a fucking police officer." The rookie immediately reevaluated his position. I quickly gave a report and explained how the chest tube was working.

I helped them to get pressure bandages on the wounds and started an IV. We got him loaded onto a stretcher, put some oxygen on him, and then he was off. He had a police escort and every intersection on the way to the vet trauma center was blocked by officers, allowing a rapid journey for Banshee. I hoped it would be rapid enough.

CHAPTER TWENTY-TWO

By now, half the Houston police force had converged on the scene. Any officer shooting draws a crowd, but a gang style hit in the middle of a nice neighborhood involving a trauma doctor, a police dog and two goons drew a circus. Every media outlet in the area had arrived, and the police department's communication team scrambled to figure out what the hell had happened, which made me a popular man.

I was coming down from the adrenaline high from the shooting and from working on Banshee. My hands trembled, and I felt emotionally exhausted as I replayed the shooting over and over in my mind. What could I have done differently? Two men were dead, and Banshee fought for his life. I had to conclude that if I had tried to retreat, I would probably be dead.

I held off telling my story until Skinny Jeans arrived, because I wanted to tell it only once. Lenny arrived first, quickly followed by Jane. She stood there, taking in everything. "I suppose you have a story to explain this mess, and why the fuck you think it's our mess to deal with?" Jane had a way of being direct.

I bravely confessed everything briefly, the tattoo, the visit to the tattoo parlor, checking out The U, learning the girl's name and address, and leaving my card with a dancer at The U.

Seething, Jane said, "I don't suppose you know anything about an anonymous call last night giving us the girl's name and address?"

"I can honestly say I did not make any call with that information last night."

Jane shook her head in annoyed disbelief, but did not press the issue. The information had advanced her case, however it was obtained. "You recognize this ugly motherfucker?" Jane asked Lenny as she walked over to the first body.

"Bohdan looked a little better yesterday. Not much better, but a little better."

"You know this guy?" I asked, surprised.

"We were out at The U yesterday, and he wouldn't let us in the place without a warrant," Jane explained. "I was looking forward to cuffing him myself, but this will work just as well. Looks like he was firing a Mac 10. Last time I checked, unregistered machine guns are illegal in Texas. At least now we can get that warrant."

Jane continued to circle the dead body. "Looks like he won't be calling me or anyone else a cunt ever again." That turned more than a few heads, but everyone had the good sense not to respond. "Get started on that warrant."

Lenny leaned over the bodies and looked at them more closely. "How many rounds you fire, Doc?"

"I fired four on the first shooter. Not sure how many Carl fired at the second shooter."

"I fired three at the second shooter, Sir." I wasn't used to this concise and confident version of Carl.

"Why four shots, Doc?"

"Big guys at twenty yards with automatic weapons. Wanted to make sure they went down and stayed down."

Lenny shook his head. "Four out of four rounds on target at twenty yards while being shot at by two machine guns. Nice shooting. And your buddy went three for three. Your street must do pretty well in neighborhood shooting contests." He made a note in his notebook and walked away.

Jane met my eyes. "So, you killed the bad guys and saved the police dog. You are full of surprises, Doc."

Tom's arrival forestalled any more questions from Jane. "Where is he? How is he? What happened?" I had never seen Tom so panicked.

"The goons from last night tried to gun us down in the street. Banshee attacked one while I was dealing with the other. He saved me. Second guy had the drop on me. Without Banshee and Carl, it would be me on the ground."

"Which one of these fuckers shot Banshee?"

"That one. "I pointed at the body of the shooter on the left side.

"Fucker has no idea how lucky he is to be dead already. How bad is Banshee?"

"Pretty bad, Tom. Three shots to the vest at close range. Two of them penetrated. One in the chest and one in the belly. Significant bleeding. Gonna depend on what the surgeon finds. Let's go check on him."

Before we left, I turned to Carl, who quietly observed everything. "I owe you a big thank you. Without your help, I would be dead on the sidewalk."

Carl nodded. "Go check on the dog. We'll talk later."

Skinny Jeans allowed me to go with Tom while they processed the scene, but promised more questions were coming my way. Carl headed directly to the station for his interview.

We arrived at the vet hospital several minutes later to find ten officers milling about, not sure what to do. When an officer is shot, fellow officers hang around to support the family and provide protection. No one was sure what to do with a shot K9 officer.

Tom thanked them and dismissed them. The lady at the front told us that Banshee was still in surgery and to have a seat. Similar to a hospital with uncomfortable chairs, outdated magazines and a TV stuck on a channel no one wanted to watch, the two hour wait seemed like a couple days.

Finally, the surgeon appeared with a relieved reassurance, always a good sign unless the surgeon is a psychopath. "Banshee is gonna be alright. The abdomen wound hit his left kidney. Significant damage and bleeding, so we decided to remove it. None of the other organs were hit."

Tom started to speak, but the surgeon held up his hand. "Relax. Like humans, a dog does not need two kidneys. I expect him to make a full recovery. The bullet that caused the chest wound bounced off a rib and tore through a lung. The damage to the lung was not significant, but it caused a pneumothorax. Whoever put in that makeshift chest tube saved his life. No way he would have survived the trip to surgery without it. He will need some time to recover, but he is gonna make it."

Tom had tears in his eyes as he thanked the surgeon. I myself wasn't crying, but I did have some dust in my eyes that made them water. The surgeon led us back to see Banshee.

Lying on his side with his midsection covered in bandages along with a chest tube and a drain and glassy-eyed from all the drugs, his tail thumped lethargically when he saw us. Tom nuzzled his face to reassure him and received a single kiss for his efforts. Dust came back, and my eyes watered again.

We spent a few minutes rubbing his ears and headed to the station house. Time to face some questions and hopefully, get some answers.

CHAPTER TWENTY-THREE

Skinny Jeans finished their work at the scene, and Tom and I headed to the station house to meet them. I felt nervous when they put me in an interview room, a ten by ten-foot cube with no windows other than a small rectangle at eye level across the door. They bolted the desk and chairs to the floor in an impossibly uncomfortable position. The bare, harshly lit walls held two cameras in opposite corners. Sweat and fear from previous interrogations permeated the air. Most intimidating was that the door lacked a handle on the inside, so that I could open it only from the outside. Although I did not think I had done anything wrong, the room caused me to sweat, but they hadn't cuffed me and had left the door open, so I hoped this would be a friendly interview. Lenny strolled in, which was a good sign. Jane was the ball buster in interviews.

He turned on a recorder and stated names and dates for the record. Before he could begin, I asked, "Do I need a lawyer?"

"For the record, we will not be charging you or your neighbor with any crimes. Pretty much every house in view has a home security camera that captured the entire scene. It was a legitimate shoot in self-defense. You are welcome to call a lawyer, but this interview is only to collect information from you as a witness. You are not being charged with anything."

Relieved, I talked through the events of the shooting, then the events of the last few days leading up to it. He jumped from topic to topic, but I kept my answers short and focused. I disclosed everything, except Jean's making the anonymous call; no reason to get her involved. She might be more dangerous than the Ukrainians.

Jane came into the room only once, when I mentioned my conversation with Linda. "Let's go back to this devil character. What did you call him?"

"Dyyavola," I replied.

"Care to spell that for me?" Lenny asked.

"It's Ukrainian for devil. You'll have to look it up." Lenny underlined something in his notebook, and Jane continued.

"So Linda said this devil guy is in charge? The idiot in charge of all these other idiots?"

"That's correct."

"And she didn't say anything else about him?"

"Not really. She was terrified of him, said he was evil and that no one knew his real name."

"Sounds like the type of guy who might murder a girl and send a couple of hit men after a doctor." She turned to Lenny. "This Dyyavola character is now number one on our list. We need to figure out who he is and talk to him. He doesn't sound like the type of guy that will let this slide."

"Well, that is reassuring as hell," I quipped.

Jane leaned forward and looked at me earnestly. "Doc, I gotta be clear. This thing worries me, and I don't worry easily. It's really fucking rare to have someone send two guys out to shoot a doctor in the middle of a friendly neighborhood. Only a psycho does something like that, and psychos don't give up easily. I need to let you know that we'll have to keep the Glock in evidence."

"I have another Glock and a shotgun."

She nodded. "You're free to go, but don't leave the city without notifying us. Keep your head on a swivel and stay safe out there."

Lenny closed his notebook. "The way he shoots, we should probably warn the Ukrainians to be careful."

"Go home and get some rest, Doc. We got work to do," Jane ordered, as she escorted me out of the oppressive room. I hadn't realized how constrained I felt in there until I experienced the freedom of leaving it. I made a note not to end up back in an interrogation room ever again.

•   •   •

Lenny and Jane compared notes again. "Well, this has turned into a real shit show," Jane sighed.

Lenny rifled through his notebook, which had quickly filled up. "You got that right. We got a torture and murder of a young girl, the attempted murders of a police dog and a doctor, and two dead Ukrainians. Something tells me we are going to be hearing from on high soon."

"Sooner than you think," Captain Shriver quipped as he walked in with Lieutenant Adams. Captain Bill Shriver had been with the department for twenty-eight years. After working his way up from patrol through major crimes and homicide to his current position as a captain, he was affectionately known as Captain BS, never said to his face. Whilst his nickname suggested otherwise, Captain Shriver was, in fact, a hard man who did not accept bullshit from anyone and always made his thoughts clear.

Jane and Lenny stood, but were quickly waved back to their seats as the Captain drew up a chair. "Probably not a big surprise, but the Chief is interested in this one. It's now a priority to get some resolution. What do we have?"

Jane looked at Lenny, who referred to his notebook. Jane replied, "I'll get straight to the point, Captain. We don't have much. Before today, we had an isolated gruesome murder of a young lady, but we had no suspects or leads. Now we have crazy Ukrainians shooting up a nice neighborhood. Unfortunately, both suspects are dead."

The Captain waved that off. "Saves us time and resources prosecuting their dumb asses. Let's focus on who is in charge of this whole thing. The girl and the goons both worked at The U, so let's focus all of our efforts on that shithole. Someone over there knows something, so let's go in hard and fast and lean on everybody to see who cracks first. I want answers, and I want them soon."

"We will make it happen, Sir," Jane assured him.

"And who the hell is this AJ Docker character, messing in our investigation and acting like he is living in the OK Corral? You tell that young man to stop interfering in this or I will throw his ass in jail until I am caught up on my paperwork. And I am currently two years behind on reports. Is that clear?"

"Yes, Sir," Skinny Jeans replied in unison. The Lieutenant chimed in, "Perfectly clear, Sir. We will make sure he stays out of this and get a team together to search The U."

The Captain stood up, indicating that the meeting was over. He filed out of the room, and the Lieutenant evaluated Skinny Jeans. "Questions?" He asked.

"No, Sir," Jane replied.

"We will sort this out, Sir," Lenny assured him. The Lieutenant nodded and left the room.

"You forgot to tell him about our other suspects, the Jethro twins," Lenny teased.

"The least promising suspects in Houston. I think we can officially write them off and focus all of our energies on The U. Call the judge, and get the warrant."

"Already on it. Let's go pick it up."

CHAPTER TWENTY-FOUR

Tom offered me a ride home, and on the way, we stopped to check on Banshee. Sedated and sleeping comfortably for the night, he was doing as well as we could hope. Without complications, he would recover fully.

We settled back into his truck, and I talked him into a stop at IHOP. Who knew shooting bad guys and answering questions could make me so hungry?

We walked in and Little D greeted me from the grill. "Evening, Doc. Or should I say, Doc Holliday?" He chuckled with a deep, rich laugh.

We slid into a booth and Tom commented, "You know that one might stick to you. Doc Holliday." He guffawed loudly.

Gladys came over. "Well, well, well. If it ain't our hero? And here with a handsome police friend. Is he single?"

"He's single by the choices of his first two wives. Not up to your standards, Gladys. You deserve better than a mall cop." Tom rolled his eyes and ordered two eggs over easy, toast and bacon. Gladys smiled and left.

"She didn't take your order." Tom noted.

"It's okay. I have a standing order here. Now, what the fuck are we gonna do about this mess?"

"I spoke to Jane and the Chief. They're willing to turn their heads on our previous activities unofficially investigating the murder, but they don't want any more interference. We stay out of the way and leave it to Skinny Jeans." Tom presented the idea tentatively, expecting a negative reaction.

The emotional impact of the night caught up to me, and I pounded the table and looked at him fiercely. "Not gonna happen. Not after what they did to Jenny and then coming after me on my street."

Tom seemed to have been hoping for that reaction and matched my intensity. "Someone sent those two motherfuckers who shot my dog. Everyone involved is gonna pay for that."

"All right, so we are agreed. We're still on the case."

"Agreed. What's our next step?"

"Next step is to finish this delicious food, go home and shower and sleep for about twelve hours. After that, I have no fucking idea, but I'm taking tomorrow off."

"You and me both."

•　　•　　•

Dyyavola spoke quietly, which forebode seething anger. "This doctor shoots Bohdan and Yakiv? And they miss doctor and only shoot dog? And not even kill dog?" A prolonged and vile Ukrainian curse followed.

"We must clean up club. Police be here soon and tear this place apart. Move everything to warehouse. No one knows about that place. Make sure no drugs or guns here. Put some drugs and gun in Bohdan's apartment where they will be found. And warn girls anyone who talks will be chopped up into little pieces. Anyone mentions me gets chopped up in even smaller pieces. You now in charge Fedir. Do not fuck up."

Fedir nodded and left to carry out the instructions before the police arrived.

• • •

Jane and Lenny drove rapidly to pick up the warrant. "Doc is lucky to still be walking and talking. Taking on two guys with machine guns with only a pistol and a dog is not a fair fight," Lenny observed.

"He wasn't lucky. He was prepared. He went jogging with his gun on him, because he knew trouble might come, and he maintained situational awareness."

"How about that shooting? I couldn't hit four out of four at that distance with rounds coming back at me."

"Again, it's preparation. He practiced that move at the range over and over. He knew in his mind what he would do in that situation. So, when it happened, he didn't need to think, only react. Might be something to that BAFERD title after all."

Lenny closed his notebook. "The two shooters lived together, and we have a search warrant for their apartment and for The U. Do you want to hit them tonight or wait until the morning?"

Jane thought for a minute. "Let's hit their apartment tonight. I doubt we will find anything important, but you never know until you look. The club will have to wait until tomorrow when we have a full team. I'm too tired to deal with all of this overnight, and we need some more info before we go charging into The U, anyway."

"The warrant is ready, so let's get it done."

Jane and Lenny arrived at the Ukrainians' apartment thirty minutes later with a forensics team and some extra muscle. They were not expecting trouble, but they needed to be prepared for the possibility after the shooting.

The landlord once again let them in, and the first thing they noted was the overwhelming mess. "I guess this place doesn't come with maid service." Lenny said as he pulled his shirt up over his nose. The place smelled nasty. Reeking, dirty clothes covered the floor, and dirty dishes and half eaten rotting containers of food grew mold. "Maybe the bathrooms will be cleaner."

Jane did not want to think about it. "Okay team, let's go."

It took only about thirty minutes to go through the place. "We got two handguns and a little bit of coke. Wasn't able to find their college diplomas. No phones, no computers, and no address books. If you ask me, someone already cleared out the good stuff and left us the coke and guns. I don't think this thing is over yet." Lenny sighed.

Jane nodded. "Definitely more to this. Wrap it up. We got one more stop tonight, and then we are gonna visit The U tomorrow."

CHAPTER TWENTY-FIVE

I arrived home around midnight to a blissfully quiet street. The reporters and most of the yellow tape had disappeared. Carl's warm interior lighting brightly lit the living room with open blinds, as he paced around his couch. I knocked on his door lightly, mindful of disturbing the quiet. "Carl, it's Doc." I didn't want him shooting me through the door.

Carl smiled as he opened the door, looking calmer than usual. "Evening, Doc."

"Good evening, Carl. You got a minute to talk?"

"Sure, come on. Can I get you a drink?"

"I'll take some water, please." I wandered through Carl's house curiously. We had lived next to each other for two years, and I saw him outside four or five times a week, but I had never been inside his home. Not sure what I expected, but the house was meticulously neat and cleaner than I would have guessed. My eyes rested on a picture of Carl in a military uniform next to a set of ribbons and medals, including a Congressional Medal of Honor. The surprises kept coming this evening.

"Let's sit out back. Mosquitoes should be asleep by now," Carl suggested.

We sat back in lounge chairs next to the pool. Carl turned on the waterfalls, giving a peaceful background noise that blocked out the noise of the city. The comfortable silence lasted a full minute.

"Interesting day today. I should start with a thank you for saving my life," I offered.

Carl looked embarrassed. "No big thing. You would have done the same for me. That's what neighbors do. They help each other out."

"True, but usually help is something like borrowing a power tool or holding a ladder. Shooting a gangster wielding a machine gun is above and beyond."

"Well, in all fairness, the gun was pointed at you, and I shot him in the back. I was most worried about missing and hitting you accidentally."

For the first time, I thought about the geometry and realized he was correct. If he had missed the Ukrainian, I was directly in the line of fire. That realization gave me a fresh case of the shakes.

He noticed and managed a brief chuckle. "Don't worry. I don't miss from inside twenty-five yards. Ever."

"I saw the medals. You were in the army?"

"Yes, Sir. Served twenty-one years. Most of it on tours in Afghanistan. Left as an E7 Sergeant First Class. I ran a platoon of fifty soldiers and made sure the lieutenants didn't get everyone killed."

"Why haven't you ever mentioned your military experience?"

Carl considered for a moment. "A lot of bad things happened to good people over there, and I lost a lot of friends along the way. Easier to move forward with my new life without looking back. I work from home now on my computer, and life is simpler."

"I don't mean to be nosy, but I am pretty sure one of those medals I saw is a Congressional Medal of Honor. I assume there is a story behind that."

Carl remained still and got a faraway look in his eyes. "There is for damn sure a story. We were over in Afghanistan on routine patrol.

There were six of us in total. I was leading the group to a village we had visited twenty times before, a friendly village that reported Taliban movements to us, and we provided protection for them. Not a place we were expecting trouble."

He shook his head as the memories flooded back. "The IED went off when we were about seventy meters from the village. If they had waited until we were in the village, they would have had us surrounded. But they hit us early when they were still hiding in the village, so our flanks and back were clear. The initial blast took out two of our guys. Scooter and T-bo never had a chance. The rest of us were not in good shape. Two guys were unconscious. Slick Willy had shrapnel in both arms and wasn't mobile. I was in the best shape with a broken femur and some minor cuts.

"The situation was dire. The Taliban started firing their AK 47s at us, and we had nowhere to go. Fortunately, most of them couldn't hit the broadside of a barn at five feet, but they had a lot of ammo. Everyone was on full automatic, and there was lead flying everywhere. Willy grabbed one guy, and I grabbed the other, and we hunkered down behind our vehicle. Willy got on the radio and called for help, but the choppers were fourteen minutes out.

"Fourteen minutes doesn't sound very long. It's only 840 seconds, but it was the longest 840 seconds of my life. I returned fire in controlled bursts and dropped some Hajis. But every time one went down, another would pop up. Willy helped as best he could, but he could barely hold a weapon with his injuries. I fired every round from all six of my mags, and the choppers were still eleven minutes out."

"Willy started handing me his mags and the mags from the other two guys. I had 720 rounds total, and I fired every one of them at them sons of bitches. The Taliban made a few charges, but each time I stopped them. With the choppers still two minutes out, I went through the last of the mags we had on us. There were still some more in the vehicle and on Scooter and T-bo, but getting them would be a slow process with my broken leg and expose me to murderous fire. But there was no choice. If I stayed still, we died.

"So, I jumped up and threw myself into the vehicle. I still remember the feel and sound of those two bone edges grinding together. Good for a nice shot of adrenaline. And I needed it since I was hit twice by enemy fire, one in the shoulder and one in the arm. I was down to one good arm, but that was enough to reload and keep firing until the choppers arrived. Final count was over 1000 rounds expended and eighteen dead Taliban. We lost Scooter and T-bo that day, but the rest of us made it out with some scars and a hell of a story."

This was surreal. I had never known this side of Carl. "That's fucking incredible. They should make a movie out of your story. You're a real live hero."

Carl laughed and refilled his drink. "No movies. And I am not a hero. I was a scared peckerhead with a lot of training and a lot of weapons. When the choice is to fight or die, it's easy to fight. And I would prefer to keep this quiet. I shared this with you because we fought together today, and we are now brothers. You understand the toll that violence and death take from people, but the average Joe on the street cannot comprehend the burden I carry."

I certainly respected those feelings. "You have my word. This stays between us," and I tipped my glass of water at him. "I assume that you always carry a weapon on you these days."

Carl reached to his back and pulled out another handgun. "One thing I learned in the Stan, always have a weapon on you. I carry from morning to bedtime. Better to have a gun and never need it than to need a gun and not have it."

"Well, I sure am glad you were around today. Things would have been different without your help. You okay with what happened today?"

Carl laughed. "Shooting that piece of shit? Don't worry about me. I feel worse about stepping on a bug. From the moment they got out of the van, it was clear they were looking for trouble. They picked the wrong street. Hopefully, their buddies have the good sense to stay away, but I doubt it."

"I don't mean to be impolite, but this is a totally different side of you than what I normally see. I mean, usually you seem a bit goofy out there in your front yard."

Carl laughed generously. "You caught me, Doc. All that time I was screwing around outside, I am watching people and looking for patterns. The Sans Box makes you a little paranoid. Helps me to sleep at night if I've made some regular patrols of the area each day. And the goofy part is an act to put people at ease. When people underestimate you, it gives you an advantage."

I certainly would not make the mistake of underestimating Carl again. "I assume you are gonna be okay if they come back?"

"My biggest problem if they come back will be scraping them off my driveway when I'm done. Unless they call in artillery fire or bring a tank, I'm pretty sure I'll have the advantage."

"Good to know. Good night, Carl, and thanks, again. Let me know if I can ever do anything for you."

"Please, keep all of this quiet, and we can call it even. Good night, Doc."

CHAPTER TWENTY-SIX

At home, plopped on the couch, I hit the play button on my music system and left it on shuffle. I wanted to see what the universe wanted me to hear, apparently The Gambler by Kenny Rogers. "Know when to hold 'em, know when to fold 'em. Know when to walk away and know when to run." The lyrics seemed appropriate for my mood.

Alone for the first time since the shooting, I carefully processed what had happened. In my job I see too much death, but they die because of illness or injuries that occurred before they got to the ER. They didn't die because of me.

My whole adult life has been about learning to save lives, not take them. Although my practice at the gun range prepared me to take a life, and at some level, I must have known it was a possibility, I never expected it to happen. I didn't feel good about the shooting, but surprised myself that I didn't feel bad about it, either. The more I thought about it, the more confused I felt. In the end, the best I could come up with was being okay with it, accepting it. I did not ask for it to happen, and I did what was necessary to survive. Here in my house and not in the morgue seemed fair to me.

I turned off the lights and collapsed in bed. A shower could wait for the morning.

• • •

Back in the ER, Skinny Jeans met with Jean. As usual, Jane interrogated, and Lenny took notes.

"I want to be clear that Doc is not going to be charged with anything. We want some background info on him, and everyone says you know him the best. What can you tell us about him?" Jane asked.

"I can tell you a whole lot. Question is, what will I tell you. Doc is a very private person and doesn't like his private business in the open," Jean replied.

"Fair enough. You have my word. None of this goes in the report. We want to understand who we are dealing with," Jane replied, glancing at Lenny, who closed his notebook and put it away.

Jean sighed. "Okay, but this stays between us. Doc is a complicated character. He grew up with a mom who was drunk all the time, and he learned to fend for himself early on. Because of that, he doesn't trust many people and relies on himself to get by. He is book smart, like most doctors, but he's also streetwise. Doc notices everything and misses nothing going on around him. He processes information faster than most and makes decisions quickly, like he has already worked through scenarios in his head and can react by instinct when shit happens. That makes him a great ER doctor."

"You said his mom was a drunk. Any concern that he's one as well?" Lenny asked.

Jean laughed. "Doc ain't had a drink in his adult life. He quit drinking in high school. He saw what it did to his mom, and he wanted no part of that for himself."

"Talk to me about this girl. Why is he doing all this for a girl he didn't even know?" Jane asked.

"Doc is a champion for the vulnerable. He always goes the extra mile for someone who is being taken advantage of. If he gets a case where a child or mental health patient is wronged, he stays on it until the situation is fixed.

"Many years ago, we had this dad come in with his son who had a simple broken arm from a fall. Nothing major, but the dad was distraught. Doc learned the dad had recently been laid off, and they were homeless, living out of their car. Dad was from Pakistan where he used to run a medical lab, but the family had to flee from escalating violence in the area. He didn't know much English and couldn't get a decent job in Houston.

"Doc brought the family into his home and arranged for the dad to get some English lessons and for the son to get enrolled in school. He made some calls and got the dad a job in the hospital lab department. Today, Mr. Bukhari runs the hospital lab and that young boy is in his second year of medical school."

"I imagine Mr. Bukhari is grateful," Lenny observed.

"You bet your ass he is. ER gets priority for lab results every day since he's been in charge. Pisses off the rest of the hospital, but nothing they can do about it. Doc quietly goes out of his way to help people and asks for nothing in return. But what he gets is loyalty. A whole bunch of folks around here are loyal to Doc because of all the kind things he has done.

"He doesn't have any family, so he considers these patients to be his nieces and nephews that he needs to watch out for. He would make a hell of a dad if he ever settled down."

"So, no regular girlfriend in the picture?" Jane asked.

Jean laughed for a full ten seconds before she could answer. "What day of the week is it and I will tell you who the lucky gal is. He dates for fun, but has never had a serious relationship. And before you ask, they all know, and they all adore him."

"How do you think he will handle the shooting? Gonna mess him up or not?" Lenny asked.

"Doc will be fine." Jean smiled as she thought of him.

Jane looked at her closely. "You really admire the guy, don't you?"

"I have been here for twenty-six years and have seen a lot of docs come and go. Most of them, the job gets the better of them. Day after day of violence and gore and grief gets to most people. It changes them. They can become bitter, angry, or selfish. But not Doc. He stays the same no matter what this place throws at him. He keeps everyone sane when we should all be in the loony bin. In a room full of BAFERD's, he is the most BAFERD of them all. He is a good man, and we need him around here. You guys need to catch the assholes coming for him. I will take it personally if something bad happens to him."

"Thanks for your time. I can assure you, we will get those mother-fuckers," Lenny stated, and he and Jane headed for the door.

CHAPTER TWENTY-SEVEN

A rare eleven hours of sleep left me feeling recharged in the morning. I showered and dressed, ate some breakfast, and then made some plans. These guys were not going away, and I still had not figured out what had happened to Jenny. I had the day off, so I headed over to the golf range to hit some balls and clarify my thoughts. In a shocking development, Carl was hanging around outside when I went to the car.

"You going golfing?" Carl asked. I guess we were back to our goofy Carl character on patrol. Even though no one was there to see our act, I played along.

"Nah. Just thought it would be good to have these in my car in case those guys come back and I run out of bullets," as I put my clubs in the trunk.

"Okay. How's the dog?"

"He's gonna make it. He had a collapsed lung and a lacerated kidney, but he'll recover. Thanks again for your help yesterday, Carl. He would not have survived without the supplies you grabbed from my house."

Carl swelled up with pride. "We make a pretty good team, don't we, Doc?"

"We certainly do, Carl. We certainly do. Have a good day and stay safe."

"Okay, Doc, you too. Hey, what do you think of the trees? They look great, don't they?" he said, pointing at his cuboid monstrosities. "I can do your trees as well if you want."

"Please don't touch my trees, Carl. Would be a shame to have to shoot another person this week. Have a good day."

• • •

The Hermann Park golf course driving range, a large park right next to the Medical Center and to Ben Taub Hospital, and an oasis in the city, offered beautiful park space and cheap rounds of golf. At night, it transformed into a good place to buy drugs or get mugged.

I bought a bucket of balls and headed to the mats. I started with my 8-iron, taking aim at a flag 157 yards away. My swing went on autopilot as I worked through the events of the last few days. I remembered Jenny's first visit to get her arm fixed, when she seemed so sad and yet so hopeful. Then, a few hours later, they dropped her at our entry, beaten to death. No, not beaten to death, beaten and tortured, but the AVM killed her.

So, her death was unexpected and came before she could tell them the information they wanted. But what information? And who was "them?" Someone had to be behind all of this. Bohdan and the other shooter were low-level lackeys sent to do a chore, certainly not in charge. Someone gave orders, someone powerful enough to control and order men like Bohdan to kill, cruel enough to torture someone like Jenny for information, and desperate enough to have her dropped off at the ER after her unexpected death. Was this Dyyavola character that powerful? The key was at The U, but I couldn't get within a hundred feet of the front door.

A voice I recognized interrupted my musings. "Hey, mister, you need anything to take the edge off?"

I turned to find myself face to face with Squirrel, not his real name, but an obvious choice with his slight frame, constant twitching, and beady eyes. A well-known dealer and user of methamphetamines, the fact that he was still alive defied the odds. Peddling meth on the streets of Houston is about as violent a lifestyle as he could choose. On any given day, we might see Squirrel for an overdose or for getting his ass kicked in a fight, many of which he started, and none of which he won. Most involved only fists and kicks, but occasionally, bottles, bats and other solid objects caused more damage. He had been knifed a few times and shot once in the arm. He had no interest in rehab or in changing his lifestyle. He needed a miracle to survive another year on the streets.

"Hey, Doc, is that you?" A perk of a job in the emergency room is that crack heads and sociopaths know your name and recognize you on the street.

I leaned casually on my club.

"Squirrel, my man, you're looking good. Haven't seen you in a while."

"Yeah, it's been a good run. Haven't lost a fight in weeks."

"Don't you get tired of all that fighting?"

"Part of the job, man. The important thing is not to quit each time you have a setback. Keep doing your deals and moving forward. Ignore the beat downs and enjoy the crank."

"You stay safe out there. I don't want to see you in the ER any time soon for fighting or overdose. And I'll pass on the meth for today. Do you really sell much of that stuff on the golf course? Wouldn't think that meth and golf are a likely combination."

Squirrel smiled and showed off his three remaining teeth. The poor guy could floss with a small rope if ever so inclined. "You would be surprised how far a motherfucker can hit a golf ball when they're cranked up. Of course, they can't putt for shit, but they don't care when they're flying that high. Okay, Doc, you be careful, too. I heard some crazy fucking foreigners were shooting up a nice neighborhood trying to whack some dumb ass doctor yesterday."

"Thanks, Squirrel. I'll be careful." Squirrel sauntered off, looking for his next customer, as I pondered the irony of receiving life advice from a meth head named Squirrel at a golf range. I had to admit it was pretty good advice, to keep moving forward and don't quit.

By the time I finished my bucket of balls, I had a plan.

• • •

Lenny sat down in Jane's office and peered at her across her desk. A picture of her family from last Christmas radiated joy from a transported memory. Working with her every day on violent crime, Lenny often forgot that she was a mom to two young daughters. Pulling himself back to grim reality, Lenny summarized his findings. "So far we got nothing on the ownership. Place was bought years ago, fully paid in cash. Owner is some LLC with offshore owners. Computer nerds are tracking it, but they said not to count on their finding anything. It leads offshore and disappears into a mess of different companies. Long and short, we got no idea who owns the place."

Jane sighed. "Are they up to date on taxes?"

"They pay them like clockwork each year. Comes from a check drawn on the corporate name, but that account is a dead end as well."

"So, we got a skanky bar with unknown ownership with one female and two male employees dead in the last few days. Seems like a dangerous place to work. How do you want to handle it?" Jane asked.

"I say we go in hard. We have ten uniforms ready to search the place top to bottom and to talk to everyone in there. We divide up all the employees and pressure them one on one until someone cracks. We threaten to come back every day until we get what we need. Someone has to squeak eventually. We got the warrant. Let's get going."

"Okay, let's go this afternoon when some folks are there. Do you think we are gonna get anything out of this?"

"Hopefully, at least one useful lead. More likely some nasty contact disease, but hopefully a lead."

• • •

I met Tom at the vet hospital that afternoon to spend some time with Banshee, who looked pathetic with the chest tube, IV and bandages. He still liked his ears and belly scratched, though.

"Shame they had to shave your dog. Maybe you can use some of that dog hair as a weave to fill in that mustache. Looking a little patchy," I commented.

"Women dig this mustache," Tom said as he stroked his mustache.

"Yeah, but men dig it more." This earned a typical one finger response. "Heard about any progress on who is behind all of this?" Doc asked.

"Not a damn thing. Finance nerds are trying to figure out who owns the place, but they keep running into dead ends. No one will talk. We got nothing."

"Kind of hard to solve the problem when we don't know who is causing it."

"We might have had a lead if you didn't kill all the witnesses."

"True. To be fair, I only killed one witness, but it probably kept you out of prison. I would hate to think what you would do to the guy who shot Banshee if he were still alive."

"You're probably right. That guy could have had a very bad accident at the jail."

"What do we have going for next steps?"

"Skinny Jeans is gonna hit the place this afternoon. We need to see if we can figure out who is in charge. Until we get that guy, no one is safe."

"We need to get Banshee healthy. Then none of them will be safe."

Banshee thumped his tail in agreement.

CHAPTER TWENTY-EIGHT

Lenny and Jane pulled up outside The U at 5 pm with a warrant and ten officers. Fedir met them at the door wearing jeans and a stained white muscle shirt. His eyes lit up as he leered at Jane in her dark blue pantsuit. "Welcome to The U. You want table together to enjoy the evening? Or maybe you want to dance for all your coworkers. Amateur night is on Tuesday, but we let you up on stage if you want to make some money."

The officers bristled, but Jane held up a hand to calm them. Accustomed to ignorant shitheads like Fedir, she was well equipped to handle it. "You know, I was gonna make this quick and easy, mostly because I don't want to spend so much time here, but since you want to play the part of an asshole, I think we're gonna take our time." She turned to the officers. "No one leaves until they're all interviewed. Employees can come in, but no customers until I say so." She turned back to Fedir. "I'll start with you since you are in charge, and therefore maybe the least stupid one here. Gonna be a long evening. Where's your office?"

Jane took one officer with her to follow Fedir to an office that contained a desk with a few drawers, a shelf unit with scattered papers and a bunch of junk on it, and an upholstered couch that likely had been a solid beige, but now showed a pattern of stains best not contemplated. She briefly wondered if only one set of gloves had strength enough to protect from whatever that couch harbored.

Jane sat at the desk and went through the drawers. "I don't suppose you have any employee files or corporate records lying around for me to review?" Jane asked sarcastically. Fedir answered when Jane cut him off. "It was a rhetorical question you fucking imbecile. Go sit on the couch, don't touch anything, and don't say a fucking word until I ask you a question." Jane meant for the couch sitting to be a punishment, but Fedir, oblivious to the stains, sprawled comfortably on the couch. "Fucking nasty," Jane observed.

The desk and shelf unit contained nothing of interest. Various bills and receipts, some recent and some from years past with some random notes and doodles littered every surface with the usual collection of pens, paper clips and a stapler commonly found in an office. Nothing useful.

"Where's your computer?" Jane asked Fedir. He looked confused. "Your computer. Where is the fucking computer you use?"

"Fedir does not have a computer. Fedir does not need a computer. Fedir smart and uses brain to run business." He tapped his exceptionally round head to clarify.

"I may tap that brain of yours with a fucking baton if you keep bullshitting me." She held up the end of the cord that was plugged into the wall. "If you don't have a computer, then why the fuck do you have an Internet connection in this office?"

Fedir shrugged. "Cord was there when I took job. I no use the cord. Maybe one day I clean up office and throw out cord. Until then, cord stays in wall." Jane doubted cleaning day was coming soon.

"Who is Dyyavola?" she asked him.

He shrugged his shoulders. "I do not know any devils."

"Not an actual devil. Dyyavola. The guy in charge here."

"Fedir in charge here, not devil."

She peppered him with questions, but he gave up nothing useful.

Lenny had no better luck downstairs. The men clammed up and played stupid, just like Fedir. None of them knew anything and just worked there. The girls shared their names and identification cards, but stuck to the story that Fedir was in charge. They were clearly terrified, and refused to say anything beyond Fedir being in charge. All were offered an opportunity to leave with protection, and some thought hard, but in the end, no one was willing to say anything.

Finally, Lenny whispered to Jane. "We got nothing. Everybody knows the shooters, but no one has any idea why they might have been hunting a doctor last night. Everyone says Fedir is in charge, and they have never met any other bosses. No one knows this Dyyavola character. And everyone is scared."

"Sounds like someone has been coaching witnesses. Probably told to stay in line or end up like Jenny. I got nothing from Fedir. He played stupid the entire time, although it may not have been much of an act for him. Search turned up nothing illegal, unless you count filth as a criminal offense. The only thing we found of any interest was a certificate from the health department from seven years ago authorizing them to open. Hard to believe this place ever passed a health inspection. You're right, we got nothing."

"You think this Fedir guy could actually be in charge?"

"No way. Fedir can barely handle being in charge of getting himself dressed in the morning. He's a fucking idiot who has been told what to say. We haven't met the real boss yet."

"Surveillance? We shook the tree. Let's see if it causes them to make any mistakes."

"Set it up. Round the clock on this place until I say stop. I want eyes on all entrances and pictures of everyone coming and going. Something's got to break."

They made their way to the front door where a smiling Fedir met them. "Thank you for visiting. And offer still stands if you would like to shake your police titties on stage. Would be very popular with guests."

Jane smiled as she stepped up to Fedir. "I will keep that in mind. But the only way these titties are shaking on stage is if I get up there with you and beat the shit out of you. They would bounce every single time I kicked your tiny little balls another inch into your guts. In fact, we can go on stage now if you want." She stared at him from inches away as he processed the challenge.

"Fuck you, stupid cunt. Leave." An angry Fedir backed away and slammed the door.

"The last guy who called you a cunt was dead within 24 hours," Lenny observed.

"With any luck, that pattern will continue." As they were walking to the car, Jane asked, "How much do you think I could make shaking my police titties on stage?"

Lenny kept walking. "No fucking comment."

. . .

Later that night, Fedir reported to Dyyavola. "Police come, but they find nothing. No one talks. We are good for now, but they are probably watching."

"Let them watch. We give them nothing to see. What have you learned? How will we kill this rodent?"

"Is going to be tough, Boss. Everyone on the street is very aware after what happened. No way we can park or walk in the neighborhood. Too dangerous. And the cops will be watching us."

"Then we get him at work."

"No way, Boss. Metal detectors at door and cops everywhere."

"Then what is plan?"

"We run him down and shoot him in his car. Oleksander and Mykta can drive and shoot and get away fast."

The Boss almost smiled. "This will work. Tell them no more mistakes. Big bonus for each if they kill him. If they fail, I burn their cars. And they will be in trunk when I do it."

Fedir left to deliver the news.

CHAPTER TWENTY-NINE

Refreshed after a day off, I arrived at the ER to muted applause from the staff, probably because those two thugs did not make it to the ER; two more gunshot wounds is a lot of work.

A fourth-year medical student rotating through the ER presented my first patient. "What do we have this morning, Dr. Jones?"

"This is a previously healthy 17-year-old male who was accidentally hit by a BB in the chest. Apparently, his brother was fooling around. The BB gun went off, and he was hit on the left side of the chest. He is in no distress, vitals are stable, and he is breathing normally. There is a small puncture wound on the left chest wall, but no active bleeding. They got a chest X-ray, which was normal, so I want to send him home."

"Sounds reasonable, except where is the BB?"

The student looked at me blankly. "I don't know. But it's not on the chest X-ray, so he should be able to go home."

I pulled up the X-ray. BB's are metal and show up clearly on X-ray. "You've told me where the BB isn't, but not where it is. Let's go talk to this young man and solve the case of the missing BB."

We entered the room, and before I could say a word, the father started in. "Doctor, I ain't no medical genius. But my boy got shot with a high-powered BB and has a hole in his chest. I checked him all over and he ain't got no other holes in him. So that BB went in and did not come out. I know your fancy X-ray says it's not in there, but it is!"

I liked him right away. "Well, Sir, I have to agree with you, except for one point. My fancy X-ray says it's not in the chest, so I'm sure it is not in the chest. But like you, I am also sure it is in his body somewhere, and you are going to be amazed when we find out where it is." I turned to the student, "Order X-rays of the abdomen and pelvis, and I bet we get an answer."

Fifteen minutes later, the student pulled up an X-ray that showed a bright white ball in the right lower pelvis. "I assume that is the BB, but I can't explain how it got to his pelvis."

I smiled and had him stand up. "So, our patient was shot about here," I poked him in the left side of the chest. "What is beneath the skin right here?"

"Chest wall, ribs, lungs and heart."

"Okay, which part of the heart is anterior?"

"The left ventricle."

"What would happen to a small BB that penetrated the left ventricle? Would it be pushed along by the blood, out into the aorta and continue downstream until it finally got stuck in a smaller vessel like the femoral artery?"

The student looked amazed. "He has a hole in his heart?"

"I am betting he does. But a tiny little hole that sealed up after the BB went through. He probably has a little bleeding around the heart that will heal on its own. We will need cardiology to see him and vascular to go get the BB out. Great case."

"Sorry I screwed up. I was ready to send him home."

"That's why they call this a teaching rotation. But here's something you need to remember: when something doesn't make sense, keep searching for the answer. It is one in a million that the BB could end up in his femoral artery with no other symptoms. I've never seen that before and will probably never see a case like that again. But the teaching point is, don't stop looking until you find the answer. That's what makes a good doctor. Now go find him a bed and start the paperwork."

•   •   •

"Loser alert, coming down the hall." Jean called out.

"Okay, everybody look like you're hot and complain about the heat," I said.

"How am I supposed to look like I'm hot?" Deb asked.

"It's hard to do in scrubs, but you can pull it off Deb. Showtime everybody."

"HUHA to you, Doc," Lou said as he strolled in.

"And a fine HUHA to you as well, VP Lou. How can us lowly practitioners of medicine help you today?"

"Excuse me, fellas, I am overheating. I need to go cool down," Deb said with her best Scarlett O'Hara impersonation. Drama queen.

"I came to check on the thermostat and see how things are going down here. Volumes are still down from where they need to be," Lou said as he inspected the thermostat.

"Volumes are down and temperatures are up. Looks like nobody is happy in the ER. Any chance we can turn the temperature back down in here? Seventy-four is too hot."

"Doesn't feel bad at all to me. Seventy-four is just right. What are we gonna do about the lower volumes?"

"I have been thinking about that. One of our nurses has the flu. I was gonna send her over to the all-you-can-eat Chinese buffet twice a day and get her to sneeze on as many dishes as possible. With the number of customers they have, we should see flu cases increase over the next two weeks."

Lou looked incredulous. "You're not really going to do that, are you?"

"Already started. I would avoid Chinese food in the near future. Now, is there anything else I can help you with?"

"No, it seems like everything else is calm at the moment. I hope everything remains quiet."

"No, no, no. You never say the Q word down here. Something bad always happens when you say the Q word. Next bad thing is on you, Lou."

"I am a man of reason. I do not put much faith in silly superstitions. Certainly you don't believe in this nonsense."

"I am a man of reason and live by science. But one of the most powerful negative forces in the world occurs when someone says the Q word in the ER. Something bad will happen. Never fails."

Jean arrived at the nursing station. "Did I hear someone say the Q word?" She shook a finger at Lou. "You will answer to me if something bad happens today. Now I need to find Mr. Ramirez. He disappeared from his room ten minutes ago, and no one saw him leave."

Suddenly, a man dressed in a patient gown crashed through the ceiling, screaming until he hit the hard floor. He landed near the nursing station in a pile of wires, ceiling tiles and dust that continued to float down like snowflakes from the ruined ceiling grid.

Everyone was stunned into silence, except for Jean, who took the whole thing in stride like it happened every day. She approached the patient and helped him to stand up. She got him dusted off and turned him to face us. "I would like you to meet Mr. Ramirez. He arrived here this morning drunk with an arm injury. He disappeared from his room ten minutes ago, and apparently, did so by climbing up into the ceiling like some Mission Impossible ninja. Unfortunately, he's too drunk to fight gravity, and now has made a mess in my ER."

Jean handed him off to another nurse. "Get him back in his room and let's get him checked for any new injuries. And tell the cops what happened."

She turned toward a tech. "Call IT to get down here and sort out these wires, and have housekeeping come clean up this mess."

Next, she turned her attention to Lou, who remained speechless. Jean put her finger back in his face. "And as for you, Mr. Vice President, don't ever say the Q word in my ER again." She turned on her heel and left a stunned Lou staring after her.

I put my arm around his shoulder. "You really are part of the ER family now, Lou. Jean does that to everyone."

Lou regained some composure. "I'm not sure any employee should talk to me like that."

"Free advice, Lou. Walk away and let it go."

Lou looked like he was about to argue, as Jean bellowed orders on her way back to registration. "I think it is time for me to go back to my office. HUHA, Doc."

"HUHA to you, Lou."

• • •

Tom came by later in the shift with an update. "Banshee's doing a lot better. Drain is pulled, and they're weaning him off of the pain meds. He's getting that spark back in his eyes. Gonna be able to go home in about a week."

"Great news." I held out my hand, and Finn put a buck in it.

Tom exploded out of his chair. "You bet against my dog making it?"

Finn held his hands up as I explained. "Finn bet Banshee would be home by the weekend. I had the over."

Tom apologized. "Sorry about that. Do you ever win a fucking bet around here?"

Finn laughed. "I think I won one last spring when I bet the pool ball stuck in that guy's rectum would be an odd number. It was the seven ball, if I remember correctly."

"What if it had been a cue ball?" Tom asked.

"Then it would have been a push," Deb replied. Deb was the final adjudicator on all betting controversies. I pulled No Clue into an empty exam room and closed the door.

"Did they find anything at Jenny's house or at The U?"

"Nope. Someone tore the place apart. Not searched, torn apart. Walls ripped open, floor torn up. Someone was looking for something and apparently didn't find it. Either that, or they were really angry. Skinny Jeans didn't find a thing."

"How about her family? Anything there?"

"Nope. She was an only child who left Arkansas when she was eighteen. Dad left a long time ago, and mom died last year. No siblings and no other relatives we could find. She was alone in the world."

"That sucks. Poor thing. I assume the medical examiner is holding her body?"

"Yep. Until we can confirm she has no relatives, they'll hold on to her."

"And Skinny Jeans has no clue who did this?"

"Not a clue. Everyone at The U is too scared to talk to us. But this ain't over. Bastards shot my dog. No rest until they all go down for this."

"For once, you make sense."

CHAPTER THIRTY

"C'mon Deb, we need to get upstairs for the meeting."

"We have time. It doesn't start for another fifteen minutes."

"We got things to do before it starts. Leave your coat. I have a feeling it'll be warm up there. And grab that can of orange soda. Let's go."

We hustled to the 14th floor conference room, a beautiful room with a large mahogany table and $20,000 worth of padded chairs, where all the bigwigs had their meetings. It felt uncomfortably hot.

"Damn it, don't they have AC up here?" Deb complained.

"They do, and it's set on 68. But they're not aware that I bribed Mike from engineering to switch control of this thermostat with the one in the ER. So, every time he turns this down, the ER gets cooler."

"And every time they turn it up in the ER, this room gets hotter. I knew there was a reason we keep you around."

"Hurry up, and grab a couple of cold orange sodas from the fridge, hide the rest of the cold ones and put the warm can from the ER in the fridge. But shake it up real good first."

"And why am I doing this?"

"Because Lou always likes a cold orange soda during his meeting," I explained, as I headed for the remote that controlled the blinds. I raised two sets of blinds, allowing the sun to shine in on the table and chairs on the far side. Then I opened the remote, turned the batteries around, and put the remote back in the center of the table. Deb and I took two seats in the shade, opened our ice-cold orange sodas, and waited for the others to arrive.

Folks trickled in, with Lou the last to arrive, believing that his time was more important than everyone else's. He took one step into the room, noticed the heat, and immediately headed for the thermostat to turn it down another degree. Deb nudged me and whispered, "Gonna be a cool day in the ER."

Lou headed to the fridge to grab his orange soda before taking his seat at the center of the table, directly in the middle of the sunbeam. A sane man would have taken his jacket off, but Lou probably showered in a suit. Sweat already shined on his forehead as he reached for the remote to close the blinds. After an amusing but futile fifteen seconds of his trying to lower the blinds, I suggested it might work better if he were closer to the blinds. This elicited a grunt from Lou and a kick from under the table from Deb. Lou walked around the table and spent another thirty seconds trying to coax the blinds down before giving up and returning to his seat. All eyes were on him as he opened his orange soda and sprayed it all over the table, soaking his papers. Now the meeting was ready to start.

The ER overview meeting, a monthly multi-disciplinary meeting that featured reports from various departments, was typically a time-wasting yawn fest, and this one proceeded without surprises until Lou put up a slide on the financials. Of course, it didn't load right away, because Lou was a big fan of PowerPoint and added many useless graphics to his presentations. It wouldn't do to have a slide pop up with clear numbers available for immediate analysis. He preferred time wasting, swirling effects with random numbers popping out at various times until finally, the spreadsheet materialized. Lou paused in case anyone wanted to compliment his PowerPoint skills. No one did. Anyone who spent that much time on a PowerPoint slide needed a fucking hobby.

"Some good news to report on the financial front," Lou began. "Our year-over-year volume numbers have stagnated, which is a reflection of mediocre work by the marketing department." The VP of Marketing squirmed, but bit her tongue. "However, since I have taken over the revenue cycle management, our billing and collections have shown a steady increase over the last year and are now up 21.3% over the previous year."

I sat up a little straighter and actually paid attention. Deb turned toward me, puzzled, but I shrugged and waited for him to proceed.

"These changes reflect an improvement in chart review, efficiency of billing generation, and more aggressive collection efforts from the insurers. Our average RVU per visit has increased from 2.82 RVUs to 3.65 RVUs. All told, this will lead to an $8.3 million increase in profitability for the ER this year."

Lou continued, but my mind battled these incongruous numbers. RVU stands for relative value unit, an attempt by insurers to differentiate the relative value of different medical procedures and exams. It is supposed to be based on complexity and time required, so that treatment of a heart attack is worth more RVUs than treatment of an ear infection. Insurance companies pay for services based on the number of RVUs. It works well in theory, but in reality, the system is corrupt, with special interest groups paying millions to lobbyists to get their services valued higher. The important part about RVUs is that the average per patient is incredibly stable over time in an ER. Unless the ER adds new services, the number should remain relatively constant. The RVU number for the ER had been very consistent over the last few years, and no new services explained the changes.

I leaned over to Deb and whispered, "We have some investigating to do."

●　　●　　●

We left the meeting at the end of an otherwise dull and sweaty hour.

"Who do we know in billing?" I asked Deb. "We need to review some raw data."

"I'm pretty sure you have dated someone from every department in this hospital."

"Not true at all. Still haven't met anyone from pathology. To be honest, they don't get out of the basement very often. There has got to be someone in billing we know."

"Well, if you know her, she must be a tall blond."

I snapped my fingers. "You're a genius, Deb. Lana is in billing."

"I thought she was tired of your shit."

"She was miffed, but absence makes the heart grow fonder."

"Well, I'm headed back to the ER and will leave it to you to get the reports from Lana. I'll reserve a patient room for you in case she knees you in the nuts." She rolled her eyes and strolled away.

"No worries. My nuts and I will figure out a way to get the data."

CHAPTER THIRTY-ONE

The land of billing consisted of small, square cubicles, gray and five feet high, tall enough to see only a person's head when they stood. The room looked like an organized game of whack-a-mole as people stood up and sat back down. Everyone looked jaundiced under fluorescent fixtures in the absence of windows and natural light. What a horribly depressing place to work.

After a few minutes of searching for Lana's cubicle, I eventually wandered in the right direction to find her absorbed in her computer screen. I dropped into the single guest chair across from her small desk. As she turned toward the intrusion, her surprised expression took me in. Billing folks do not get many visitors. Her green eyes lit up when they saw me, but then smoldered with anger. "Where the hell have you been?"

Off to a rough start, but not unexpected. "Been busy in the ER, took a week off to go skiing, and then had a gunfight with some crazy Ukrainians."

Her eyes widened in realization. "That was you? I heard snippets on the news, but I didn't know that was you."

Saved by danger, I retold my story for the thousandth time, an abbreviated version that focused on the most harrowing parts. She swooned. "Doc, I am so glad you're safe after going after those horrible men to find out what happened to that poor girl." She was pretty close to tears. Time to refocus.

"It has definitely been an adventurous week, but listen, I have a problem with the ER numbers and wanted to see if you could get me some reports that might clarify the discrepancy."

Suddenly guarded, she shifted emotional gears quickly. "What sort of reports are we talking about here?"

"Nothing crazy. I need ER billing summaries by month, including visits, RVUs, diagnosis codes, and payments for the last three years. I need to understand the trends."

"Normally, that wouldn't be a problem, but someone in administration has said ER billing is off-limits to everyone except for two new girls who work the accounts. We aren't supposed to touch those ER records." She shrugged.

"I am not asking you to mess with the accounts. I only need some information, and I prefer that admin doesn't know I'm checking their numbers. Please? Name your price."

A smile twinkled in her eyes. "Let me see what I can do when no one will notice. I don't want an electronic record of my sending it out, and that will be an awful lot of paper to print. Give me a few days. I'll let you know when I have it, and I'll let you know what it will cost you. Now get out of here. I got work to do."

Back in the ER, Deb read a new patient chart. "She gonna do it for you?"

"Of course." I assured her.

Deb held out her hand, and Finn put a dollar in it. I pointedly stared at him.

"What? Someday the charm will fail, and one of these women is gonna tell you to fuck off."

"True, but not today." I picked up a new chart and skimmed it. The patient complained of back pain, and a quick check of his records revealed nine visits for back pain within the last year, but never a follow up with any recommended specialist. This meant that he was most likely a drug seeker. While illegal drugs remain an enormous problem, legal narcotics presented an even bigger one in the ER. Highly addictive, they numb negative emotions, with the bonus that no one went to prison for possession of a few Vicodin or Norco.

Drug seeking in the ER has evolved into an art form. A prescription for narcotics translated to $25 per pill on the street, and mixed with other drugs, it yielded an even higher profit.

While these drug seekers seemed to have a master's degree in bullshitting, ER docs had earned a PhD in detecting it. I entered the room and introduced myself.

"So tell me about this back pain."

He moaned in agony as he adjusted his position on the bed. "Doctor, this is killing me. It was a nice day, and I got the ladder out to clean the gutters. I always clean the gutters at this time of the year. I had it set firmly on the ground and braced against the wall. I was halfway up, about ten feet off the ground, and the ladder started slipping sideways. I think one leg started sinking into the ground, because we had a sprinkler head break there last week, and the ground was too soft. And when I fell, I tried to catch myself on the lower roof line, but that twisted my back, and I heard a pop and couldn't walk for ten minutes. I had to crawl into my house and rest before a friend brought me here." He pitifully moaned again as he repositioned on the bed.

My BS detector screeched from the complexity of the story. Drug seekers practice their stories and make up way too many details. A guy who actually fell off a ladder says so simply and to the point.

"It looks like you're allergic to some medicines," I observed.

"Yes, sir. I have really bad allergies to Tylenol, Motrin and all those non-steroidal medicines. I am not supposed to take any of them. I usually take Vicodin or Norco."

When you are "allergic," to all the non-narcotic stuff, they expect you to give them narcotics. "Sir, Vicodin and Norco both contain

Tylenol, so patients allergic to Tylenol can't have those medicines. Let me take a look at you."

On exam, he could barely move, and even the lightest touch seemed to cause excruciating pain. My bullshit meter skyrocketed. "Sir, sit tight for a moment, and I'll go get something for the pain." He smiled at the thought of morphine soon entering his system, but I wasn't headed for the nurses' station to order meds. I headed for the security office.

"Ron, pull up the security cameras from the parking garage and front entrance and go back about forty-five minutes." Ron cued up the tapes and fast-forwarded until I saw my patient easily hopping out of his car and walking toward the entrance, as he joked with his buddy. When he got to the door, he slowed down and began to limp, as if in obvious pain, with his friend calling for a wheelchair to help him out. Gotcha.

"Ron, make a copy of that and email it to me, please."

I returned to the patient's room. "Sir, I want to confirm how bad the pain is in your back. Are you able to walk at all?"

"Barely. I need help to get anywhere."

"I see. And this pain has been there for a couple of days now?"

"Yes, Sir."

I pulled out my phone and opened the link from Ron, and pressed play. "So, it looks to me like your pain didn't start until you got to our front door. You look pretty good getting out of the car. Let me be blunt. No narcotics for you today. I can get you hooked up with someone to help with rehab if you are interested, but no pain meds."

"Fuck you, asshole. I'm out of here." He jumped off the bed and stormed out of the room. In the hallway, he turned and shouted, "You're a shitty fucking doctor, and this is a shitty fucking hospital."

His outburst did not impress Jean. "Looks like another bad customer survey score for you."

"Maybe not. I did fix his back pain. Dude came in here in a wheelchair, and now he's pain free."

Jean shook her head. "When will these buffoons learn?"

"Probably never. Call the other local ERs and give them a heads up that he'll be heading over there for pain meds."

Jean smiled. "At least you didn't shoot him."

"Not today."

CHAPTER THIRTY-TWO

Oleksander and Mykta, the youngest members of the Ukrainian team in their early twenties, loved race cars, and as soon as they made enough money, they bought matching black Charger Hellcats. At $72,000, the Hellcat produced almost 800 horsepower, one of the fastest cars under $100,000. Not satisfied with only 800, they had immediately upgraded their cars to add another 110 horsepower. A mere touch of the gas pedal led to burning rubber, smoke, and a roaring engine. They melted through a set of back tires almost monthly. They had also modified the exhaust system, so that they sounded like jet airplanes when they hit the gas. Everyone within a one block radius could hear their approach.

After Fedir delivered their orders, both men enthusiastically agreed. Chasing people down in their cars and shooting their guns included two favorite activities. They both acquired fresh tires and a full gas tank. They planned to go after him that night on his way home from work, already fantasizing about the new upgrades they would buy with the money from this job.

·   ·   ·

I wrapped up my last chart at about 11 p.m. and checked out to the night crew. Aware of my increasing weariness, my last decision of the day was IHOP or straight home. Really not much of a decision. IHOP, here I come, I thought, as I looked forward to hot fries.

I jumped in my car, turned left out of the employee lot, and headed down Fannin Street to a delicious grilled cheese sandwich and fries. I probably wouldn't have noticed the two muscle cars behind me, but their souped up engines demanded attention, as they pulled out behind me. Adrenaline flowed through my body, as I watched them split apart, with one taking the left lane and the other taking the right. I gripped the wheel tighter, braced my left foot on the floor, and snugged more securely into my seat. When their windows lowered as they pulled up on each side of me, I punched the gas pedal to the floor. Immediately, automatic weapons fired from both cars, but with no chance of hitting my receding tail lights, and I hoped no innocent bystanders, either.

My Mercedes leapt forward with all four wheels gripping for traction. In the blink of an eye, it accelerated from 35 MPH to 85 MPH. Normally, acceleration like that is enough to lose anybody, but clearly, these guys had some horsepower of their own. Headlights rose in my rear-view mirror as they punched the gas, and their engines roared as they accelerated toward me. Okay, so the cars were equally fast. Time to find out whether they knew how to drive muscle cars.

I approached Braeswood at about 95 MPH, and the traffic lights were in my favor. I leaned hard on the brakes as I approached the turn, letting off gently as I turned, then releasing completely and suddenly at the apex of the turn. Coupled with acceleration, this had the effect of rotating my car to the left and getting me back on a straight line more quickly, which meant I was back to acceleration sooner. There is no faster way to make a turn in a car.

My pursuers took a different approach. They came through the intersection sideways with smoking tires. Every moment their tires burned was another moment I pulled away from them, but once they straightened out, their horsepower kicked in, and they caught up.

I had chosen Braeswood because it's curvy and runs along a currently empty bayou. My car should have an advantage on the curves, I hoped, as I sped back up to 110 MPH. Fortunately, my Mercedes had as much braking power as engine power, and I was willing to bet these guys didn't want to scratch the paint on their pretty cars.

I slowed to let them close to within fifty yards. We traveled together through a long sweeping right-hand turn, fighting for grip. I reached the end of the turn first, and on a straight stretch of road with a balanced car, I pushed my brake pedal to the floor.

Mercedes' ceramic brake pads heated up to over a thousand degrees as I pressed the pedal to the floor. The car's computer prevented any slippage during braking, and rapid deceleration threw me forward. Then I watched in the rear-view mirror as physics ran its inevitable course.

The driver on the left side nearest the bayou locked his brakes during his right turn. Although he had spent a fortune on upgrading acceleration, he had apparently spent nothing to improve his brakes, and he didn't have a computer to help modulate them. The spectacular result of his locking his brakes at 100 MPH on a sweeping turn began with his complete loss of control of the car. It slid fast and hard, slamming into the curb at 100 MPH and then bounding over the railing upside down toward the bayou.

Braes bayou, a concrete culvert thirty feet deep, channels flood water out of Houston. At the moment, it was dry because of a lack of recent rain. His car was already flipping when he hit the incline and spiraled down the slope, and flipped seven times before he smashed into the dry concrete floor. The explosion negated any chance of rescuing him.

The second car fared better. He braked more gently, keeping his car under control, then leaned hard on the brakes, stopping safely, but positioned now in front of my Mercedes. As soon as he had lit up his tires and spun around, I decided to match him and swung my car around so that now we were both accelerating the wrong way down Braeswood.

Overdue for some help, I pressed the phone button on my steering wheel and ordered, "Call emergency," and my car dialed 911. Before they could say a word, I reported. "Shots fired. High-speed chase. I am in the medical center area being pursued by a black Charger with shots fired. Second car has crashed into Braes Bayou and is on fire. I am headed to the police station on Elgin. Alert all units. Mercedes is friendly, and Charger is armed and dangerous."

The 911 operator asked questions, but I concentrated on driving and failed to answer. I wanted to make it to the station less than two minutes away without crashing or getting shot. Behind me, the Charger stayed with me turn for turn. We passed the hospital and made it to Main Street, where I hung a hard right turn. He caught up to me on the straights, but I pulled ahead in the turns. Less than a minute from the station, I hoped they had prepared for my arrival.

I stayed on the emergency phone line to update my location as we approached the station. They finally handed me off to the officer in charge at the Elgin station. I quickly explained the situation and told him we were thirty seconds out. He told me to come into the lot, stop, and stay low.

I did as I was told.

CHAPTER THIRTY-THREE

Enraged, Mykta focused only on the Mercedes that killed his friend. Through his enraged tunnel vision, he had followed at speed into the parking lot without even realizing it was a police station. Seven police cars immediately flashed their police lights and two more blocked the exit, trapping Mykta.

"You're surrounded. Turn off your car, and put your hands on the wheel," an officer commanded over his speaker.

Mykta looked around to confirm a ring of police with guns aimed at him and with the only exit blocked. He turned off his car, but left his hands in his lap. He had a simple choice: death by cops or death by Dyyavola, who would not tolerate this failure and would prolong a painful death. He chose the quickest and easiest way.

After thirty seconds of consideration and another warning from the police, Mykta raised his Mac 10 and fired at the Mercedes, the source of his demise, with an instantaneous result. No less than twenty officers opened fire on the Charger's driver. Later, a forensics team determined that over 130 shots were fired and forty-two hit Mytka. Not even Morquist could determine which bullet killed him.

Ducked down in my car, I saw none of this, but the warnings followed by gun shots shattered my rear windshield, and the immediate deluge of fired bullets echoed through my head for weeks. The barrage of return fire overwhelmed my senses and ended as suddenly as it began. In silent relief, I confirmed that I had not been hit.

"You in the Mercedes. Let me see your hands."

I slowly raised my hands, realizing I was not out of danger yet. A bunch of amped up cops out there couldn't know I was friendly. An officer spoke over his speaker. "I need you to turn off your car and put both hands out the window, and open your door from the outside with one hand.

I placed both hands outside the window and reached for the handle when I realized a problem. "My seat belt is still on, and I can't get out of the car," I shouted nervously.

The cops conferred for a second. "Keep your left hand out the window, and move your right hand slowly to unclick your belt, and then slowly put it back out the window. No sudden movements or you will be fired upon."

It felt like I took an hour for my sweaty hand to reach down and unclick my seatbelt, and another hour to get my hand back out the window. My breath whooshed from my lungs with relief, as I finally opened the door and could get on the ground to allow the cops to cuff me, my first time in police cuffs. My previous experience wearing cuffs had been voluntary and much more pleasurable.

Once again, I asked them to call Skinny Jeans. The officer in charge got Jane on the radio, and although I couldn't hear the entire conversation, the volume and rapidity of her speech indicated that she was pissed. The officer signed off and uncuffed me. Free for the moment, Jane sounded so angry that the probability of my being put back in cuffs seemed high.

The officers led me into another interrogation room and brought me a Diet Coke, leaving me alone in another square room with the same furniture bolted to the floor as in my previous interrogation. I used the tab on my can to scrape my initials into the table along with all the other miscreants' markings. I finished up when Jane stormed into the room, dressed in jeans, a University of Houston sweatshirt, and some classic Chuck Taylor canvas high tops.

"I would add destruction of police property to the charges if I thought it would do any good," she fumed, noting my scrapings. "This is beginning to be a regular thing between us. I try to go to bed, and then I get a call that your dumb ass has killed another two Ukrainians."

"Technically, I only killed one. The cops killed the other guy, and I only killed one the other day as well."

"Easy, smartass. I haven't used up my allocation of bullets yet this month. Let me hear it from the beginning."

I walked her through the evening from the moment I left work until I pulled into the parking lot.

"So, we got a high-speed chase through the medical district, a deadly crash into the bayou, and a shootout at a police station. Quite the evening."

"And the night is still young," I pointed out.

"If it didn't involve too much paperwork, I would hand you over to the Ukrainians myself. You should have called the police as soon as you noticed them," she said as she leaned back. "Lenny, turn off the tapes and come in here."

Lenny sat down across from me as Jane said, "The official interview is over. Now I need to know if you know anything else, and we need to make a plan to keep you safe."

"I honestly don't know anything else. They were probably mad at me because I was poking around about Jenny, and then they were madder after I shot two of their guys. I don't think this evening is going to make them any happier."

"You got that right. You need a place to lie low for a few days until we clean this up. This shit is way out of hand. You got a place to stay?"

"I have a lady friend who may tolerate my presence for a few days."

Jane shook her head and rolled her eyes. "Not even sure why I bothered to ask."

"You guys got a plan to end this thing?"

"We have round-the-clock surveillance on The U, and eventually, the big guy has to show his face. We'll get another warrant to search The U, and maybe one of the girls will talk this time with our plan to take them all together to a safe house. The finance guys are still tracking the accounts to look for the source of all this money. We'll keep applying pressure until that one little thread is exposed, and then we shut this thing down for good. In the meantime, keep your head down and stop killing Ukrainians," Lenny advised.

"And if you have to kill any more, do it during regular office hours. I need my beauty sleep, and the Chief is gonna bitch about all this overtime."

"Scout's honor, I will keep my head down. This is crazy. I mean, they gotta be running out of guys, right?"

• • •

At that moment, Dyyavola was down another thug as he finished beating Fedir to death in front of his remaining six men. He made them watch the hour-long beating until Fedir finally stopped breathing. Barely winded, Dyyavola turned to the surviving six.

"Fedir has failed me. Bohdan has failed me. I need new leader. Who is ready to lead?"

Given the recent misfortunes of those in leadership positions, five of them nervously fidgeted and avoided eye contact, but one boldly stepped forward. "I am ready to lead, Dyyavola."

The Ukrainian nodded. "Very good Kyrylo. You are very brave or very stupid. Maybe little of both." He looked at the other five in disappointment. "Have these little girls clean up mess while you and I go discuss plans. I pay you for your bravery. Do not disappoint me."

Kyrylo nodded at his men. "Make sure he is never found." The men got to work without question, relieved to obey their new leader.

CHAPTER THIRTY-FOUR

Tom came by the ER the next day. "Seriously, man, why didn't you call me? I missed all the fun."

"Lots of fun. Fuckface tore up my car before his suicide by cop. He hit my car thirteen times. That car is like my baby, and he shot it thirteen times!"

"Well, I should be thankful my dog only got shot three times."

"How is Banshee?"

"Much better. Should be home soon. Still moving slowly, but better each day."

"Glad to hear it."

"So, what's the next step, Doc?"

"Well, I promised Skinny Jeans I would lie low and stay out of trouble."

Tom laughed. "Well, we both know that ain't going to happen. Where are you staying these days?"

"I moved in with Gina, the respiratory therapist, for a couple of days. She has an extra room at her place."

Deb chimed in, "And you expect us to believe you are staying in her extra room?"

"Of course not. I am sharing a room with her. I wanted to point out she has an extra room. In fact, even though I am there, she still has an extra room."

Deb went back to work.

"Tom, I got nothing. They are going to roust The U and their apartments today and probably get nothing. They set up surveillance on The U to see if they can figure out who is in charge. For the moment, I am lying low."

Tom sat quietly for a moment before announcing, "I have an idea."

"Four of the most dangerous words that could come out of your mouth. I am going to regret it, but let's hear it."

"What if we catch up with that girl Linda you talked to at The U the first night? If we can talk to her outside of the club, she might be more willing to share some information."

I sat back and pondered how to handle this. It was actually a superb idea, but I didn't want Tom to know that. "You mean follow her home from work and sneak up on her? It might work as long as she's not living with a bunch of Ukrainians. Given the lack of alternatives, it might be our best bet," hedging as much as I could.

Tom smiled. "It's a great fucking idea, and you know it. Admit it."

"I will concede it is by far the best idea on a list of one. Let's go tonight. I'll drive my rental, and don't worry, I have insurance on that one too. See you at one o'clock."

• • •

Skinny Jeans had warrants in hand first thing in the morning and hit Oleksander's and Mykta's apartment first. They lived in the same complex as Bohdan had and apparently had used the same interior decorator. Once again, they found two handguns and some drugs, but no computers, phones, or worthwhile information.

The trip back out to The U proved slightly more interesting. On presenting the warrant, Jane demanded that someone go get Fedir. A moment later, a different man stood in front of her. "I said I wanted Fedir. I need to talk to the guy in charge. Now, go get him."

"Fedir no work here anymore. Kyrylo is now in charge," the man replied calmly.

Lenny glanced at Jane. "We were here two days ago, and Fedir was in charge. Where the hell is he?"

"Fedir no work here anymore. I am in charge."

"Yeah, we got that the first time you said it. Why was Fedir fired?"

Kyrylo shrugged his shoulders. "Kyrylo does not know. Kyrylo is in charge now."

"Holy fucking hell. Why do all these guys talk about themselves in the third person? It's annoying enough they have nothing to say."

"Lenny does not know. Kyrylo is now in charge," Lenny responded in the monotone of the Ukrainian, that earned him a hint of a smile from Jane.

"All right. Y'all know the drill. Search the place, and let's interview everybody," Jane announced.

The search and interviews went faster the second time, and an hour later, Jane and Lenny met to compare notes. "Did you get anything out of him?" Lenny asked.

Jane responded in a Ukrainian monotone. "Kyrylo does not know. Kyrylo is in charge now." She gave an enormous sigh. "Please tell me you got something."

Lenny triumphantly held up a plastic bag with a piece of paper inside. "This little gem fell behind the file cabinet in the main office. It was a bitch to move, but worth it. It's a bank statement from an account we haven't seen before. Check out the balance."

Jane leaned forward to see the paper better and gave a low whistle. "$387,000 and change is an impressive balance for this shithole."

"I thought so, too. The finance guys should be able to start a new trace on this money, which will hopefully lead us back to the head honcho. Only the main man will have access to that kind of cash."

"Strong work. Anything else under the cabinet?"

"Three used condoms and a dead mouse."

Jane gave a short laugh. "I am gonna go out on a limb and say those will not solve the case for us." She turned serious again. "I hate this fucking case. Do you really think Fedir is gone?"

Lenny thought for a moment. "I think he's gone, but I don't think it was willingly, and I do think it's permanent. Doesn't seem like the type of place where they fire you and give you a severance package."

"Maybe they sent him back to the Ukraine for some reason."

"My money is that he's dead and buried somewhere around here. Guys like him don't get to leave, ever. And besides, he has the highest risk factor for death."

Jane looked at him quizzically. "What risk factor? You mean working for a Ukrainian mob?"

Lenny laughed and closed his notebook. "No. His risk factor was calling you a fucking cunt the other day."

Jane scoffed and stood up from the chair. "True. Spread the word that calling me a cunt is bad for your health. Let's get out of this place."

CHAPTER THIRTY-FIVE

Tom stopped by at one o'clock in the morning, and by 1:30 we shared a clear view of The U's front door from my dark rental car parked in the shadows facing the road. We stayed out of the sight lines of the surveillance team, and both of us had handguns within easy reach. Tom had thoughtfully brought a shotgun as well in case things got exciting.

We settled in to watch the last customers of the night stumble to their cars. "There is pretty much a 100% incidence of drunk driving leaving that lot," Tom noted.

"I can see by your indifference that it offends you greatly."

"It actually does. When this is all over, I'm gonna ask the Captain to set up a sobriety checkpoint down the street and arrest all of these assholes."

"When this is all over, this place will be shut down for good."

"True enough. Maybe I will ask the Captain if we can stop by and burn the place to the ground ourselves."

"Think he would go for it?"

"He might. Captain gets pissed off pretty easy some days. May see burning this down as therapeutic."

"And I thought the ER was fucked up. Pay attention. Girls are coming out." Exhausted, they trudged in groups of two and three, presumably for safety, toward their cars. After hugs and goodbyes, some hopped into overcrowded cars to leave together, but Linda climbed into a used silver Toyota alone.

"All right, Tom, the chase is on. Keep your eyes peeled for any unwanted attention."

We pulled out behind her and followed at a safe distance. She drove the speed limit, and after about fifteen minutes, she led us to another nondescript apartment complex of dubious quality. "Stay in the car and keep me covered. I'll approach her alone. With that mustache, you look too much like one of her clients." Tom signaled his ok with a single finger.

As she parked, I hopped out of my car and headed quickly toward her. I needed to be close enough to speak to her, but not too close to scare her. About fifteen feet away, she noticed me and startled. She reached one hand into her purse as she stood straighter and looked around for other threats. Clearly, she had some experience with danger on the street.

I stopped and held up two empty hands. "Whoa, Linda, it's me, Doc. The guy who took care of Jenny in the ER. I just want to talk. That's it, just talk."

Linda relaxed a little, but kept her hand in her purse. "What do you want?"

"I just have some questions about Jenny. I'm working with the police to figure out what happened to her. She deserves justice, and I want to make sure whoever did this can never hurt anyone again. I need more information."

She looked around furtively. "It's not safe to talk around here. Follow me. And any bullshit, and you will be visiting the ER as a patient yourself."

I backed away slowly as Linda got back into her car and pulled back out onto the road. We followed her for about ten minutes until she pulled into an IHOP, not my IHOP, but I took it as a good sign.

"Who the fuck is he?" she asked, pointing at Tom in the parking lot.

"He's a friend helping out." I didn't mention that he was also a cop.

She looked us over, then headed for the door. "Nice mustache. You look like a cop with that thing. You're buying."

Linda looked exhausted after a long shift at the club with long hair that had frizzed and tangled from the humidity in the club. The outline of dried sweat lined her face, and her smeared makeup made her look like she had cried. "You've pissed off a lot of people this week. I could make some serious money turning you over to them."

"That may be true. Or you might end up like Jenny for talking to the enemy. Your employers don't seem to be the most reasonable people."

"There's a fucking understatement. They're monsters. All of them."

"So why not leave? Why not get in your car and drive away?" Tom asked.

"I have thought about it a thousand times. Every day I think about it, but if we run, he will hurt our families and our best friends among the other girls, and not with just a few slaps. Sadistic crazy shit like in a horror movie. I can't do that to my friends and family. And if you get caught..." Her terrified eyes filled with tears.

These guys were hardly geniuses, but their savagery made up for their simplicity. The girls were not wearing chains, but were effectively imprisoned anyway.

"Linda, we're trying to shut these guys down for good. They killed Jenny and have come after me twice, but we don't even know who is in charge. Who is calling the shots? You mentioned Dyyavola the other day, but we can't find any evidence that he even exists."

She sat quietly for a moment, kneading her hands restlessly, clearly anxious. Finally, she spoke. "Dyyavola exists. He's the biggest monster of them all. He works out of the office upstairs, and we never see him in the rest of the building. We don't know if he has some secret exit up there, but we never see him coming or going through the front or back door. On the first day of work, each girl has to go up to his office for a training session. And whenever he wants, he can call you back in. It's never pleasant."

No further details were necessary. "Does this guy have a name?"

"That is the weird part. We are only allowed to call him Dyyavola. Anything else gets you a punishment. No one ever calls him by a name. As far as I know, no one knows his name."

Tom looked at me and shook his head. The one piece of information we really wanted from this meeting was the guy's name.

"So why did he kill Jenny?" I asked.

This brought a fresh wave of tears, and Tom and I ate a few bites in silence while she composed herself. "It doesn't make any sense. They are horrible to us, but we make them a ton of money. Even when they hurt us, they make sure we can still work. And Jenny was one of the special ones who got sent out on projects outside of the club. She would have been extra valuable to them."

Tom leaned forward. "What were these outside projects?"

"They probably threatened her about telling anyone, but she did say that she had to meet businessmen, usually at a swanky hotel. She felt glad to escape the scum at the club three or four times a month. The rest of the time, she worked alongside us."

"When was the last time she went on one of these trips? Did she ever tell you any details about them?"

"The last time was probably about a week before she died. I remember because she was excited about going back to the Four Seasons. She always loved going to the Four Seasons."

Tom leaned forward. "Which day last week?"

Linda thought for a moment. "Maybe Tuesday or Wednesday. I'm not sure."

"How about the name of the guy she met? Did she ever mention any names?"

"Nah, she referred to them as 'Johns.' We stay away from names in our business." She took a few bites of food, as Tom sat back in frustration.

"Wait a minute. She did mention the last guy's name, because she found it so funny. She made a joke out of it." She thought for a moment as we both held our breath. "Giovanni, that's it. Giovanni the Italian Lover is what she called him."

"Any chance she mentioned a last name?"

"Nope. Just Giovanni the Italian Lover." She laughed sadly as she softly sang it to herself.

Tom looked over at me and nodded. Finally, something to work with.

"Anything else you can tell us about Jenny?"

"She was special. All the girls have had a bad time in life before ending up here, and most of them have given up hope. But Jenny was different. She was smart and always optimistic, no matter how bad things got. She always said she would figure out a way to get all of us out of that place. From anyone else, it would sound ridiculous, but from her it was almost believable."

"Sounds like she was special to a lot of people," I said.

Linda wept again. "She was a rock for most of us. She kept us sane when things got really bad. She was always looking out for the other girls. I am not sure how we are gonna keep going without her."

Tom and I looked at each other. "Linda, I can promise we are going to get these guys and get every one of you out of that place." Tom said.

"I hope so," she said as she got up. "But you will have to do it without any more help from me. If they catch me talking to you guys, I'll end up like Jenny. Good night and good luck. And thanks for breakfast." With that, she hurried away to her car.

Tom smiled. "We got nothing on the devil man, but we need to track down Giovanni from the Four Seasons last week. I want to know what was so special about these meetings."

"Do we hand it over to Skinny Jeans?"

Tom shook his head vigorously. "They won't have any cause to get a warrant to track this guy down, but you and I can do it in our free time. All we have to do is hack the system and find this guy."

"Unless you've been taking some online courses I don't know about, we're shit out of luck. I can't hack, and you can barely type."

Tom grinned. "I know a guy, and you're going to love him."

"This sounds special," I said dubiously.

"We gotta do something soon to help those girls," Tom noted.

"We will." I nodded across the table with hopeful determination, but in the pit of my stomach, I feared for all those girls.

·   ·   ·

Back in her car, Linda had second thoughts about speaking to Doc. More than anything in the world, she wanted all of those men to be arrested, and for her and her friends to be free again to start over, but she was terrified what would happen to her if Dyyavola found out she had been talking to anyone. The punishment for breaking the rules was swift and brutal, but nothing would change unless someone spoke up.

Linda cried alone in her car, as she realized how scared and alone she felt. She didn't have the courage to carry on without Jenny, and she wouldn't be able to stand up to Dyyavola if he questioned her again. It all came down to Doc. If he couldn't stop Dyyavola, she was going to end up like Jenny. She had run out of tears by the time she made it back to her apartment.

CHAPTER THIRTY-SIX

Tom and I finished and paid, each of us silent with our own thoughts, and headed back out to my car. Tom pulled out his phone and opened his list of contacts.

"Who you calling at this hour?"

"Brian Tarson. He's the guy who is gonna get us information about Giovanni."

"You do realize it's almost three in the morning? Maybe wait for a decent hour to call."

"This is a decent hour for him," Tom chuckled.

"Odd working hours."

"Well, Brian is an odd guy. He's a 21-year-old hacker who lives in a converted warehouse with enough computer equipment to launch a small war. He's paranoid, has bad ADHD, and lives on energy drinks, Adderall, and junk food. The kid is absolutely brilliant and can hack anything. The District Attorney has tried to prosecute him multiple times, but he always walks, because we can't find an expert smart enough to explain what he's doing."

"And you think this guy will help us?"

"Positive."

"He must really like you."

"No, he pretty much hates everyone, but he has a soft spot for dogs, and ever since they met on one of his arrests, he is fascinated by Banshee."

Tom started to call, but paused before tapping the final number. "Couple of rules you need to know. He hates his name. If you say Brian or Tarson, he will hang up. You have to call him The BT. If you leave out 'The,' he'll hang up, and don't waste his time. If you waste his time, he'll hang up."

Tom tapped the number, and The BT answered on the first ring. "Who the fuck is this? You got three seconds."

"Officer Nocal. Need a favor."

"How's Banshee?"

"Getting better each day."

"Good. Bring him by some time. I'm ready."

"Four Seasons last week. A guy named Giovanni checked in. I need his full name and contact info and anything else useful you can dig up."

Before Tom finished speaking, we could hear him clacking on a keyboard in the background. It sounded like he had thirty-seven fingers working simultaneously on five keyboards.

"Dude can type," I muttered to Tom.

The typing stopped instantly. "Who's there with you?" The BT demanded.

"My friend, Doc. He's cool. Banshee likes him."

"Okay." The mad typing resumed.

In under a minute, we had an answer. "Giovanni Romanelli. Date of birth 5-15-83. What else?"

I shook my head in wonder at how quickly he had gotten the information. "I need a picture and contact information."

"Sending you a picture now," as Tom's phone dinged with an incoming message. "Dude lives in Dallas, but comes here every other week. Probably work." There was a slight pause as he typed some more. "Definitely work related. Uses a corporate AMEX for charges."

"When is his next visit?"

"You're in luck. He checked in yesterday for two nights. He is in room 528. Junior Suite. Nice." More typing. "Look for him in the hotel bar after seven. He usually gets a few drinks while he stays there. Prefers a vodka gimlet. Shitty drink."

"One last thing. Does he have a family?"

Fifteen seconds of typing later, "Wife of eight years and three kids under five."

Tom pumped his fist in celebration. "Thanks, The BT. What do I owe you?"

"Bring Banshee by. And bring some Flamin' Hot Cheetos, too." He hung up without another word.

I realized I had been holding my breath as the high-speed conversation took place. "That dude is fucking intense."

"Actually, that was pretty calm for him. You should see him when he really gets worked up."

"How the hell can he get all of that information so quickly?"

"He tried to explain it to me once. He said everything is online these days, and therefore, everything is connected. If you know how to navigate the virtual tunnels that connect these sites, you can get anywhere on the internet. He claimed there is literally no information connected to the internet that he couldn't access eventually if he wanted to. I believe him."

"Remind me to delete all my social media when I get home."

Tom and I studied the picture The BT had sent. Giovanni Romanelli could indeed be classified as an Italian Lover. Dark brown eyes peered back at us under a full head of messy jet black hair. His strong angular jaw showed off stubble long enough to be accidental, but short enough to be intentional. His smile shined with a set of teeth usually found in dental whitening ads.

"Good looking guy," Tom observed.

I had to agree. "Want me to set you up on a date with him?"

Tom laughed out loud. "No, but you're gonna be sitting in that bar later tonight waiting for him."

"What's the plan?" I asked cautiously.

Tom ticked points off on his fingers. "We know he is here on business. We know that on his last trip, he met with an escort who has since been murdered, and we know he has a lovely wife and three kids at home. I'm pretty sure if you explain those three things to him in the right way, he will be more than willing to talk to you in return for your silence."

I nodded as I thought it through. The plan definitely had possibilities. "All right. I'll do it. You coming along?'

"No way. I'm official, and if Jane found out, she would throw the book at me.

"What about me?

"You're a private citizen striking up a conversation with an incredibly hot Italian guy in a hotel bar. Perfectly normal."

CHAPTER THIRTY-SEVEN

Later that morning, Jane worked at her desk when Lenny knocked and walked in with a young, statuesque brunette. "Jane, this is Heather. Heather, this is Detective Ormund."

Jane stood and offered her hand as she took the measure of Heather. In her mid-twenties, she stood about 5'7" with another three inches added from her heels, worn with a perfectly tailored black straight skirt. Her blouse had two buttons undone to highlight a simple gold necklace. She maintained eye contact throughout her firm handshake. Heather was a very confident young woman.

"Please, have a seat, and call me Jane."

"Heather is with our internet financial crimes team and has discovered some interesting information from that paper we found at The U," Lenny explained.

"Thank you," Heather began, as she handed a small folder to each of them. "Our initial evaluation of The U disclosed nothing interesting with normal business accounts with revenue coming in and bills being paid. This typical activity is summarized in Section 1 of the report. You can look at it later, but I want to focus on the information in Section 2."

Everyone flipped to the appropriate page as Heather continued. "The bank statement only had the one account which contained over $387,000, much more cash than this business could generate from normal activities. The bank is well known to cater to clients with illegal cash flows and to help them launder their money. We are still trying to track down the owner of the account, but it's hidden behind a network of offshore entities and unlikely to be uncovered."

Heather countered Jane's deepening frown with a reassuring smile. "Don't worry. We can't trace the owners, but we can trace the money. Money has to come from somewhere and leaves a trail. The bad guys try to erase it as much as possible, but it's impossible to erase the trail completely. We were able to trace the money backwards until we finally found the source, Bitcoin."

Noting Jane's confusion, Heather may as well have said the money came from aliens, or yellow elephants, or jello. "Let's take a step back and talk about Bitcoin. What do you know about it?"

"Almost nothing," Jane admitted.

"You're not alone. Bitcoin was the first digital currency ever created back in 2009. It is only digital, which means it exists only in computer code, without actual coins or bills you can hold in your hand."

"That doesn't sound very safe."

"Safer than you might imagine. Most of our traditional finances are virtual as well. When we transfer funds, or pay by PayPal or Venmo, or use credit cards, no actual money changes hands. It is all done virtually. We trust that the money we send will arrive at its intended location, but most of us don't worry about how it happens."

Jane nodded thoughtfully. "I never thought of it that way."

"Most people don't. The difference between Bitcoin and other digital currencies is that they are decentralized, which means no one organization or individual is in charge."

"Wait a minute. How can it work when no one is in charge?" Jane demanded.

Heather responded with her own question. "Tell me, who owns and operates the internet? It's the biggest and most valuable asset on the planet. Who is in charge?"

"I never really thought about it," Jane admitted.

"The answer is that no one is in charge. It is a decentralized platform, and anyone who speaks the common computer language can add content to the internet or find content. Anyone can connect a server to the internet and add content, which is how the internet grows. People control the airwaves that access the internet, but no one controls the internet. Bitcoin is exactly the same."

"If no one is in charge, how does it help us to know that the money comes from Bitcoin?"

"Because the digital ledger of each account is public. When you put money in a bank or in an investment institution and make trades, those trades are confidential. When you buy or trade Bitcoin, that trade is on a public ledger that everyone can see."

"So there's no privacy?"

"Actually, the exact opposite. Bitcoin is much more private. Every account has a unique numeric identifier that is used in all trades and is visible on the public ledger, but the identity of the account holder is private. Some exchanges require account holders to validate their identity, but many exchanges, especially foreign ones, allow anonymous accounts. There is literally no identifying information attached to those accounts. That means that whoever has the account number and password controls the funds."

"So if you lose the password?"

"You are absolutely fucked. The money is gone forever like it never existed. There is no one to help you access your account or recover the funds. It is literally the same as setting a pile of cash on fire."

"Now that we understand Bitcoin, why don't you tell her the good part?" Lenny interjected.

Heather smiled. "The good part is that we traced this money back to a Bitcoin account on an exchange in Eastern Europe, and while we do not know the identity of the holder, we can see every transaction.

This account has had regular large infusions of Bitcoin deposits for the last seven years and relatively minimal withdrawals for cash. Over that time, the account has grown to approximately 20,000 Bitcoins," Heather said excitedly.

Jane asked tentatively, "Is that a lot?"

Heather pulled out her phone and swiped to a new screen. "Bitcoin is currently trading at about $60,000 per coin."

Jane tried to do the math in her head. "Is that $120 million?"

"Close, you missed a zero. It is actually $1.2 billion."

Lenny smiled broadly as Jane's jaw hit the floor. "Let me make sure I have this correct. You're saying that information on the bank statement traces the money back to an account worth over a billion dollars?"

"Yes, ma'am, with 100% certainty."

Jane turned to Lenny. "Who else knows about this?"

"Only the three of us."

"Keep it that way for now." She turned to Heather. "Incredible work. Thank you. Keep monitoring those accounts and let me know if there are any changes. Not a word of this to anyone, please. If word gets out, the Feds will steal this case." She turned back to Lenny with a huge smile. "Let's go see if we can find ourselves a billion dollars."

CHAPTER THIRTY-EIGHT

At seven that night, I rolled up to the Four Seasons' valet in my rental car. Not knowing exactly what to wear when meeting a handsome Italian man in a hotel bar, I went with a sports coat, jeans, and cowboy boots. That look could pass for well dressed in most social situations in Texas.

I ambled to the bar of golden granite framed with mahogany. Subtle lighting combined with the dark wood and classical music to create a sophisticated ambience. Half full of couples and business groups enjoying food and drinks, their low murmurings mingled with the sonorous tones. I chose an empty seat and waited for Giovanni to arrive.

The bartender seemed impressed enough with my appearance, but thoroughly unimpressed with my order of a Sprite. In a fair world, my job that night would be to get information out of her instead of Giovanni. I made a note to return here another night to talk with her, as I settled in to wait. Luckily, a TV played an NBA game to help me pass the time.

I waited only twenty minutes for his arrival. With The BT's photo, I knew I had the right guy and no doubt he played the part of the Italian Lover. He wore a silk, three-piece suit with shiny black shoes. As I watched him in the mirror, his shiny black hair framed his whiskery dark skin that accentuated his perfect bright smile. The guy looked like he had an army of assistants who did nothing but polish him. He glided to the bar and gracefully slid into his seat. He must have been a real regular, because the bartender brought him a drink without his asking.

Despite how weird it probably looked, I grabbed my drink and moved down two seats to sit next to him. Startled, he studied my face, trying to recognize me. The bartender stopped wiping down the counter to watch curiously.

I held out my hand. "Giovanni, right? My name's Doc. Nice to meet you."

Giovanni shook my hand and asked, "Do I know you?"

"No, sir. We have a mutual friend."

"And who might that be?"

"A young lady named Jenny. I believe you spent an evening with her on your last trip here."

His dark skin paled and his eyes widened in alarm. He furtively scanned the bar, apparently evaluating his options. He looked like he was about to make a run for it.

I put my arm firmly on his. "Relax, I'm not your enemy. I need some information. How about we move over to a booth, where we can talk more privately."

He stared into my eyes on the edge of panic, and I cooly held his gaze. He finally nodded once, grabbed his drink, and led me to a quiet booth in a corner. I followed with my Sprite.

"Explain to me exactly who you are and what you want."

"It's a bit complicated. I'm an ER doctor and took care of Jenny for a wrist injury earlier this week. Later that day, she was tortured, and beaten to death, and dumped at my ER."

Giovanni gasped and made the sign of the cross. "Certainly you do not think I had anything to do with this!"

I held up my hands. "No, we have a pretty good idea who did it, but we don't know why, and we don't have any proof. So, I'm tracking down her movements to see what we can learn."

"How did you manage to track me down?"

"Jenny mentioned she had spent a night with you to one of the other girls at work, and she passed the information on to me."

"Who else knows about me and Jenny?"

"For right now, only me and my partner."

"For right now? Do you have intentions of sharing this information?"

"I know you have a wife and three kids. I know you are a big time executive at your financial firm, and I know your life will be complicated if this information gets out. I do not want to complicate your life. I want some information, and then I'll go away forever."

Giovanni muttered something in Italian under his breath. "I have your word that this will stay quiet?"

"You have my word."

"Then ask your questions." Giovanni was all business now.

"How did you meet up with Jenny?"

"There are websites where traveling executives can go to find... companionship while on the road. The girls are guaranteed to be clean and discreet. I set up a meeting with Jenny through the site."

Giovanni told me about the website, and I entered the information into my phone. "How did the evening go?"

He shrugged. "The evening went how evenings such as this go. We had a nice dinner and then retired to my suite for the usual after dinner activities."

"That's it? Just dinner and sex?"

"That was it. Dinner and lovemaking, and she left in the morning. I did not find out about her other activities until two days later."

I raised an eyebrow. "Other activities?"

Giovanni became much more agitated as he spoke. "I do not wish to speak ill of the dead," as he crossed himself again, "but this bitch, she tried to ruin my life. While I slept, she did something to my computer. When I returned to the office and logged in, my computer spread a virus to the entire network. Suddenly, we all received ransom messages. They wanted us to pay two million dollars, or they would make all of our information public on the internet, including all of our clients' personal and account information, all of our company's financial data and emails. Everything." He shook his head and looked like he was about to cry.

"Did you go to the authorities?"

"Nope. They were clear. Any contact with the authorities and the information would be released."

"How do you know Jenny was responsible?"

"Because they sent a message to me telling me I was responsible for the hack, and if I did not convince my company to pay the ransom, they would make sure everyone knew that it was my fault, and they would make sure my wife knew about Jenny. They would ruin my life."

"So what happened?"

He sighed and shook his head. "We paid. There was no choice. If that data got out, we would have been ruined, and my marriage would be over."

"How was the payment made? Did someone drop off a suitcase of money in a dark parking garage?"

Giovanni flashed those shiny white teeth. "You've been watching too many movies. We paid in Bitcoin, anonymous, instantaneous, and untraceable Bitcoin. Within fifteen minutes of payment, they erased the virus completely from our system, like the whole thing never happened."

"Sorry to dredge up the bad memories, but thanks for telling me. I'm not sure how this all fits together, but maybe it'll help stop these people."

"You're welcome. I assume that there will be no need to mention my part in this travesty?"

"None at all. Take care, Giovanni."

Back at the bar, I closed out my tab. The bartender came over with a smile as she handed me the bill. "Looks like you struck out with your man friend over there. You should have stayed at the bar and made a move on me instead," she said with a wink.

"Would you believe me if I told you that was just a business meeting?"

She pondered the thought for a moment and then reached into her shirt for a card. "I might be able to be convinced. Call me sometime, and we can discuss it further."

I pocketed the card and left.

As soon as I was in the car, I called Tom to share the news and figure out our next step.

"You're not gonna believe what I learned tonight," was my greeting when Tom answered.

"Let me guess. You learned that you're attracted to hot Italian men."

"No, but I will admit he's good looking. Jenny wasn't only sleeping with these guys. She planted a ransom virus on his computer while he slept, and then someone blackmailed his firm. Want to guess how much Giovanni's firm paid to keep their information private?"

"Hell if I know. A hundred grand?"

"Nice guess. Try two million dollars."

Tom audibly gasped. "Are you shitting me? Two million bucks? I need to start blackmailing some companies."

"You and me both. Listen, we gotta let Skinny Jeans know about this. Two million bucks is a helluva reason to kill someone."

"Yeah, you're right. They need to know about this. The question is how to tell them without facing real consequences at work. I've been ordered to stay out of this."

"I'll tell them in the morning and keep you out of it."

Tom protested, but I cut him off. "You can't be part of this. You're a cop who disobeyed a direct order way up the chain. I'm just a private citizen being an asshole in my free time. She'll yell at me, but that'll be the end of it."

"Thanks, man, and good luck tomorrow. If I don't ever talk to you again, it was nice knowing you."

"Thanks for the vote of confidence. Goodnight, Tom."

"Goodnight, Doc."

I drove home, hoping Jane's appreciation would outweigh her anger.

CHAPTER THIRTY-NINE

The next morning, I called Jane, and she told me to be in her office at 10 a.m. sharp. I showed up at 9:55 a.m. to get on her good side, but it didn't work. Jane seethed as she called me into her office, and coupled with the black pantsuit she was wearing, she personified the Grim Reaper.

Lenny, already seated, pointed me to the other chair in front of Jane's desk. "You said you have some information to share. This suggests to me that you have continued to investigate this case despite my explicit order to stay away. How am I doing?" Her unblinking eyes stabbed through me.

I swallowed hard. "Pretty accurate so far."

She leaned forward over her desk. "Let me make myself one hundred percent clear. You come clean with everything you know right here, right now, or I will charge you with obstruction. No more fucking around. Start talking."

I took a deep breath. "I met with Linda, one of Jenny's friends, two nights ago. I followed her home from the club, and she agreed to meet me at IHOP." Jane turned redder with each sentence. "We talked for a while, but she had only one useful bit of information, that Jenny sometimes went on special jobs to high end hotels. She didn't know why the jobs were special, or why they chose Jenny, but she had mentioned to Linda a guy named Giovanni who she met at The Four Seasons the week before she died."

I paused for a moment as Jane's softening eyes bored into me. "Using resources I would rather not discuss in detail, I discovered the identity of the man and learned that he was currently staying at the hotel. So last night, I waited in the bar and talked with the guy."

Jane let out an explosive breath, controlling her anger as I related the details of my chat with the Italian businessman.

Jane sat straighter in her chair, but leaned back and asked, "Are you positive he paid the ransom in Bitcoin?"

"Yes. I'm sure he said two million dollars in Bitcoin."

"First, I am majorly pissed at you still. The only reason you are walking out that door without cuffs is because you brought me useful information, and I do appreciate your coming to me with this. What I am about to tell you is confidential. If you share it with anybody, even that low life Nocal, I will personally shoot you in both kneecaps. Understood?'

"Yes, ma'am."

"We discovered financial information that led us to an account with a large amount of Bitcoin, but we had no idea how they earned them. The extortion piece makes sense and explains the source of the money. Now that we know the crime, we still need to identify the head honcho, this devil guy."

I went back through my story and answered all of their questions in as much detail as I could recall. They agreed to keep Giovanni's role in this quiet for the time being, and I was able to keep Tom and The BT's involvement out of the conversation. Finally, Jane stood up and came around the desk. "Seriously, thank you for your help. Now please, get the fuck out of here and stay out of my case."

"Yes, ma'am," I scrambled out of the office, thinking that the meeting went well.

• • •

Back in the ER for my afternoon shift, I called Tom between patients to update him on the meeting with Jane and Lenny.

"Thanks, again. Sounds like a good decision to keep my name out of it," he observed.

"Good for you anyway," I replied.

"Listen, I got an idea."

"Those dangerous words again. You're the only one with worse ideas than mine."

"That may be true, but we need some more info, and we got no other leads right now. So why don't we stop by and visit the surveillance guys tonight? One of my buddies is covering overnight, and we can get the scoop from him without Lenny or Jane hearing about it."

"I don't know, Tom. Jane was looking for a reason to arrest me, or maybe shoot me in the leg, but she's definitely pissed."

"Come on, we'll make it friendly. We can bring them coffee and donuts. We'll stop by late, when the club closes, as that's the most likely time to see something. They're a block away. It'll be safe. What do you say?"

"Gina will be disappointed."

"Gina will still be there when you get back."

"True, but she'll be disappointed. I'll be done at one o'clock again tonight. Come by then."

As I hung up, Finn walked by with his hand held out and a smile on his face. Deb sheepishly placed a dollar in his hand, and Finn continued on his way.

I stared at Deb until she relented. "He bet me you would get another Ukrainian this week. First bet I have lost to him in months. I blame you." Deb did not like to lose.

CHAPTER FORTY

Lou took the call after lunch. There was no greeting. "We have a problem. Doc is asking questions about ER billing."

"Has he gotten anywhere?"

"Not sure, but I am sure he's popular around here. Everyone knows him, and his recent heroics have made him a star. We have to assume someone will get him some data."

"No way you can stop it?"

"Not without drawing even more attention. We need you to shut this down."

"Okay, I planned for this possibility. I'll handle it. Just keep your head down and keep working."

•   •   •

Although the rest of my shift proved routine, I had an eight-year-old with a wrought-iron fence pole through his thigh. Apparently, his Mensa qualified parents thought that pushing the trampoline into the corner of the yard against the spiked fence maximized the play area.

Whoever would have thought that children bouncing wildly on a trampoline next to sharpened metal spikes might be a bad idea? Morphine and a good surgeon could fix it, though, and he would have a badass scar to prove he was raised by imbeciles.

Tom came by as I completed my charts. "Good day for you today. Pretty sure you haven't killed anyone yet."

"Nope, today was all about saving lives, or at least doing no harm. I assume I got my tax dollars' worth out of your protecting and serving today?"

"Absolutely. I shut down a ring of napkin thieves at the food court today. Actually, a couple of old ladies took a few extra napkins for home, but we threw the book at them. They should be locked up for the next ten years or so," Tom said proudly.

"Strong fucking work. Amazing you're not the Chief of Police, yet."

We took Tom's truck, since it would blend in better. With the surveillance set up in an old abandoned building about a block away, they had eyes on the front and sides and had planted some cameras in the back. No one could come or go without their knowledge. Tom phoned ahead to let them know that we were bringing donuts to avoid any drama.

"Officer Nocal showing up with some donuts. First useful thing he has done for the department in twenty years," Tom's friend from the Houston Police Department announced.

"Still more productive than your career. Doc, this is Officer Turner who holds the record for most years on the police force without solving a single crime. Officer Turner was kicked in the head by a goat when he was young and isn't all there. We keep him around as a mascot and let him do important work like night surveillance."

"Some of that is actually true," he said, as he bit into a jelly donut. "I was kicked in the head by a goat, but it happened when I was trying to get Tom off the goat. They're apparently attracted to his mustache, and Tom never turns down an offer from a farm animal." He turned his attention to me. "So, you're the famous Doc who whacked four Ukrainians this week?"

"Technically, I only whacked two of them. My neighbor and your fellow officers got the other two."

"Well, we're giving you credit for four, and if our count is correct, only six more Ukrainians remain. At the pace you're going, you should have this cleared up by next week."

Cops were nothing if not pragmatic. Tom and Turner shared a few more stories and donuts, and then Officer Turner shared the report. "We got nothing. Been here for four days, and every day is the same. The girls and employees show up about four. The goons arrive in the next hour, and by five o'clock, all six of them are inside. Then a bunch of drunk idiots come in and out until closing at two. The girls leave soon after. The staff and goons turn off the lights and are out of there by 2:30. The goons head home to their apartments. Boring."

"So, you haven't seen anyone else coming or going? Someone has to be in charge of the place."

"Nothing. Just a bunch of verified fucking losers."

"Anyone carrying anything out? The money has to go somewhere," Tom added.

Turner shrugged. "We watch. Someone else has to make sense out of all this. But I can tell you nobody who looks to be in charge is coming or going, and no one is leaving with any money, at least that we can see. Unless something happens, this is our last night."

We sat in silence as two in the morning approached when the last customers straggled to their cars. Then the girls came out, and finally, the staff left the building.

"Should be just the big guys left." Two minutes later, the lights blinked out, and the two big guys exited, locking the door before they got in their cars and left. Their hands were empty.

"Just like the last few nights. Now comes the exciting part where we stare at an empty, dark building until our relief shows up in the morning. You guys are welcome to stay, but the show is over for now."

I was the only one still staring at The U, when a faint light glowed in the back of the warehouse next door. Only a dim light crept around the edges of a blacked-out window. I would never have seen it except for the total darkness of the surrounding area. I was about to mention it, but blinked, and the light vanished.

CHAPTER FORTY-ONE

The next day, I stabilized a guy who ran a circular saw through his thigh when he tried to cut a board by bracing it on his leg. Another patient tried to jump over his friend's convertible while it drove by at 30 MPH after watching a guy do it on YouTube. Potential orthopedic sponsorship of such videos went through my mind, as he predictably had a broken shoulder and femur. The spectacular video of his getting hit by the car had gone viral on Instagram. More business for us in the near future, which reminded me of Lou.

A greeting of HUHA from VP Lou highlighted my afternoon. I should have charged Finn a dollar for each time he said it. I would be retired and on a beach somewhere instead of listening to his stupidity.

"Well, HUHA, and good afternoon to you, VP Lou. How can us lowly ER peons help the mighty administration team advance their cause today?"

His dumb ass actually smiled. His ego couldn't allow him to imagine that I could be mocking him.

"Doc, is there somewhere more private we could talk?"

Deb and I simultaneously raised our eyebrows, and she shot me a warning glance, but I was already on high alert.

"Sure thing. Let's grab an empty exam room." I figured he would be uncomfortable in the smaller setting rather than in his usual conference room. I would take any advantage.

We went into exam room eight, and I lifted myself onto the bed. Lou looked around and noted, "Why is the furniture layout in this room reversed from all the others?" as he leaned up against the counter and crossed his arms.

"Well, this is the room set aside for gynecological exams. We get a lot of sexually transmitted disease cases, and this layout allows for more privacy during the exam."

Lou straightened and looked back at the counter, making sure not to touch anything in the room. "Good to know. I understand you have some questions about the ER billings after our last meeting."

I wasn't sure what he knew, and I still didn't know what was going on. "I commented to Deb that they showed an impressive turnaround in less than a year. I want to understand how it happened, so I can congratulate our team."

Lou stared at me, as if trying to detect a lie. I stared back, like I knew. It felt like a Clint Eastwood movie, and all we needed was a soundtrack to make the moment more intense. I wasn't sure what he expected, but I had all day, and no way would I lose a staring contest to this fool. Eventually, he relented.

"I want to make clear that any questions about the billing numbers need to be addressed directly to me and only to me. Do you have any questions about our current billing practices?"

I smiled and played stupid. "No, sir, not really. Since you've got it handled and working so well, then it's one less thing for me to worry about. Unless you ask, I'll stay out of the billing realm. Anything else?"

"No, that should cover it for today. Have a good afternoon." He waited for me to get the door for him, maybe because he felt important or maybe because he was afraid of getting chlamydia from the handle. I opened the door and swept my arm grandly. "After you, and a very HUHA afternoon to you, VP Lou."

Lou did not appreciate my rhymes and left without another word. I made a mental note to check in with Lana about those reports.

• • •

My shift ended after midnight, and I had three choices. I could go back to a nice, warm bed with Gina. Choice number two was IHOP for a nice warm meal, and then a warm bed with Gina, and choice number three was to do something really stupid. I went with the third option, of course.

I settled into my rental car, a basic Mercedes model, fortunately painted black, and headed for The U. I knew surveillance had been pulled earlier in the day, and I had a hunch about that light in the warehouse next door, but I didn't want to get everyone worked up for nothing.

I drove to the original abandoned warehouse that the surveillance team had used and crept to the second floor. I sat down to wait. In the quiet solitude, I had some time to think about what I was doing. It might seem crazy, but I needed to get this problem resolved, or I would look over my shoulder for the rest of my life.

At about 1:45 am, the last stragglers left the club, and as usual, the girls and staff followed. Finally, the lights went out, and the two big uglies came out the front door, locked it, and left in their cars, leaving The U dark and silent.

If I was wrong, nothing further would happen. If I was right, a light would come on in the warehouse next door in the next couple of minutes.

Time drags by slowly when sitting in an abandoned building in the middle of the night in a bad area of town controlled by murderous Ukrainians. Three minutes later, the same faint light leaked from a blacked-out window in the warehouse next door. I hate being right sometimes.

The intelligent thing would have been to leave and let Skinny Jeans know about my suspicions in the morning, but they were already mad at me and would be furious if they found out I was nosing around down here. I needed to be sure before I said anything, which meant getting closer.

I was prepared in that I had worn dark clothing, but that was the extent of my plan. I decided to take a quick look to confirm my suspicions, and then I would be out of there.

I hurried downstairs and toward the warehouse, where the dim light still crept around a darkened window. I stayed in the shadows as much as possible, but about two hundred windows looked down on me. Anyone sitting up there could detect movement, and I would be an easy target, but why would someone be looking out a window of an abandoned warehouse at 2:30 in the morning?

I finally leaned to the side of the warehouse and rested for a moment. This spy shit was way more stressful than working in the ER. I took a deep breath through my nose and peered through a window. It was dark, but I got the sense of a wide-open area like you would find in any warehouse, definitely with no lights or signs of life.

The illuminated room was about halfway down the building on the second floor. I tiptoed slowly past the rubble piled up outside, curious how old tires, a washing machine, and a computer monitor ended up there.

I rose again to look through the dark window. Clearly, this area had a second floor above it, likely some sort of office area for the warehouse. I couldn't see how to access it from where I was.

A little further down the building, I found a broken door and decided that a quick peek inside would be helpful. I carefully snuck inside and stopped to listen. I heard movement upstairs, but no voices. I didn't want to move, fearing noise from stepping on the debris on the floor. Without some light, I would likely run into something and make enough noise to wake the dead. In my first intelligent choice of my outing, I retreated and called it an evening. I slowly made my way outside, along the front of the building, and back to my car. I hurried in and took off for Gina's place, as I made a mental list of equipment I would need for the following night.

CHAPTER FORTY-TWO

After a long, restorative sleep, I went back to Lana in accounting to check on my reports. Her playful smile and a stack of papers greeted me.

"Good afternoon. Are those for me?"

"They might be. Depends what I get in return."

I enjoy these types of negotiations. "I was thinking the going rate for a stack of unauthorized billing reports is one dinner at Three Forks with steak, lobster, crab cakes, wine and dessert," I offered with my most tempting smile.

She pondered my offer for a moment. "I'll take the dinner, but dessert is on me at my place."

The woman knew how to negotiate. "Deal. Saturday night around seven?"

She pushed the reports to me. "Deal. Now get out of here before I get in trouble."

I grabbed the reports and hustled to the elevator.

I dropped them off in my office. The hospital provided me with a nine by nine-foot cube with no windows and shitty lighting. I did not try to decorate it, because I made every effort to stay out of there. The depressing room had one drawer with a lock. I threw Lana's reports into it, covered them with some random documents, and locked the drawer and the office on my way out.

I headed to the medical school. All faculty members had to publish research or teach to keep their appointments. While I understand the value of research, the thought of actually doing it ranks somewhere below walking barefoot on broken glass. I had suffered through a research project to complete my fellowship and vowed never to do it again.

The medical school had tried to get me to teach one of the usual topics, like airway management, sepsis, or fluid resuscitation, but I had come up with an entirely new course about the business aspects of medicine, which turned out to be very popular.

I arrived at the lecture hall to find fifty eager young students waiting breathlessly for me to opine on the business of medicine. Actually, they were milling about in small groups that largely ignored me as I walked in.

Natural groupings formed based on where students sat in lectures. The best students sat front and center, diligently taking notes on every word spoken for the hour. These future doctors had the highest grades and seemed destined to become dermatologists, anesthesiologists, or ophthalmologists. The students in the back of the room paid attention to the lectures, but also constantly evaluated everything else going on in the room. Trauma surgeons, ER doctors, and ICU doctors come from the back rows. The middle of the room tended toward internal medicine, pediatrics, and other specialties.

"All right, sit down, and let's get started. Administration will dock my pay if we don't start on time."

Before I could get any further, a student in the front row stood up and stated, "Doctor Docker, I was not able to find the slides for this lecture online. Can you please distribute a copy for the class?"

"First of all, call me Doc. Anyone who calls me Doctor Docker gets a C. Second, there are no slides for this class." The students in front audibly gasped and a smattering of applause and cheers hailed from the students in the back. "In this class, we are going to think and discuss, not memorize. You guys spend way too much of your time memorizing in school and not enough time thinking. In fact, you can close your computers, stop taking notes, and think about our discussions, and you will do fine in this class." The students in back enthusiastically slammed their computers shut while the ones in front warily kept them open.

"Let's start with the basics. Is medicine more about the money or the mission?"

A student in the second row spoke up. "Medicine has to be about the mission first, to do no harm, prevent disease, and minimize pain and suffering. If you are not mission first in medicine, then you are in it for the wrong reasons."

"Thank you very much. Any other opinions out there?"

"Money comes first," shouted a voice from the back of the room.

"Tell me why."

"Mostly because I need to pay off all of these damn student loans." That produced another smattering of applause. "And because money equals mission, and no money equals no mission."

"No money equals no mission. That is profound, young man. If I ever decide to make a slide, I might put that on the first one. I hate to disappoint some of you idealists, but that young man in the back is correct. In medicine, money comes before the mission. So if you want to be successful in medicine, you need to understand where the money is coming from and where it is going."

"Focusing on money in medicine is evil," an indignant student commented.

A debate brewed. Maybe my class would be meaningful after all. "Money is neither good nor evil. What you decide to do with money is good or evil. Money is power. The more money you have, the more power you have to help people or to hurt people. Good people with money do great things for society. Bad people with money are dangerous to society. If you want to do a lot of good in medicine, you have to control a lot of money."

I scanned the audience and saw an amazing thing. They were thinking. Most lectures in medical school involve understanding and memorizing, but these fledgling doctors were actually thinking.

"Let's shift gears. How much money is spent each year on medical care in the United States?"

"Three trillion dollars?" came a timid response from the class.

"Not bad. It's closer to $3.8 trillion. That equates to almost twenty percent of the United States' gross domestic product. That means one out of every five dollars spent in the US is spent on health care. Now going back to our equation of money equals power. Is healthcare powerful in the US? Hell, yes. Healthcare spending is one of the largest drivers of our economy, certainly an issue relevant to this class."

At that moment, a door opened in the back and a figure slinked into the room. The suit immediately eliminated the possibility of a student, and as he moved into the light, I recognized the beady eyes and furtive movements of my good friend VP Lou. No idea why he crashed my lecture, but I could not squander the opportunity.

"Class, what is the fastest growing category of healthcare expenditures? I will give you a hint. It is not a real good use of funds."

The crowd shouted answers. "Pharmacology, research, new buildings, new technologies."

I let them go on for a few minutes, but no one guessed correctly. "Surprisingly, and depressingly, the answer is healthcare administrative costs." This drew a murmur of dismay from the crowd. "Administrative costs are now thirty-four percent of all healthcare costs. One out of three dollars is spent on administrators. Every hospital has an entire floor of thirty- something MBAs who are Vice President of this or that. Most of them don't know anything about medicine, yet they make the important decisions that directly affect patient care. In your medical career, you will butt heads with some of these VPs." Lou gave me his death stare, and I returned it.

"But some of these administrators have to be good at their jobs, don't they?" asked a student up front.

"I admire your optimism. Clearly a pediatrician in the making. Of course, some of them are useful and good at their jobs. In fact, we are lucky enough to have one in our midst today. Lou, can you please introduce yourself and explain your role to these young, impressionable minds?"

Clearly surprised, Lou collected himself as the class turned toward him. "Thank you. I am Lou Gallagher, and I am the Vice President of Internal Operations and Efficiency at Ben Taub Hospital."

"Would you like to come down here and explain to these impressionable students how the role of Vice President of Internal Operations and Efficiencies improves the lives of medical providers and patients at the hospital?" I threw the challenge spontaneously, but also with curiosity.

Lou looked uncomfortable. "I appreciate the offer and would love to discuss my role with the students, but unfortunately, I have a meeting soon. Perhaps I can attend a future lecture."

"Perhaps that opportunity will be available in the future. Please don't let us keep you from important hospital meetings. Lou Gallagher, everybody."

Lou cracked a half smile at their smattering of applause. His eyes never left mine until he turned to exit.

"All right, class, where were we?"

CHAPTER FORTY-THREE

It took two days to gather everything I needed for my next excursion; I had to wait for an overnight delivery from my online order. James Bond may have had Q, but I had Amazon.

I left work at ten, so that I could arrive early. I drove to my favorite abandoned building and sat in my car thinking about what I was about to do. I could still call Tom or Skinny Jeans and let them handle it, but I wasn't sure what I had discovered, if anything at all. Besides, they would take too long to collect any information, since they had to follow the rules. I'd take a quick peek to gather information, and then give it to them.

Mind made up, I grabbed my bag and made my way to my chosen observation post. At this earlier time, the parking lot bustled with more activity, concealing me more effectively. With my gear prepared, I walked to the warehouse. Five minutes later, I was back at the broken door.

I stopped to put on my night vision goggles. They don't actually create any light, but they enhance available light by about 20,000 times. With only a small amount of light filtering in through the windows, I could make out the details of the room.

Long abandoned equipment populated the open area blanketed with dust, undisturbed for a long time. To my right, the main floor ceiling reached forty feet. Straight ahead, a staircase led to the second floor, where I had seen the dim light on previous evenings. Tonight, only darkness and silence greeted me. I stood still for five minutes to make absolutely sure I was alone in the building.

I moved cautiously toward the stairs and noticed many fresh footprints had disturbed the dust. I added mine and climbed the stairs to find a stout steel door at the top. I tried the handle, but it was locked solid. With the steel frame, it would take explosives to open this door. Unfortunately, Amazon had not brought me any explosives. Dead end.

I moved back down the stairs and followed the footprints to a large pile of equipment about forty feet away, where they abruptly ended, confirming my suspicion that a tunnel connected to The U next door. Now how to access the tunnel?

I searched in vain for fifteen minutes, finding no way to move the equipment. I figured it had to be something simple, given the Ukrainians' performances so far, but I couldn't find it. I needed to know where that tunnel came out in The U, and why previous searches had missed it.

I waited. I had about three hours if the established patterns held. I moved to another pile of equipment, thirty feet away to the right, and found myself a small space behind it that left me mostly concealed and offered a good sight line to the tunnel entrance. Then I settled in to get comfortable, a relative term while sitting on rusty equipment covered with layers of dirt, grime, and God knew what else. I thought back to my microbiology class and about all the different bacteria I could be exposed to. Then I thought about my infectious disease rotation and which antibiotics I might need after this.

Sounds of someone emerging from the tunnel interrupted my musings. I had not even heard the tunnel door open. I peeked around the equipment to see that the tunnel entrance was indeed hidden by the equipment, but it had silently slid to the side to reveal an enormous man climbing out. Unsure if the light amplification goggles played tricks on me, I gauged this guy made the previous Ukrainians look like gangly teenagers. This had to be Dyyavola.

He climbed out of the tunnel, quite agile for a man the size of a walk-in freezer. He took a few steps to a rusty 55-gallon drum nearby, lifted the lid, did something I couldn't see, and the equipment slid noiselessly over the tunnel entry. One mystery solved. These guys may have sucked at assassinating doctors, but they certainly knew how to build a secret entrance to a tunnel.

The giant lumbered up the steps, which surprisingly did not collapse under him. At the top, he took a key from his pocket, pushed through the open door, clanged the heavy metal door closed, and threw a deadbolt.

I needed to wait until The U emptied to get into the tunnel. I settled back into my hiding place and thought about what I would do when I got inside.

• • •

At ten minutes after two, the tunnel slid open to disgorge four more guys with flashlights. They spoke in hushed tones and chuckled. One of them carried a large backpack on his shoulder. They closed the tunnel and climbed the stairs to the office.

I waited ten minutes to make sure no one else was coming and silently threw a simple switch on the 55-gallon drum. I rushed to climb down to the tunnel, hoping the switch to close the entrance would not be hidden on the inside, and luckily, it wasn't. At the bottom of a ten-foot ladder, another switch closed the opening above me. At least I knew how to get out.

The tunnel was pitch dark, and I couldn't see anything. Light amplification works only if there is some source of light. I took out a red-light flashlight and clicked it on. The seven by seven foot square concrete structure tunneled straight toward The U. It likely had carried utilities between the buildings at some point, but that equipment had long ago been removed. The long, straight tunnel made hiding impossible.

I stepped forward quickly and silently. Fifty feet in, the tunnel branched into a smaller hallway to the right. I turned off my light and listened only to silence. This branch led away from The U, but I wanted to get a quick look. I took off my light amplification gear and turned on my regular flashlight. Even pointed away from me, it almost blinded me, as I had been in the dark for so long. After my eyes adjusted, I could see a smaller tunnel leading straight off into the distance. I turned off my light and turned my attention back to the main tunnel. Time to see where it ended.

I paused when I heard a noise ahead, the skittering and intermittent squeak from a rat. I panicked a little. I hate rats, and I had an image of my getting hurt in this tunnel and dying in the dark alone surrounded by an army of them. As I imagined them gnawing on me, a rat rushed by and brushed against my leg. I yelped and jumped high enough to hit my head on the low ceiling. I turned on my flashlight and scanned all around for my imagined army of rats, but only one tail receded in the distance. I calmed myself and moved forward.

In less than a minute, I reached the end of the tunnel with another steel ladder heading straight up. When I got to the top, I faced another blank ceiling with a convenient switch next to it. I prayed no one was on the other side, flipped the switch, and the cover slid open.

No one rushed me or shot at me, a positive sign, so I climbed out. I found myself in an office, presumably upstairs in The U. A bookcase, which had opened silently when I flipped the switch, hid the tunnel entrance. It was the kind of secret entrance you saw in every Scooby Doo episode, but I had to commend them on their workmanship.

My heart still pounded from my meeting with the rat as I made my way further into the office. I wanted to do a quick search and get out. I already had the information about the tunnel and the location of Dyyavola to give Jane, but I wanted to see if I could find any evidence in the desk that would help with the case. I figured the more I gave her, the less angry she would be. I was going through the desk drawers when I heard noises coming from the open tunnel door.

My first thought was that the rat was coming back with friends to get me, but that thought disappeared quickly with the sound of human voices. I ran to the tunnel entrance to see multiple flashlight beams headed my way.

My fear of rats quickly swelled to terror of Ukrainians. My heart pounded and sweat oozed from my hands as I went through my options, none of which were good. With no way to seal the tunnel entrance and no way for me to close the bookcase without being seen, their voices, now clearly audible now, reached the base of the ladder. Out of options, I left the bookcase open and sprinted into the club to hide. Hopefully, I would be lucky, and the guys would think they had left the bookcase open accidentally.

Turned out, it was not my lucky night.

CHAPTER FORTY-FOUR

As I rushed into the club, I heard the surprise and anger in their voices as they discovered the open bookcase. I stopped down the hall, where I could still hear them, but could easily escape downstairs. I didn't want to make noise or run outside and set off the alarm.

An argument ensued, half in English and half in Ukrainian. I followed the general gist, as they blamed each other for the open bookcase. Without reaching a consensus, they soon realized that one of them would have to tell Dyyavola, which led to another argument, as neither wanted to be the bearer of bad news. Eventually, one of them called to inform him. It must have been my imagination, but I swear I felt the building shake with the fury of Dyyavola. Several "yes, sirs," followed by his disconnection of the call led to a plan. "He wants the place searched top to bottom. The others are coming over, but we need to get started."

Bad news. I had enjoyed a good game of hide and seek as a youngster, but the loser did not get killed by a psychotic giant. With my goggles on, I slipped quietly downstairs to find a hiding place. The lights momentarily blinded me as they came on, and I got a good look at my options. None of them were great. The main floor was pretty open, with only a stage, a bar and some booths and tables. I ran to the kitchen, hoping for more options, and maybe even an exit.

Unsurprisingly, the kitchen was filthy. I made a note to let the health inspector know they should stop by with extra citation books. Time evaporated like steam in summer heat, and the door to the outside was chained shut. The fire chief should come by with his citation book as well. The supply closet, packed with junk and expired food, afforded no space. The freezer was cold and too crowded. I briefly considered the ceiling, but the thought of Mr. Ramirez falling through the ceiling grid in the ER ruined that idea.

As the voices neared, I decided on the pizza oven, about six feet wide and two feet high, probably big enough for me to squeeze inside. I opened the door and was grateful to feel no residual heat from the service earlier. I crawled inside on my stomach but quickly realized I would not be able to turn over in there. So I backed out, laid on my back and scooched back in. I stirred up a lot of dust and hoped I wouldn't sneeze. I finally got all the way inside, reached out, and closed the door silently.

The darkness was absolute. I am not prone to claustrophobia, but the darkness, the cold, hard metal surrounding me, and the Ukrainians hunting me fueled my anxiety. I recognized that I was hyperventilating, and sweat trickled from my forehead as I imagined them blocking the door and cooking me alive in here, or throwing rats in here with me. My imagination ran wild, sending me into a full-blown fit of terror.

Not that it made any difference in the absolute darkness, but I closed my eyes and focused on my breathing. Slow, deep breaths in and out through the mouth. Nothing through the nose. I imagined my last ski run at Jackson Hole. Every turn with a crisp, perfect edge cutting through the snow. I calmed down.

My hard earned serenity shattered as two goons barged into the kitchen, still yelling at each other in a curious mix of English and Ukrainian, clear about what they thought of the order to search the place. They banged around the kitchen, opening and slamming doors as they checked everywhere. My heart nearly jumped out of my throat when one of them banged on the outside of the oven with a metal pan. The echo inside was deafening. It turned out he was abusing kitchenware to vent his frustration. Better for him to beat on the oven door than on me.

After two very long minutes, they left the kitchen to continue their search. I realized I had been holding my breath, and I took a deep breath for the first time in what seemed like ten minutes. The inhalation of soot almost sent me into a coughing fit, but I was able to suppress the urge. I again focused on my breathing until it slowed to a normal rate. I looked at my watch to see only 2:53 in the morning. Somehow, I had entered the tunnel only twelve minutes ago, definitely the longest twelve minutes of my life. I figured they would complete their search in the next few minutes, but I decided to be cautious and wait in the oven a full half hour before I left.

The long thirty minutes gave me time to think about everything that had led me here. I was sure that the giant I had seen earlier was the boss that Linda had described. He traveled via the tunnels and was never seen going in or out of the building. I was also sure that the office next door was his base of operations and would produce plenty of evidence. I also hoped that once in custody, the girls would break their silence and testify against that vicious animal. He needed to be behind bars for the murder of Jenny and for all the other crimes against these women, and probably against countless other people.

Speaking of animals, I needed to finish up with that weasel, Lou. Some financial fuckery was going on, and I would love to be the one to catch that smug son of a bitch. I vowed to go through the billing reports later that day. I should see if I could arrange for Lou to share a cell with that crazy giant next door. No, even Lou didn't deserve such a fate.

After thirty minutes, I carefully climbed out of the oven and surveyed my situation. Covered in soot and alone in a club owned by a bunch of guys who wanted to kill me, no way I could risk exiting through the tunnel, which left the front and back doors. With the back door chained, I had to use the front door. I figured I could run out and get into my car and out of the parking lot before anyone could respond to the alarm. It seemed like a good plan. Well, it was my only option.

I helped myself to a Diet Coke from the fridge and prepared myself to run. The front door was exposed, but close to my car. I figured that speed was better than stealth in this situation. I turned the deadbolt, then put my hand on the crash bar. I took a deep breath, pushed the bar, and raced out the door. Instantly, the alarm blared, but I sprinted for my car. Fifteen seconds got me across the parking lot and out of the glare of the main lights. Another fifteen seconds brought me to my surveillance building. I rounded the corner and ran for my car with my keys in my hand. I yanked open the car door. Scrambled inside, and put my key in the ignition. In 20 minutes, I would be at Gina's, enjoying a well-deserved hot shower, followed by Gina's warm bed.

A bright light stabbed into my eyes and a gunshot shattered my front windshield, interrupting my celebratory thoughts.

I froze as a Ukrainian approached my window. "Dyyavola told us to search for extra cars around here when we no find you in the club. Dyyavola is smart. You are dumb. If you have gun then gently throw it out window now or you die."

"Okay, okay," I said as I put my hands up in the air. "I have a gun on my left hip, and I am going to release it and give it to you real slow." With my left hand, I slowly reached for my gun, while with my right hand, I hit speed dial for Tom and threw the phone on the floor. I hoped he was sober, and that he would answer and could hear me.

"Here you go," I said, as I gently tossed my gun out the window. The goon smiled, but his poor dentition ruined the sentiment. Apparently, The U did not provide a good dental plan.

"Now get out of car slowly," he ordered.

I needed to speak to the phone while I was still in the car, so Tom could hear me. "Okay. No need to point the gun at me. I will go with you back in The U or to the warehouse next door or wherever you want me to go. Please don't shoot. I am all alone here, and don't have any backup, so I don't want any trouble." I slowly climbed out of the car to face a violent death.

The goon sneered as he shined the light on my face. "Well, well. It looks like doctor is sticking nose in places it does not belong. Dyyavola will be very happy to see you. Turn around and put hands on car. My friends come to help in case you want to cause trouble."

He made a call from his cell phone as he covered me. While we waited for his friends, I tried to pass more information to Tom. I could only hope that he was awake and could hear me. "Are you taking me back to The U or to the warehouse next door? I don't want to get shot. I am out here all alone and will keep quiet."

I pretended to be frightened to justify raising my voice. Although truth be told, the cold fear was genuine. "How many other guys are coming here with guns? Wait, wait. I don't want to go back to The U or to the warehouse to the east of the club. Let me go, please. I can pay you."

Through it all, the Ukrainian laughed, occasionally telling me to shut the fuck up. Eventually, two more goons arrived and laughed at my soot-covered self. They quickly searched me and relieved me of all my equipment before marching me back toward the office. No one asked about my phone, still lying on the car floor with an open line.

• • •

Tom rolled over to look at the clock when his phone chirped. "Almost four o'clock? Someone better be fucking dead, or I swear to God I will kill them." He reached for the phone. It took him a moment to focus and realize he was overhearing a conversation on an open line. He missed some phrases, but clearly someone had a gun pointed at Doc at The U. The voices disappeared, but in case the voices came back, he put the call on hold and used another line to call Jane.

"Jane, we got a problem."

CHAPTER FORTY-FIVE

They marched me directly to the office in the warehouse, up the stairs and through the steel door. Now, with six of them, I knew resistance would be futile and could only hope Tom heard my message. I passed through an outer room with some sofas, a small table, and a kitchenette. They shoved me through another steel door into a surprisingly nice office.

"Dyyavola, look who we found," one goon swaggered after me.

Dyyavola stood up and seemed to keep rising. The giant I had seen earlier. Up close, he was even bigger. Easily six and a half feet tall and well over three hundred pounds, with no evidence of fat, his arms and neck strained his flannel shirt, and his jeans struggled to contain his massive legs. His wrists were bigger than my thighs. He probably ate a small pony each day for breakfast, bones and all. His eyes sparkled in anticipation of violence and bored right through me.

"Bring him closer. So, you are the famous Doc who has been causing so much trouble for me. Explain why I should not kill you right now."

I wasn't sure if this was a rhetorical question, but I answered. "Because there is still a chance to get to know each other better and become best friends?"

Apparently, the wrong answer, as his oversized fist plowed into my solar plexus, knocking the wind out of me. The big man was fast. I hadn't even seen the punch coming.

My knowledge of pathophysiology did not help me breathe. Immediately, I gasped for air on the floor like a dying guppy. I briefly wondered if the single punch had permanently stopped my breathing. After what seemed like an hour, but was probably only thirty seconds, I could take shallow breaths. A minute later, I drew an actual breath and got back on my feet. The giant glared unblinkingly at me as the other men laughed.

"Tie him up in the chair and leave us alone." Two goons each grabbed an arm, threw me in a chair and zip tied my hands to the back of the chair, tightly, probably one of the few things these idiots could do well. Their work completed, they left to go fry some ants with a magnifying glass or to enjoy some other equally important cruelty.

Alone with Dyyavola, he continued his unbroken stare. I decided a more nuanced approach was in order. I could not tolerate many more punches from this beast.

"I ask one more time. Why not I just snap your neck right now?" He flexed his fingers. Confident that those massive hands could break my neck effortlessly, I also knew that the neck was fairly fragile. Time to think fast.

"First, the cops know I was coming out to visit you, and if I disappear, they will come looking for me, and they will find you."

A hearty laugh emanated from the giant. "Cops come here all the time, and every time I have excuse with many witnesses to say I am not here. You must do better, or I snap your neck." He cracked his knuckles one by one, each sounding like a two by four snapping.

I needed to buy some time for Tom to show up with the cavalry. The nuns in fifth grade told me it was never okay to lie, but I hoped they would understand my need to stall. "I may have information about the girl, and I can tell you what the police know about your operation."

Seemingly interested, his eyebrows went up. "Tell me what police know about me."

"Well, they know you are into drugs, guns, and pimping out girls. Your principal business is sex trafficking. You run a gang of Ukrainian thugs that terrorize these girls and force them to work for you."

He leaned back and roared with laughter.

"I have bigger body than you, bigger brain than you, and most importantly, bigger balls than you. Police know nothing of my business. Whores and guns and drugs are little business. I tell you secret. My real business is none of those." Another fit of laughter ensued.

Come on, Tom, please show up. "I know. Your real business is blackmail."

Instantly, his laughter ceased, and his mass lunged toward me. I could not believe how fast this immense man could move. Directly in front of me, he leaned over, put his hands on the arms of the chair and roared, "How do you know about blackmail?" Inches from my face, his rancid breath covered me in a film, as droplets of spit flew all over my face.

This guy was truly insane, but I was interested in his confession. Unsure I would live to report it, I was damn sure it would buy me some more time.

"The cops found a paper behind the file cabinet in the office that showed a bank account number. They traced that account to other accounts, and they all traced back to one account that contains a large amount of Bitcoin."

Dyyavola roared something unintelligible and brought his massive fist down on a table next to me, shattering it. He continued to rage around the office, yelling in Ukrainian and punching various solid objects, but miraculously, not me, yet.

I took the opportunity of his tantrum to work on the zip ties holding my wrists in place. A certain cop friend had given me a small flexible file to wear in my watch wristband a few months ago, explaining its handiness for escaping zip ties. I had added it to my equipment for to-night at the last minute. I dragged the four inch flexible file with the serrated edge from my watchband. With my hands slippery with sweat, I had to concentrate hard not to drop it. If it fell to the floor, I doubted the giant would pick it up and give it back to me.

I finally got the strip free and positioned it over one of the zip ties to drag it back and forth. I couldn't generate much force, as it was pinched between two fingers at each edge, but I felt it cutting slowly across the tie with each pass. Slow and steady.

Dyyavola paused his path of destruction and turned back to me. "You told me how you find account with bitcoin, but how did you know I make bitcoin by blackmail?" He approached my chair once again. "Tell Dyyavola now how you know about blackmail or I crush your eyeball." He placed a massive finger on my right eye and applied slow, steady pressure.

I had only a few seconds to come up with a lie to explain how we knew about the blackmail without telling him about Linda. No way would I give up Linda. My voice stammered as I replied as slowly as I could. "Some financial firm reported last week that their computers had been hacked, and that they were being blackmailed. They didn't want to press charges, because they were afraid their information would be released. So the cops kept it quiet, but looked into it. They figured out which computer had been infected first, and they traced the movements back to a guy who met with an escort at his hotel. They got the security tapes and recognized Jenny. That's how the cops put it all together." My entire story was bullshit, but apparently it convinced him. Dyyavola re-leased pressure on my eye and resumed pacing the room like a caged predator.

I worked furiously to saw through the zip ties. Dyyavola was be-coming more unhinged by the moment, and I needed more time. I had to keep him talking. "From what I hear, you guys made a lot of money with the blackmail."

Dyyavola pounded his chest as he spoke. "Dyyavola smartest of them all. I do blackmail for many years and save all the Bitcoin. Dyyavola collected over 20,000 bitcoins." He beamed with furious pride.

I continued to saw on my bindings as I did the math in my head. Twenty thousand bitcoins at $60,000 each was $1.2 billion. "You're a fucking billionaire!"

His large hand slammed down on the desk again. "I was a billionaire, but that fucking bitch whore stole half my coins." He slammed the desk a few more times, and amazingly, it endured. Obviously, a sensitive subject, but I needed to keep him talking while I kept at the restraints.

"How did she manage that?"

"Dyyavola was careless and made mistake. Underestimated whore. Whore snuck in my office at club, found password, and transferred 10,000 coins to her account, but we caught her before she could leave town. I knew account number but not her new password to get coins back. Started to beat her to get answer, and she passed out and would not wake up. Took her to hospital so you can save her, and you fucked up and she died. Password die with her, and now I cannot get coins back. Dyyavola blames you for this." His fury refocused on me.

I didn't think a discussion about AVM and mortality with stress would be appreciated, but I needed to keep him talking. "Is that why your office is in this room now?"

"You like? Steel walls, steel floor, steel ceiling. Cost many coins, but takes a tank to get in here. And new computer is better. Password is no written down, only in my big brain. Need password and thumbprint to open account, and must repeat every ten minutes or account closes. Need my thumbprint to transfer coins, so only I can do it now. Much safer." He held up his thumb, and I briefly wondered where you would find a print reader for a thumb that size.

He logged into his computer, carefully pressed his thumb down on the thumb reader, and turned the screen toward me to show a crypto account with one of the more popular exchanges. Under holdings, I could see that his wallet held 10,258 Bitcoin, currently worth about

$613 million dollars. In the corner, a clock counted down from ten minutes when he would be logged out automatically if he did not engage the thumb reader again. I needed more time. "You are the first guy I ever met who made a billion dollars. How did you end up here?"

The beast actually looked thoughtful for a moment. I figured it might take neurons a little while to communicate across the space of that massive head. He leaned against his desk and shared his story.

"I was born in Ukraine. When I young, soldiers come to house. They rape mother and sisters, and kill whole family. They break my arms, but leave me alive to tell my story to others. I only eight years old at time. Little child with pencil arms. Weak. I cannot help family. Just watch what happens.

"Neighbor help me heal arms. Then I decide to get big and hunt soldiers who kill my family. I work in fields and grow strong. Eat much. Get big. At thirteen, I find first soldier, and one night he walking home drunk, and I beat him to death in alley. I use only these." He held up his massive hands.

"Over next two years, I kill five more soldiers. Last one is one in charge. He died more slowly than others. I take him out in field and take two days for him to die. He did not die like a man."

"Others come look for me, and I find my way to Black Sea. I work on boat and go to Istanbul. There I find work on new boat and go to America, and I start new life. Old life is gone. Old name is gone. No more family. No more friends. Now I am Dyyavola. Too much talk." He abruptly stood up and picked up a hammer and chisel from his desk. "Time for you to get Ukrainian manicure."

CHAPTER FORTY-SIX

I'm not overly familiar with manicure options around the world, but it didn't appear that the Ukrainians did things like other countries did. I thought of poor Jenny, and his explanation sated my curiosity.

"In Ukrainian manicure, I take chisel and place on little finger near last joint and…" BANG! He drove the hammer down onto the chisel and drove it about half an inch into the desk. "Much bleeding, so I take hot metal and press on wound to stop bleeding. I do this for all ten fingers, then I repeat on middle joints of all fingers, then on remaining joint in finger. BANG! The hammer dropped again. "But thumb is very hard, usually takes two hits. My best score is thirty hits for all twenty-eight joints. Maybe with you I am perfect this time. Whole thing takes four to six hours, depending on how much you pass out."

I have seen some fucked up things in the ER, but the idea of bloody and burnt nubbins for hands, if I even survived this ordeal, made me move the file that much faster. The zip ties cut into my skin as I sawed at them, but fear induced by the colossus in front of me intensified more than the discomfort of the file cutting my skin. Almost through a zip tie, but still locked in a steel room with a psychotic giant holding a hammer, I had to rely on my limited martial arts and defense classes, and defeat already seeped into my mind.

"That is day number one. Many things planned for next days. Strong man like you may last a few weeks, a lot longer than the whore." He laughed.

My file finally snapped the zip tie. I had been thinking about my options. Normally, I would strike the neck, but his thick neck prevented me from stunning him with a single blow. A good kick to the nuts temporarily incapacitates any man, but it's a low percentage shot. A slight turn to the side would deflect my kick, which would lead us to a one-on-one fight. Usually, I like these odds, but I placed my chances at zero of surviving a fight with this behemoth.

Only one option I could think of had the slightest chance of success. Normally, I wouldn't even consider trying it, but when the option is to try and fail or to wait around for a Ukrainian manicure, trying and failing does not seem so bad. My mind made up, I prepared for my last stand. All I needed was for him to move a little closer. Appealing to his greed seemed like the best bet.

I pretended to break down, which hardly required acting skills. "Please, please don't hurt me," I sobbed. "I'll do anything to help you get the money back. Anything, just don't hurt me."

Dyyavola snickered. "Disappointing. You will not die like man. Dyyavola does not need your help."

I went for broke. "Seriously, I'll do anything. You can have these papers I found in Jenny's apartment. Maybe there is something on them to help you find the password."

Dyyavola spun in place and fixed his eyes on me. "What papers?"

"I found some papers in Jenny's apartment. They have a bunch of writing on them. I have a picture of them on my phone in my back pocket. Maybe that will help."

His eyes lit up with hope, and he dropped his hammer as he eagerly approached my chair. I sat up straighter, braced my legs, and reviewed everything that had to happen for my plan to work. I would have only one chance to live through this. He leaned in to check my pockets.

My legs unleashed all the power they had to launch my body from the chair like a sprinter starting a race, as I called on every ounce of strength to accelerate myself toward Dyyavola. I held my head back and tensed my neck muscles to accelerate my head forward. My eyes locked onto the bridge of Dyyavola's nose, but my target was three inches behind his nose.

Dyyavola still bent forward to reach for my phone that he imagined must be in my pocket. My head whipped forward. I timed this acceleration perfectly, and the arch of my forehead crashed into the bridge of his nose. The skull is the strongest bone in the body, and an arch is one of the strongest structures in nature. The nose is composed of delicate bones and cartilage.

The tremendous impact resulted in a series of fractures, but they happened so quickly that they combined into one large crack that reverberated through my head. His nose instantly crumbled under the force of the impact. My forehead continued to drive into his face, crushing his cheekbone and orbital rim. The whole right side of his cheek and orbit collapsed into his sinuses, while the arch of my forehead remained intact. Eventually, my momentum expired, but the crushing damage debilitated him.

I had hoped to at least knock him out with that shot, but the wounded giant seemed only as stunned as I was from the impact, but I had been prepared for it and juiced up on adrenaline. The surprised giant had not had time for his own adrenaline to kick in, and I had a momentary advantage.

I had rehearsed the move in my head repeatedly while I sawed at the zip ties. I dove under his arm, stood up behind him, swept his knees, wrapped my arm around his throat, and fell backward. I locked my right arm tight under his neck, hooked my left arm over my right wrist, and pulled with every ounce of strength I could muster. The three hundred pounds of crazy Ukrainian falling on my chest made me struggle to breathe, but I needed him on the ground where he could not use his bulk against me. I lie there flat on the ground with the giant flat on top of me and with my arm wrapped around his throat, squeezing like my life depended on it, which it did.

Dyyavola had recovered from his initial shock, and his adrenaline fueled anger pumped through his body. I felt him tense up for an attack, and I knew this was the moment of truth. If I couldn't maintain my grip around his throat, I would die.

He bunched his muscles to break my grip, and his anger melted into panic. My arm wrapped around his throat compressed his carotid arteries on both sides, effectively cutting off blood flow to his brain. Even a psychopath needs oxygen in the brain to function. His efforts quickly became feeble as his brain depleted the last of the oxygen. Finally, his body went limp.

If I let up, blood would flow through the carotid arteries and into his brain again. In about thirty seconds, he would wake up, and within a minute, he would be clear-headed, or as clear-headed as a psychopath can be.

Grateful for my own panicked adrenaline rush, I lay there on my back breathing shallow breaths with the dead weight on top of me and kept the pressure on his neck. No more blood or oxygen would ever make it back to his brain. I am not proud of it, but I held that pressure for at least four long minutes, the time it takes for brain cells to die. With no messages going out to the rest of the body, eventually all the cells die, and blood stops pumping. I thought of Jenny and of all the suffering he had caused, as I held pressure and counted the 240 long seconds. Exhausted, I finally released him and rolled his lifeless body off of me.

CHAPTER FORTY-SEVEN

My first instinct was to make sure I locked the office door. I didn't want to have to explain to six angry goons that the boss had tripped and died. With the steel bolts in place, I finally felt secure.

I headed for the desk to call for help and noticed the computer screen, still logged into his crypto account. The timer showed three minutes before his session ended. I remembered his saying no one could access the coins but him once it logged out, and it seemed like a waste to let $613 million disappear into the ether. Since I had a small account with some crypto in it, I opened the transfer application on his account and initiated a transfer of the 10,258 bitcoins to my digital account. I punched in all the information and hit transfer with forty-five seconds left on the clock, but instead of transfer complete, I received a prompt to verify with thumbprint. I looked at his lifeless body across the room, realizing I couldn't make the thumb reader reach his hand, and I definitely couldn't drag his mass over to the computer in time.

Sitting in front of me was the Ukrainian manicure tool set. I would like to say I hesitated, but the pragmatist in me knew he wouldn't need his thumb anymore. With the clock running down, I grabbed the hammer and chisel and rushed to his side. I laid his right hand flat on the floor, placed the chisel at the base of his thumb, and without further thought, struck the chisel with the hammer as hard as I could. He may have had trouble with thumbs, but I had a better understanding of anatomy. The thumb came off with one clean blow. I picked it up and rushed back to the computer. With five seconds left, I pressed the thumb on the pad and waited for the message.

"Identity verified. Transfer complete." His account changed to zero in front of my eyes. I opened my account and had to refresh twice before I saw the bitcoins arrive in my wallet. Even after paying the $350,000 transfer fee to the host site, I still had over $613 million in my account, not a bad payment for all the trouble they'd put me through.

I didn't have a moment to celebrate my newfound wealth, as it was time to get the authorities involved. I still had six angry idiots with guns sitting outside my door. When they figured out that Dyyavola was dead and had only nine fingers and a crushed face, they should feel relieved, but might react violently anyway. What to do with the thumb? I laid it next to the bloody hand to worry about that later.

I picked up the phone on the desk and called Tom. Before I could say more than his name, he yelled into the phone, "Where the hell are you, Doc? We found your car. Are you okay? Where are you?!"

I had never heard Tom sound so anxious. Tempted to scream and hang up for the fun of it, my grown up side took over. "Well, you might want to try Dyyavola's office. I am sitting at his desk and calling from his phone."

"Are you fucking crazy? Get out of there. If he finds you, he'll kill you."

"Not a huge concern at the moment. He is right in front of me, but won't be hurting anyone ever again."

"Don't tell me you killed him?"

"For the moment, let's say he had an unfortunate fall."

"Ok, so I got breaking and entering and 'causing a fall' that presumably led to death. Any other crimes I need to be aware of?"

"There was some minor desecration of a corpse, and I stole $600 million, but that should about cover it."

"What the fuck, Doc? I left you alone for only a few hours."

"What can I say? I use my time efficiently."

Suddenly, a fresh voice responded. "If you two are done fucking around, maybe you can give me some useful information before I decide to shoot both of you." Jane must have really tired of these middle of the night calls.

"Here's what you need to know. I am locked in his office, which is also a steel safe room. It's in a warehouse east of The U. The office is upstairs, but the front door is solid steel, and six goons with guns and limited intelligence are guarding it. You're gonna need to bring SWAT and talk these guys out of the house. I'm gonna wait in here with the dead Ukrainian. Oh, and tell some FBI guys that I got some info here they'll love."

"Anything else you need besides a SWAT team and FBI agents?" Jane's sarcasm made me laugh a little, and the tension melted from me.

"Some ibuprofen and an ice pack would be nice."

"Fuck you, Doc. You are out of favors. Stay there, and keep this line open."

"Yes, ma'am," I said to an apparently deserted line.

I collapsed into the desk chair, and I realized how much my head hurt. Adrenaline had masked pain initially, but now the adrenaline dropped and the aching intensified. I gently felt my forehead and detected the swelling already. I would be sporting an impressive bruise and two black eyes soon.

I looked around the office. Five cellular phones and one satellite phone occupied a drawer that would interest somebody. A few stacks of money, which looked to be about $70,000 in cash, haphazardly littered the bottom of a deeper drawer. Some Ukrainian porn magazines looked used enough that I chose not to touch them. The bottom drawer held a leather journal with hand written scribbles dating back to 2008. Although written in Ukrainian, the notes clearly listed names, dates, and dollar amounts. If I had to guess, it was a list of all the blackmail victims accumulated over the years.

• • •

A SWAT team eventually surrounded the place. Tom gave me a play-by-play of the entire process over the phone. The goons made a big show of being tough for several minutes, but after they called the office to check in with the boss, I politely explained the situation. They banged on the reinforced steel door for five minutes, trying to break it down, but it stood strong, and they didn't even dent it. Within an hour, they gave themselves up to the waiting officers, probably the first good decision they had made in a while.

Tom finally told me it was safe for me to unlock the office door. I debated asking him for the secret code word, but hunger gnawed at me; my headache had worsened; and Dyyavola reeked. I opened the door to find five tactical officers with guns pointed at me. They rushed past me with a brave and bold entry into an office populated by a friendly and a dead guy.

Jane approached, shaking her head. "You look like you got your ass kicked pretty good." She turned to the other officers in the room. "Please note that Doc was already bruised when we entered. I don't want him claiming I kicked his ass for creating this clusterfuck," she said as she surveyed the room. I had significant swelling and bruising on my forehead, and I was still covered in soot from hiding in the pizza oven. I must have looked like a pretty big mess.

"This? This is nothing. Just a little bump on my head. You should see the other guy, a Ukrainian giant I ran into accidentally."

We walked around the desk to view Dyyavola lying dead on the floor with his thumb next to him in a pool of dried blood and with half of his face caved in. His skin had already turned gray. On the desk were the leather journal, six phones, and some neatly piled cash all lined up in a row.

"Looks like you got the motherfucker," Lenny deadpanned as he made notes in his book.

Jane turned to Lenny. "I hope you brought an extra notebook, because there is no way this story fits into only one. Okay, everyone, clear this room until the evidence team processes it. Let's meet in that front room and go through this story when the Feds get here. I only want to hear this thing once."

We went out into the lounge area outside the office, and I collapsed onto a dirty couch. Tom brought me two Cokes. I looked at him quizzically, and he said, "One to drink and one to put on your forehead. Looking more ugly than usual." I placed one against my forehead, and the cool metal relieved my bruised skin.

Some paramedics stopped by and cleared me, using the time-honored test of shining a bright light in my eyes, which did nothing to help my headache, but I finally got a dose of ibuprofen and acetaminophen to take the edge off. After a few more minutes, the Feds arrived.

CHAPTER FORTY-EIGHT

As I talked about Banshee's recovery with Tom, a couple of dark suits zeroed in on me. "I am Special Agent Keller, and this is Special Agent Hixon. What in the hell do we have going on here, and why am I in this nasty office at five o'clock in the morning?"

Special Agent Keller, a tall African American woman, left no doubt that she was in charge. Special Agent Hixon personified a garden variety agent straight out of central casting, a white male about six feet tall and perfectly fit in a dark suit with a white shirt and matching white teeth. He probably wore FBI cologne, but I passed on sniffing him for the moment.

Special Agent Keller's stern demeanor and no-nonsense approach reminded me of Jane, who I suspected didn't like me much, so I turned on all the charm. "Good morning, Special Agent. Name is AJ Docker, but you can call me Doc. I can explain what has led us here."

"Don't believe a fucking word this guy says," Jane stormed into the room. She had spent the last twenty minutes in the office with the evidence team. "This is the third night this week he has killed a Ukrainian. I told you to keep regular hours from now on."

She turned to the FBI agents. "I'm Detective Ormund. So we're clear. This is my scene and my case. We invited you as a courtesy because of some information that Doc discovered which might be relevant to you, but for the moment, you are observers." Jane death stared Special Agent Keller, whose expression remained unchanged. Tensions ran high. While the thought of a fight between these two officers intrigued me, it had already been a long night.

"Everybody chill for a moment. Let me tell my story, and you can hash it out later."

Jane looked around incredulously. "You have a story to explain all of this? I can't fucking wait to hear it." Lenny pulled out his notebook.

"One hell of a story, ma'am," and I gave a complete summary of events leading up to the carnage. Since the FBI agents were new to the case, I started on the night Jenny came into the ER dead from a brain bleed. I walked them through my trip to The U, my shootout with Bohdan and his friend, the car chase and the aftermath at the police station, and my talks with Linda and Giovanni that led to the visit with the surveillance team a couple nights ago. At this part of the story, Tom flinched under Jane's icy stare.

"Which brings us to tonight." I explained how I had hid in the warehouse, found the hidden tunnel, and used it to access the club. I described how they discovered my presence and how I hid in the pizza oven before they captured me in my car, as I called Tom to tell him where I was.

"First fucking smart thing you did all night," Jane commented.

Other cops had gathered to listen as I finished up my story. The threat of a Ukrainian manicure raised some eyebrows, but not as many as the information related to extortion and $1.2 billion dollars in bitcoins. By the time I got to the fight with Dyyavola and the severing of his thumb to transfer the money, the small crowd looked at me incredulously, even though they had seen the dead Ukrainian with only nine fingers and half a face left. Their stunned faces accentuated the awkward silence.

Lenny finally spoke. "You stated that you were able to remove the thumb with one blow from the hammer and chisel. Is that correct?"

"Yes, sir." He duly made a notation in his notebook and looked around the room.

Special Agent Keller found her voice next. "I understand you cut off his thumb in order to transfer the money before his account locked, but you failed to mention one little detail. Where did you send the money?"

I had genuinely forgotten to mention where the money went. I held up my phone and opened my app. "I sent it to my account, the only one I have access to. Looks like I have $614,500,000 in Bitcoin, which made about a million dollars in the last hour. Crime really does pay well."

Lenny stifled a laugh, but the Feds looked like they were about to throw me in a supermax prison in Colorado. "And if you look at that journal on the desk, you can see a list of names, dates and amounts. I reckon it's information about the people who have been blackmailed over the years. A lot of it is in Ukrainian, but I am pretty sure it is a meticulous record of where all the money came from."

Special Agent Hixon put on some gloves and walked into the office, returning in a moment with the journal. He leafed through it briefly, then nodded at his partner before returning it to the desk.

"Detective Ormund, we are going to need that ledger." Special Agent Keller moved forward to get right up in my face. "And you, Dr. Smartass, are gonna give me every single one of those bitcoins. Let me be clear. If I find one coin missing, I will throw you in a cell for the rest of your damn life. Do you understand me?"

I understood that it had been a long day, my head hurt, my ribs hurt from the giant hitting me and falling on me; I was hungry and covered in soot; and now she was busting my balls. "Let me be clear, Special Agent. I have had a bad fucking week. These assholes have tried to kill me three times and almost killed Banshee. I had a fight to the death tonight with a guy twice my size. I cut his thumb off and transferred that money to my account so it would be safe. If I wanted to steal it, I wouldn't have said a word about it, because you guys never even knew it existed. I found it; I saved it; and I will happily turn it over to you, but I am one of the good guys, so back the fuck off."

Special Agent Keller slowly backed up with a trace of a smile. "My apologies. It's been a long day for all of us." She turned to Jane. "The scene is yours, but the extortion is federal jurisdiction. I will need the ledger transferred to us, and I will make sure you have a copy. I will arrange the transfer of the coins to FBI accounts. Is that satisfactory?"

Lenny jumped in, "We'll process it and make it happen. Anything else you guys need?"

"Yeah, like a thumb or some Ukrainian porn mags?" I added helpfully.

Special Agent Keller actually cracked a genuine smile for the first time that morning. "I'm pretty sure that oversized thumbs and Ukrainian porn mags fall under local jurisdiction, not federal. We'll get out of your way. I'll be back to get those bitcoins transferred to us. In the meantime, I need to hold on to your phone until they are in our possession."

I was too tired to care and handed her my phone before they promptly left the room. Skinny Jeans smiled at me. "You act like you've dealt with the Feds before," Jane said.

"Never met one, but they wear suits and are kind of assholes, so I treated them like a hospital executive. Seems like all the suits act the same." This observation led to a round of laughter and lightened the mood.

The paramedics returned to take another quick look at me, but like any doctor, I had already diagnosed myself with a need for rest, ice, and ibuprofen. If the pain got worse, I could upgrade to a massage, vodka and Vicodin. I just wanted to go home. Turns out, if you are kidnapped, beaten, kill an international extortionist, desecrate his corpse and steal his money, everyone seems to have questions, but in the end, no charges were filed against me.

Special Agents Keller and Hixon showed back up and handed me a slip of paper. "Would you please transfer all the Ukrainians' Bitcoin to this account?"

I asked Skinny Jeans to witness as I opened my app and accessed my account. There it was, 10,258 Bitcoins, now worth only $612,000,000. The market had gone down a little in the last few hours. I entered the new account number and had everyone double check it, then triple check it. Once it was sent, it could not be retrieved. When it was all set my finger hovered over the send button. It wasn't my money, and I had only had it in my account for a short while, but I would be lying if I said it would not be missed.

I turned to Special Agent Keller and pointed to my phone. "If you want it, you can hit send." She decisively hit the send button.

And just like that, the coins disappeared. A few nervous moments passed when the coins were neither in my account nor in theirs, but Agent Hixon was on the phone with the home office, and after a nerve-wracking several seconds, nodded, and confirmed receipt of the money into their account.

Time for a shower, and some much needed sleep.

CHAPTER FORTY-NINE

The pink sunrise bathed Houston gloriously, prescient of a new start for all those traumatized girls. With my rental car entered into evidence, Tom drove me home. Carl greeted me from the front yard, apparently still on constant patrol since the shootings.

"Damn, Doc! Looks like you had an eventful evening."

Genuinely glad to see him, his understatement made me smile. I had been up for over twenty-four hours, my clothes were saturated with soot, and the bruising darkened across my forehead and around both eyes. "Ran into the Ukrainian boss last night, Carl."

He looked me up and down again. "Well, I hope you gave better than you got."

"I certainly like to think so. I may look like shit, but he is in the medical examiner's freezer waiting for someone to bury him."

Carl shook his head in admiration. "Any story where you live to tell the tale has a good ending. It looks to me like you're about to fall over and pass out. I definitely want to hear the story, but why don't you get some sleep first?"

"Thanks, Carl. It is a helluva story, and I don't think you need to worry about watching out for Ukrainians anymore. They are gonna be locked up for a while."

"Good to know, but I'm always on patrol. Never know when the next crazy ends up on this street. You sleep tight, and I will keep watch."

And I knew he would. I walked into my house feeling safe for the first time in a week.

. . .

Special Agents Hixon and Keller's first step with the ledger was to find a local agent who spoke Ukrainian, which turned out to be easier than expected. With the help of a translator, they transferred all the information in the ledger to a spreadsheet.

Two hours later, clear totals emerged. The Ukrainians had extorted over $97 million in the last eight years, but because of the exponential growth in value of Bitcoin, the total had grown to almost $1.2 billion. They could see that 10,000 bitcoins were missing from the total, presumably the ones that Jenny had stolen.

"There is gonna be a hell of a surplus, even after we track down and repay all the victims," Agent Hixon noted.

"You ain't kidding. We can give them all interest, and there will still be a few hundred million left over, even if we don't find the other 10,000 coins," Agent Keller agreed.

"I assume the Director is gonna want to keep all of this surplus."

Keller laughed. "The Director wants a receipt and explanation if we order extra bacon at breakfast. I'm sure the surplus has already made it into his discretionary account to fund some special project."

"What about the other 10,000 bitcoins the girl stole? Any leads on that? Six hundred million buys a lot of bacon for the Director."

"Computer nerds are working on it. The transactions are all open source, so they can see exactly when it happened and where the money was sent. They have already done some voodoo to figure out which exchange hosted Jenny's account. They are confident they have the account number from the notes scribbled in the Ukrainian's journal. He must have gotten that info before she died, but no password. The Ukrainian clearly didn't have it, or he would have transferred the amount back to his account. So right now, we are class A fucked on the missing coins."

"Can't the computer guys hack her password?"

"The exchange has pretty robust security. Three tries, and then the account is locked for twenty-four hours and needs to be unlocked with a password reset to the email. Would take about a million years to crack it at that pace. We have a team digging into her life and into all of her other accounts to see if we can get a hint on her password, but unless we get a break, that money stays where it is."

"Hard to believe $600 million can be sitting in that account on a public ledger, and no one can get it."

"Welcome to the crypto world. Decentralized money living in the ether ceases to exist, because no one can recover a password. We can monitor the account, and we will know if the money moves, but we will have no idea where it goes. Once it leaves that account, it is gone for good."

Hixon sighed. "Well, I am going to guess three passwords a day. Better odds than Powerball."

"Good luck with that. I am going to stick to the lottery. It's a lot less work."

•   •   •

The six remaining Ukrainians who had been taken into custody were held without bail on charges of prostitution, extortion, drugs, weapons, and new charges were added as evidence teams processed the crime scenes. After the interviews with all the dancers at The U, charges of sexual assault expanded the growing list. The women were offered counseling, rehab, help with relocation, and job training, paid for through a victims' compensation fund. Scars from the abuse would never fade completely, but they had opportunities for new lives and for reconnections with loved ones they had not seen in years.

The remaining mystery was the identity of Dyyavola, lying in the morgue.

"Tell me you have something," Jane demanded as Lenny came into her office and sat in his usual chair, opened his notebook with a flourish, skimmed some pages, looked up and stated, "We ain't got shit. No one knows who the hell this guy is."

Jane stared at him incredulously as he continued. "Fingerprints are not on file locally, nationally or internationally. FBI is scouring their files, but so far has nothing. We reached out to Interpol, but early results are not promising. No one has a file on this guy."

"How the hell did he embezzle that much money over that much time, run guns, drugs and girls, and never show up on anyone's radar? How is that possible?" Jane fumed.

Lenny was thoughtful for a moment. "Most criminals are caught when they spend their money in a flashy way. They buy mansions or expensive cars and attract attention. People talk, and eventually, law enforcement looks into it. This guy never really spent his money. It sat there and kept growing in value. Even his own guys probably had no idea how much money he had. They would have killed him for it if they knew."

"What about these assholes in custody? Are we really supposed to believe no one knows who this guy is?"

"They have all been interviewed multiple times, and the stories consistently match. They each got a call one day from a guy who offered them work at a generous rate. They took the jobs and were told to call him Dyyavola. He never talked about his past and never mentioned his name. Dental work and accent indicate that he was Ukrainian, but INS has no record of his arrival here. Homeland Security has nothing. The best information we have is from what he told Doc, which is still nothing to identify him. The guy is a fucking ghost."

Jane shook her head. "A fucking reclusive billionaire Ukrainian ghost, scariest ghost story of all time. We'll see if anyone claims his body in the next ninety days. If not, he'll be the wealthiest man to ever get an unmarked grave."

Lenny closed his notebook. "Happy to put an end to this case." He stuffed the worn notebook into his pocket and pulled out a fresh one. "What's up next?"

Jane smiled. "Funny you should ask. Just got a call about a gang-banger shot in a drug dispute. Let's go." She stood up and grabbed her jacket.

"Finally, something easy." Lenny followed her out of the office.

CHAPTER FIFTY

The media could not get enough of my story, but only for one day. Fortunately, a naked man with a bow and arrow shut down a major freeway for two hours, and my story was old news. There is a time and place for crazy, and this episode was perfectly timed.

Despite his best efforts, Tom could not convince the staff to call me Doc Holliday. With my best efforts, I was able to convince them to call him Mall Cop Nocal. Don't mess with me on my home turf.

A couple of days later, I invited Tom, Lenny and Jane to dinner to thank them for their help and to apologize for the trouble I had caused. I chose a pizza place with a wood-fired oven, since it was my treat, and I had developed a new aversion to traditional pizza ovens.

"A toast to the successful conclusion of our first case together," I raised my glass of sprite.

"And hopefully our last case together," Jane said pointedly to a round of laughter. "The whole gang is locked up without bail. We have them on prostitution, drugs, extortion, assault and accessory to murder. The girls were all willing to testify in exchange for no charges, rehab, and some help to resettle."

"The Feds are tracking down each extortion victim to return their money. Gonna take some time, but the recovered funds are fifty times the original amount extorted, so the Feds are happy to have the surplus. There is even talk of a reward for you, kind of a collector's fee."

I doubted that would happen, as they had to be painfully aware of better places to use the funds. "What about the leader? What have we learned about him?"

"Still no ID on him. Morquist can't even ID him yet. I believe he said this is the 283rd autopsy he has done on someone with no ID, but the first Ukrainian with no ID."

"He also mentioned this was the heaviest person with no ID he has ever autopsied at 343 pounds," Lenny added. "He was all kinds of excited about the firsts on this case."

"No worries. As long as he doesn't have an angry brother looking for revenge, I don't really care what his name is. Are we sure he is the one who killed Jenny?"

"Everyone confirms that he was in charge of torture. Apparently, the manicure was his thing."

I thought about that for a moment. I felt bad about killing someone, but at least I killed the right guy. "So, what about the 10,000 coins she stole? Any leads on that?"

"The Feds have her account number but not her password. They're tearing her life apart to figure it out, but so far, nothing. They're monitoring the account, but the money may be lost forever."

"Damn shame to see $600 million go to waste," Tom noted.

"I'll drink to that," Lenny said as he raised a glass. "How is Banshee doing?"

"Stronger every day. Officially retired from duty because of injuries, but doing well. Can still run down your lanky ass."

"He ain't got enough ass for the dog to grab onto," Jane observed.

Stories, laughter, and good pizza filled the evening. Time to move on from the case and all things Ukrainian, I resolved to let it go, except for the money. I kept thinking that letting $600 million disappear would be painfully wasteful.

• • •

I had put the hospital billing project off long enough, so I read through the reports that evening, three years of ER billing records, RVU's, CPT codes, and insurance statements. I'm pretty sure that in hell, projects like this never ended. I persevered through my self-inflicted mission.

I headed to IHOP for a break. Late night carbs are good for thinking, or at least, good for stopping thoughts of being hungry. I was the only one there and greeted as Doc Holliday by Little D and Gladys. The name did not stick in the ER, but I thought it might be permanent at IHOP.

Gladys brought my food, and uncharacteristically, she and Little D sat down across from me. "Well, let's hear the real story instead of that watered down version on the news."

I gave an abridged summary, and they hung on my every word. "You really choked out that big Ukrainian dude?" Little D asked.

"Yep," I said as I dipped some more fries into my little pool of ketchup.

"And that dude was bigger than me? He probably died of shame. I would die of shame if some tiny punk like you choked me out. I'm gonna keep an eye on you from now on Little Ninja Boy." He pushed himself up from our booth and sauntered back to the kitchen shaking his head.

"So, there is really $600 million sitting out there and whoever gets the password gets the money? I wish I had known Jenny. People tell servers some serious secrets."

"Maybe all her secrets stayed in her head and no one will ever know."

Gladys laughed. "Son, you don't know nothing about women. Women are always writing their shit down somewhere. And if you forget, you lose $600 million? I guarantee she wrote that thing down. This money was her key to freedom. She was gonna use it to start a whole new life. You need to look harder. That password is out there somewhere. And when you find it, I want a finder's fee for helping."

"I promise I'll keep looking." I smiled with little hope of success. I finished my last bite, left cash on the table, and headed home.

CHAPTER FIFTY-ONE

It took me two days to get through all the hospital's financial reports, but finally, a pattern emerged. After doctors fill out each patient's chart, a numeric code that corresponds to the patient's diagnosis determines the total charges and how much the health insurance company pays for each visit. The billing department reviews these codes to correct mistakes, which happen occasionally, and charges sent to the insurance company are adjusted accordingly. In the two previous years, about 4.3% of charts had been corrected after billing review.

Starting about nine months ago, that number had increased to 38% of charts being adjusted, and almost all of them increased charges to the insurance companies. Some were changed to more expensive levels of service, but the majority added procedures and tests performed in the emergency room. Either we were doing a shitload more tests in the ER these days, or we failed to charge for a shitload of tests in years past. A third explanation was that we performed the same number of tests, but the billing team had been adding fictional tests and procedures.

Billing fraud is a nightmare for everyone involved. The private insurance companies sue to get the funds back and refuse to do business with the hospital in the future. For federal money like Medicare,

Medicaid, and Veterans Administration funds, the penalties are much worse, including criminal charges and fines for the responsible individuals, who would then be prohibited from ever working in healthcare again.

Two specific coders who had been here for only nine months had submitted all the upcharges. A few calls to my friends in Human Resources revealed they had both come from a hospital in Louisiana at the same time Lou had arrived. Lou had mentioned his success with improving collections at a previous hospital, and his scheme was starting to make sense.

But what was he doing with the money? No way a snake like that was not skimming something for himself, and of course, he would have to pay the coders to alter the charts. Time to call my new friend.

"Tom, what is the number for that hacker kid?"

"You mean The BT? I assume since you are asking that you are planning to break a few laws," Tom said as he found the number.

"Only for the good of the people, a truly noble endeavor."

"Well, I want deniability, so don't tell me another word. Here's his number."

The BT answered on the first ring. "Who the fuck is this? You got three seconds." I heard him hammering away on his keyboard and crunching on his snacks. I made a note to meet him in person someday to see if he weighed less than one hundred pounds or over four hundred pounds. I couldn't imagine anything in between.

"This is Doc, Tom's friend, and I need a favor. I need a full financial background."

"How soon?"

"24 hours?"

"Easy. Cost you $500 paid in Bitcoin or Ether. Send what you got to my email."

"Okay, do you need my contact info?"

The BT laughed. "I have your cell phone number. In two minutes, I will have everything on you, including your biology grades from sophomore year."

"I will save you some time. I got an A."

"Congrats, but it looks like you got a C in calculus."

He hung up. I emailed all the information I had about Lou, transferred $500 from my crypto account, and went to bed.

I woke up to a response from The BT. No way he was going to take all day for something this simple, apparently. The email contained a list of all Lou's accounts, their histories, and assets. It took only a moment to realize Lou was living large. Beginning three years ago, he started spending money on big-ticket items, including three luxury cars, a second house and a boat, and all of it had been paid for in full with cashier's checks. His boat, The Louey Lou, was forty-two feet long and had cost well into seven figures. No way he could afford all that on a hospital VP salary. He should go to jail for giving his boat such a stupid name. Now I had to figure out how to nail him.

· · ·

That night I stopped by IHOP again, much easier than actually making food at home and cleaning up after myself.

Gladys greeted me. "Still ain't found that treasure?"

"Nope, and now I have another problem." I explained the situation with Lou.

"Damn white people with white people problems. Boy definitely needs to go to jail and learn some manners. You're not giving up on the $600 million are you?" she accused.

"Gladys, I got to be honest. I'm about out of ideas. I think that money is lost," I admitted.

"Well, it ain't gonna jump in your arms. You got to go earn it. You're a smart guy. Think, and figure it out."

I sipped my orange juice, thinking I needed to treat this like a complicated medical case in the emergency room. I pulled out my phone and looked at all the notes and pictures I had accumulated about Jenny over the last few weeks. The last picture showcased the tattoo on her arm that had started this case. I laid my phone down as my food arrived, still open to the picture. Everything clicked into place as I took the last bite of my grilled cheese sandwich.

"Fuck yes!" I yelled. Everyone in the restaurant silenced and stared at me. Little D came out from behind the counter to check out the commotion. Gladys hurried over.

"You okay, Doc?"

I jumped up and gave her a kiss right on the lips. "I am fucking perfect, and you are a fucking genius. I have to go." I ran out without remembering to pay for my food. Normally, such behavior earned a visit from Little D in the parking lot, but stunned, he let me go. I jumped in my car and tore out of the parking lot.

CHAPTER FIFTY-TWO

I banged on Tom's door twenty minutes later. I hadn't called, because I knew he would have told me not to come over. A tired, annoyed and disheveled Tom finally cracked the door open to greet me with a healthy, happy and sleek Banshee.

"Seriously, give me one fucking reason I should not shoot you in the leg right now and feed you to my dog."

"Give me five minutes, and I will give you 600 million reasons not to shoot me in the leg." I pushed inside and Banshee followed for a neck scratch. He grew stronger every day and was almost back to his old self.

Tom woke up quickly. "No way. Tell me you found the password!"

"I figured it out. Actually, it was there all along. The brilliant girl hid it in plain sight."

"What the hell are you talking about?"

"The tattoo on her arm, of the sorceress casting a spell? Remember, Anne said Jenny was particular about the sorceress, but wanted Anne to choose the random letter and number combination, and Jenny told me all of her dreams would come true with that spell?"

"Dumbass. She never said that to me. She only said it to you."

"Maybe that's why I'm the only one who figured it out. Get the report. Her account number is in there."

Tom leafed through a notebook to find the report while I logged into the crypto coin exchange. He dug up the account number, and I entered it. I opened my phone, tapped into my photos, and stretched the picture of the tattoo. I slowly entered the numbers and letters: 7Gbo4sM1hJd99.

We held our breath as I pressed enter. "Incorrect password. Please try again." I stared at the screen in disbelief. I was so sure I had it figured out. I wandered to the window. "There is no fucking way I got that wrong. That has to be the password."

Tom tapped on the keyboard, pressed enter, and pure glee lit up his face. He turned the computer around to face me. "Hey, dumbass, you have to enter it in reverse." The computer showed an account balance of 10,000 coins and $610 million. "Think they'll promote me from mall cop now?"

"Promote you? You can buy the whole damn mall if you want!" We started cheering like we had won a college football national championship. Tom opened a bottle of bourbon, and I popped a can of Sprite. Banshee shook a new toy to join the celebration.

Eventually, we calmed down, although the bourbon continued to flow steadily into Tom. "Do you think we should call the Feds now?" I asked.

Tom said, "We can call the Feds in the morning and give them the password. Let them sleep for now."

"Fuck the Feds. I got a better idea." I entered my account number and transferred 9,999 coins to it, leaving a single Bitcoin in the account. Tom laughed hysterically, and in only a little while, we passed out, Tom from bourbon and me from exhaustion.

•   •   •

In a sterile cubicle at FBI headquarters, a junior agent on the night shift received a pop-up notice on his screen, the most exciting thing to happen during his last three shifts. A monitored crypto account, one of many, displayed a large transaction. Over $600 million had transferred out of the account. Special Agent Keller had requested immediate notification of any activity on this account. He checked the clock, 2:20 in the morning.

He sighed and called, and a sleepy Agent Keller picked up on the fifth ring. "This better be fucking worth it at this hour," definitely not a night owl.

"This is Agent Cummings on night watch calling to notify you that one of your flagged accounts transferred 9,999 bitcoins to an unknown account." Normally, such late notifications resulted in a 'thank you' and the agent's going back to sleep. Not this time.

Suddenly alert, Special Agent Keller demanded, "Can you repeat that total and which account those bitcoins came from?" Cummings complied and Keller commanded. "Start taking notes. I need the Ukrainian team task force notified immediately. Everyone needs to be in the office and prepared to give a report in one hour. Notify the cyber team, too, I need that money traced. Don't wake him up, but make a note for the Director to be notified of this first thing in the morning. Any questions?"

"No, ma'am," Agent Cummings stammered.

"Get to work, and keep the line open for me. More people are gonna get called in on this one."

•   •   •

An hour later, Special Agent Keller stood in front of her team. Adrenaline and coffee had energized them, but frustration hung in the air like toxic smoke. "Talk to me, people. What do we have?"

A senior agent from the cyber division spoke up. "Not much at this time. The Ukrainian account was accessed at 2:14 a.m. After a failed login at 2:13 a.m., whoever accessed the account transferred 9,999 bitcoins to an unknown account. We are trying to trace the transaction, but so far, we have nothing, and it's unlikely we will ever be able to identify the recipient account due to the decentralized nature of the platform. We may be able to trace it to an exchange, but probably no further, and even that will take a couple of days at least."

"What about tracing whoever accessed the account? Can we trace backwards?"

"There, we may have some success. It's complicated, and we will be treading in some gray legal areas, but we are confident we can trace the IP address that accessed the account. From there, we can get an accurate geolocation of the access point which should narrow down who accessed the account. Then it will be foot soldiers on the ground identifying the person who did this."

"Better than nothing. How long will it take to get a location for us?"

"Best guess, about twenty-four hours."

"All right people, get to work. We need to be on their tail the moment we have a lead. Keep me informed immediately of any new developments. I'm briefing the Director in three hours, and I would like to tell him something better than we need another eighteen hours for our first lead. No one goes home until we find that money."

Special Agent Keller stormed out and contemplated how to tell the Director that $600 million of seized money had slipped through their fingers and that they had no clue where it was.

CHAPTER FIFTY-THREE

I woke up at about 8:30 the next morning cramped on Tom's couch with a jackhammer pounding inside my head, and I was pretty sure a bear had taken a dump in my mouth while I slept. First priority, toothpaste, and then coffee, and by the second cup, I felt human again.

Tom staggered into the kitchen a few minutes later, and I handed him a cup of coffee. "Did you have a dream that we stole another $600 million last night?"

"Not a dream at all." I handed my phone to him, which showed the money in my account.

"Good. Now you can afford to pay me fifty bucks for the bottle of bourbon we drank last night."

"I didn't drink any bourbon."

"Fine, but you made me drink, so you can pay for your half of the bottle which I had to drink. You need to report this, and keep my name out of it. I'm already in enough trouble at work, thanks to you."

"I'll call my buddy Special Agent Keller and turn it over to them, but not before I go home and shower. Gonna be another set of interviews about this one."

I drove home, savored a long, hot shower, and sat down to a delicious lunch of reheated pizza. My mind, finally clear, formed a plan. I found Special Agent Keller in my contacts and tapped to call her.

She answered immediately. "Make it quick. All hell is breaking loose here. Someone stole Jenny's money last night, and I have ten agents trying to track it down."

I swallowed hard. "You can probably call off your agents. The money is in my account."

The silence festered, and then she yelled to the room, "Stand down. That fucking doctor has the money."

She got back on the line with me. "Any particular reason you waited over eight hours to tell me?"

"Well, I figured it out in the middle of the night and didn't want to wake you."

"First thing in the morning wasn't good enough for you?"

"I may have had a small celebration and slept in," I said sheepishly.

I am sure she shook her head as she said, "Get your ass down here, ASAP! And be prepared to transfer that money to our account, or this will be your last view of sunshine for the next fifty years." She hung up without waiting for a response.

.   .   .

I arrived at the FBI building to find a junior agent waiting for me out front with a visitor's badge. Another agent said he would take care of my car. I wasn't sure if that meant valet, or he was impounding it, but since he had a gun and I had enough money to buy a fleet of cars, I let him have it.

We took an awkward elevator ride to the fifth floor and into a conference room full of grim-faced suits. I wondered if the FBI recruited people who all looked the same, or if the FBI look was part of their training. My thoughts abruptly faded when Special Agent Keller pointed at the chair across from her. "Have a seat, please. I will forgo introductions of my colleagues, but suffice it to say, these people have been searching all night for that money." Okay, so a table of people who might resent me. "Would you please explain how the money got transferred to your account?"

When I started my story at IHOP the previous evening, I thought Special Agent Hixon might blow a gasket. I explained how Gladys had encouraged me to rethink the entire case and had stirred my memory of the tattoo and what Jenny had said to me, which sent me home to try the password from her tattoo.

"And it worked? Just like that, you were in the account?" Agent Keller asked.

"Actually, it failed." This raised some eyebrows in the room. "So, I entered it a second time, backwards, and I accessed the account."

A junior agent at the end of the table had his computer out. "Who has a picture of that tattoo?" People shuffled papers, and I slid my phone down the table to him. He looked at the tattoo and started typing. A moment later he said, "We're in. Balance is one bitcoin."

Special Agent Keller glared at me. "You left me one bitcoin?"

"I wanted to make sure the FBI could take credit for the recovery."

A smattering of laughter erupted around the table. Special Agent Keller remained humorless.

"I need those other bitcoins in our account. Now!"

"No problem. All I need is my phone and a favor."

"A favor. How about as a favor, I don't lock your ass up in the nastiest cell I can find? Give me one good reason I should do you a favor."

"I got 600 million reasons you should do me a favor. Besides, you'll get all the credit for this recovery in the press, and I kind of think you'll like the favor I am asking."

Within ten minutes, I explained what I wanted. By the end, everyone seemed happy, and we had a deal.

"Agreed. Now transfer that money."

For the second time in a week, I had to transfer $600 million out of my account, and I never got to be a billionaire. Special Agent Hixon noted my sadness. "Cheer up Doc, you're joining elite company. You and maybe a couple politicians are the only people I know who stole a billion dollars and got away with it."

· · ·

Arriving in the ER the next day, I noticed a little girl crying next to her mom at registration. I stopped at the desk and bent down to the girl's eye level. "Hey sweetie, what's your name?"

She timidly replied, "Tara" between sobs.

"Well, Tara, I'm one of the doctors here, and there is nothing to be afraid of."

"What happened to your face?"

"I fell off my bike and bumped my head. Luckily, I had a helmet on and didn't get hurt. Why are you here today?"

She looked down at her pink sandals embroidered with white butterflies. Her mom answered for her. "She stuffed a cheap plastic bead up her nose, probably gonna be a $3,000 bead when I'm done with y'all."

"Tara, do you like magic?"

Tara nodded.

"Well, I know a magic trick to make beads disappear from noses. Want to see it?"

Tara nodded again, and mom stopped to watch. "I definitely want to see this trick."

"Okay, Tara. Which side of the nose is the bead on?"

Tara pointed to her right nostril.

I gently placed my finger on the left side of her nose and applied gentle pressure to block her left nasal passage.

"Now, on the count of three, I want you to blow your nose really hard. Like the world's biggest sneeze. Ready, one, two, three, and sneeze!"

Tara sneezed hard, and a red bead shot out of her nose. Tara smiled and laughed and pointed at the bead. Mom chuckled and shook her head. "How much is that going to cost us?"

I laughed back at her. "Magic is free. We only charge for medical care. Don't worry about it. She'll be fine. This happens more often than you might think."

I turned my attention back to the little girl. "Tara, it was nice to meet you, and you were very brave. Let's get a sticker for you, and then you and your mom can go home, okay? How does that sound?"

Tara jumped and nodded enthusiastically. She chose a sticker, and I headed back to the nurses' station.

"Damn, Doc, are you sure you're ready to return? You look more like a patient than a doctor with those bruises." Jean always made me feel welcome in the ER.

"Jean, I assure you I'm fit for duty. I even wrote myself a note saying I was okay to return to work. Did you miss me?"

Jean actually surprised me, as she wrapped me in a genuine hug for the first time. "I did miss you, and I'm glad you're safe. You had us all worried. Don't do that again."

"I promise not to fight with a gang of violent foreign nationals involved in extortion and murder ever again."

Jean pulled away and returned to her normal self. "Good. Now go check in with Deb. There's some intern rotating through this month who thinks he knows everything, but he's dumber than that chair over there. The only question is whether I kill him before he kills a patient. Talk some sense into him."

"I'll try. There has definitely been enough killing this week already."

It felt good to be back at the ER. Finn and Deb wanted a first-hand account of my adventures, and the other available staff listened in. Tom stopped by with Banshee to throw in his two cents. Officially retired, Banshee would always be welcome in the ER. He jumped on my lap and gave me some kisses like old times.

CHAPTER FIFTY-FOUR

Saturday arrived, showcasing sunny skies and temperatures approaching eighty. A phone call let me know everything was set up. I threw on a Tommy Bahama shirt and shorts and drove myself to the Seaside Marina in my new car. A gentle breeze rummaged through my hair as I ambled to the docks and strolled among the boats.

I found The Louey Lou exactly where The BT had said to look. The beautiful boat, actually more of a yacht, was a forty-two foot Hinckley with all the bells and whistles, including state-of-the-art propulsion and navigation. It could hold thirty people and comfortably sleep ten at a price tag north of a million dollars to own and over $75,000 a year to maintain.

I sat on a bench to admire it and was soon rewarded with the sight of Lou putzing around on deck, wearing pressed shorts and a nautical shirt that featured the name of his boat embroidered on one side and "Captain Lou" on the other. Aviator sunglasses completed the look. If you looked up "Douchebag Yacht Owner" online, this is the first picture that would pop up.

I sighed and climbed the boarding ladder to the deck. Lou coiled some rope and startled when I landed on the deck. Surprise turned to confusion when he recognized me, followed by anger. "What the hell are you doing here?"

"I was visiting some friends and noticed you on this beautiful yacht. Is this yours? Mind if I look around?" Without waiting for his answer, I climbed a ladder to the next deck, where I found a very attractive lady sunbathing topless. "Pardon me, ma'am," I said, as I politely turned to give her privacy.

Lou had stormed up after me, fuming as he glanced from me to his topless companion. "Kiki, why don't you put your suit on and head below, please?" The woman put her top on and walked toward me to descend the ladder. She licked her lips and gently brushed against me as she passed, leaving me alone on the sunny white deck with Lou.

"I don't recall your wife's name being Kiki."

The suggestion hung in the air, as Lou refused to comment. Instead, he sat down on a chair and tried to compose himself. In a much calmer voice, he enunciated, "What are you doing here?"

I sat across from him and sampled cubed pineapple from a fruit plate on the coffee table between us as I made him wait for the answer. "I heard about this boat and wanted to see it for myself. Beautiful teak wood and brass fittings throughout, with three bedrooms, if I am not mistaken. I presume Kiki uses one of the guest rooms?" I popped a fresh strawberry into my mouth.

Warily, Lou started to feel more in control. "I was fortunate enough to come from a wealthy family. Unfortunately, though, my parents are both deceased, and I used the proceeds from their estate to buy this boat." He sat back smugly, awaiting my reply.

I bit into a crisp apple slice. "That would be a great explanation, if it were true. However, your parents are neither wealthy nor deceased." I leaned forward to pull a thin folder out of my back waistband that I had hidden under my shirt. Without another word, I laid the file on the table between us and went back to munching on fruit.

Lou wrung his hands and sweat beaded on his forehead as he tried not to look at the folder. "Okay. What's in the folder?"

I casually picked it up and leafed through the pages. "If I am not mistaken, this lists all of your accounts and financial dealings for the last three years, along with a summary of ER billing records for the last year. Interesting stuff. Care to review it?"

Lou leaned forward with murder in his eyes. "Cut the bullshit. Tell me what you think you know and what you want."

I leaned back in the chair and folded my hands in front of me. "How about this for a story? Three years ago, a junior executive at a Louisiana Hospital was given oversight for ER revenue. He wanted to impress his boss, so he convinced two of his billers to inflate the ER revenue with fictional charges. The dramatic results led to his promotion. Eventually, he landed a new job in Houston. He wanted to move up to a large hospital system as part of his plan to become a CEO someday. He took a job as VP at the largest public hospital in Houston and, based on his stellar record at his previous job, he took on oversight of ER revenue.

"The first thing he did was convince his two coders from Louisiana to join his team in Houston, and with the team back together again, he began creating fictional charges again to make his department numbers shine. Along the way, he realized there was enough excess revenue to make his department shine as well as to fatten his own accounts. So now, that VP is living large and looking for a promotion to CEO of his own hospital. Did I miss anything?"

Lou sat back and matched my pose. "That's a nice story, but incomplete."

"Care to enlighten me?"

Lou smirked. "Happy to do so. You see, that VP knew there were certain people who might catch on to his activities, and the most worrisome was the Director of the ER. So he decided to make that Director a partner in his activities. He established an offshore account and each month he put $20,000 into that account to buy the Director's silence. Right now, there is an account in the Caribbean in your name with over a quarter million dollars in it, Partner." He sat back with a contented smile.

"So, as your partner, I get to keep that money?"

"Absolutely."

"And I can use the boat when I want?"

"It's yours whenever I'm not using it. I'll even throw in Kiki if you want. Do we have a deal?"

I pretended to ponder the offer, repulsive as it was.

"Doc, there's no way out. I planned this thing from start to finish. I have contingencies for each contingency. You talk, and you go down with me. You stay quiet, and we both live like this," he said, as he gestured expansively at the surrounding yacht.

"Okay, one more question. Can this boat hold ten adults comfortably?"

Lou looked puzzled as he looked around at all the open space on deck. "Of course. It can hold thirty people comfortably."

I sat back with some more apple slices, as a clatter of heavy footsteps on the main deck interrupted us. Alarmed, Lou watched the first agent climb to the deck. Special Agents Keller and Hixon appeared next and approached Lou.

Keller had the honors. "Sir, please put your hands in the air. You are under arrest for Medicare fraud and embezzling stolen funds." Keller advised him of his rights.

A stunned Lou stuttered his assent that he understood his rights. He turned toward me. "How? How did this happen?"

I unbuttoned my shirt, unclipped the microphone and receiver, and handed them to Special Agent Hixon as Keller cuffed Lou.

"You see, Lou, I figured it out when I looked through the records. It was there all the time if someone looked for it. I figured you knew that the billing records could incriminate you and that you would have a scapegoat lined up in case you were caught, and I was pretty sure the scapegoat would be me. So, I discussed it with my new best friends at the FBI, and we decided the easiest way to convict was to get a recorded confession. They thought it was unlikely you would do it, but I was sure your ego would compel you to brag about how smart you think you've been. You laid the whole thing out on tape. The trial to convict you shouldn't take very long. Special Agent Keller, how much time is VP Lou facing for all these charges?"

"Depends on the final charges, but it could be about thirty years."

"And don't forget about the forfeitures," added Special Agent Hixon.

"Good point. Those funds were federal and traveled across state lines. That means wire fraud, and seizure of all assets." Keller explained.

Lou, tearful now, wisely remained silent as he was led away.

CHAPTER FIFTY-FIVE

A week later, I arrived five minutes early to a ten o'clock meeting with the Feds downtown. Special Agents Keller and Hixon already waited in the conference room along with eight more similarly suited agents. These guys certainly liked to travel in large groups, but at least they were timely.

I grabbed a water from a mini fridge and took a seat. "Morning, everyone. So, what is this all about?" They had "invited" me, but I got the impression I had no option to decline the meeting. They had also requested that I bring my lawyer.

"We should probably wait until your lawyer gets here to start," one agent said.

"My lawyer will not be joining me today. I wanted to see what this was all about before involving my attorney."

Four sets of eyes stared back at me as the others shifted uncomfortably in their seats. At least now I knew which four were lawyers.

"Why am I not surprised? Let's proceed and get this over with," Special Agent Keller said.

One of the suits passed out some documents. "We have sold all the seized Bitcoin and converted it to cash. After transaction fees, we were left with 1.15 billion dollars in cash. Three hundred million has been set aside to repay the original amount of blackmail plus a modest interest adjustment. We have a team working to identify everyone, but it will take some time."

"That leaves $815 million in surplus cash attributed to the runup in Bitcoin pricing over the last few years. That is subject to federal seizure laws and now part of the asset forfeiture fund."

Special Agent Keller took over. "Federal law mandates a civilian reward of a maximum of ten percent of any surplus funds recovered. So, Doc, you are eligible for a reward of $81.5 million."

Special Agent Hixon piped in, "And that money is one hundred percent tax free."

I sat back and stared at them in disbelief. I am rarely at a loss for words, but then again, I am rarely given $81.5 million. I had expected a modest thank you, and maybe even a cake, but not $81.5 million.

A lawyer continued. "Additional funds may become available in the future, if we are unable to track down all the victims."

I finally stammered, "That is mighty generous."

Special Agent Keller continued, "It certainly is, and there's more. We are still investigating the fraud case at your hospital and at Lou's previous hospitals, and any funds recovered are eligible for a payment of thirty percent to the whistleblower. It will take some time to get a final number, but the total fraud is in the neighborhood of $30 million. Your share would be about nine million dollars."

Special Agent Hixon added, "Also tax free."

Special Agent Keller continued, "Our lawyers have drawn up some papers for you to review and sign, unless you'd like to have your lawyer review them first?"

It was a simple decision, because now I could actually afford some good lawyers.

Special Agent Keller actually smiled. "How does it feel to be a rich man?"

Still stunned, I couldn't find the words.

• • •

Discussing options and setting up trusts with lawyers and accountants dominated my time for the next few days. The FBI had made no public announcement about the awards, so no one knew, thankfully. With the logistics in place, I invited Tom to join me at IHOP after work.

We arrived around eleven with only a few other patrons in the restaurant. We grabbed a booth and ordered the usual. Tom opened with, "Where the hell have you been the last few days?"

"Been working on some things. Trying to make some decisions on what to do next."

"Don't tell me you're thinking about leaving?"

"Maybe it's time for a change of scenery. To be honest, the administration isn't too happy about the negative attention related to the fraud."

"Fuck them. *They* hired him."

"True, but still, I have been in Houston for twelve years now, and I want to stretch my legs and move on."

Gladys brought our loaded hot plates. "Thanks, Gladys. Can you ask Little D to come over here for a moment?"

She looked curious, but called to Little D. He finished his current order and joined her at my table. "What's up, Doc?"

"You three are the first to hear this. The FBI offered me a reward for finding all that Bitcoin, and since you guys helped me, I thought I should share it with you."

They protested, but I held up my hand to quiet them. "I couldn't have done it without you guys. Gladys, you and Little D helped me talk my way through things, and Tom, well, you mostly stayed out of the way."

Little D held up his hands. "We can't take any of that. You're the one who almost got killed."

I smiled. "The reward is a little more than I need for myself."

Gladys' eyes widened. "How much is it?"

"Actually, it is a lot more than I need. It's ten percent of the extra money seized. Total reward is $81.5 million. Tax free."

Their jaws dropped in stunned silence.

"Those motherfuckers are giving you $81.5 million?" Tom finally asked.

I reached into my pocket and pulled out three envelopes and laid them on the table. Each person had their name on an envelope. They looked at me uncertainly.

I smiled. "Go ahead and open them."

They tentatively reached out, tore open their envelopes, and pulled out a single piece of paper. "That is a letter from my attorney informing you that they have set up a trust fund for each of you in the amount of ten percent of the total reward. Each of you will get $8.15 million in a trust that you can decide how to spend. That lawyer will help you get all the details worked out, and the accounts set up."

Gladys looked at me tearfully.

"Your kids are all going to college, Gladys, and you are going to spend more time with them instead of being here five nights a week. Little D, you take care of that family of yours, too. Tom, I assume you are going to blow it on cigars, porn, alcohol and bad life decisions, but have a good time doing it."

Overjoyed at sharing their tears of joy, thank yous, and hugs, I savored the moment. Eventually, Little D and Gladys went to finish their shifts; money does not change good people.

Tom actually looked sincere for once. "Every time I'm convinced you're an asshole, you go and do a nice thing. You sure about this? I mean, you still have fifty million left for yourself. What are you going to do with it?"

Actually, I have $40.75 million for myself. I am setting aside twenty percent for a trust to help the young women who were victimized by Dyyavola. That's over $16 million to help them and other girls like them pay for counseling, rehab and education. It won't solve all of their problems, but it's a good start.

"You really are a piece of work. Most people would have kept all that money to themselves."

"It's too much. The forty is more than I will ever need to live a good life."

"Forty million dollars. What else are you gonna do with all of that money?"

I smiled, "Buy some Bitcoin."

•   •   •

The next day, I met with Deb and Jean in the ER.

"Guys, it's time for me to move on."

The protest started immediately. "I've been here for twelve years, and frankly, administration is as tired of me as I am of them. I am going to do some traveling work and see the country."

Deb said, "I'm not surprised after what happened, but we are gonna miss you, Doc."

Jean added, "So are half the single women in Houston. Gonna be a day of mourning when you leave."

Deb smiled, "But think of all the lucky women who will get to meet him on his travels."

Jean was about to respond, but I cut her off before the conversation took a turn for the worse. "I need one more thing from each of you before I go. The FBI has a whistleblower reward for disclosing fraud. It will take some time to total, but it will be in the nine million dollar range."

They stared, happy for me. "I've set it up to be dispersed in two trust funds, split fifty fifty. Jean, you control one, and Deb, you control the other. The only restriction on the funds is that Deb must use them to help providers in need, and Jean needs to use hers to help staff in need. You get to use your judgment. It can be for education or emergency funds for medical crises or disasters. I only ask you to use it wisely."

After more hugs and gratitude, I told them there was one more thing I needed from them.

CHAPTER FIFTY-SIX

On another perfectly beautiful Saturday morning, over a thousand people gathered to celebrate the life of a stranger. A large compliment from the ER, a full honor guard from the police, and many strangers who had read about the story in the paper had come to say goodbye to Jenny.

No one had claimed her body, and it wasn't right that she would be forgotten in death as she had been forgotten in life. I made arrangements with the coroner's office to have her body prepared for a proper funeral. I spoke to the police Chief, and he agreed to an honor guard. The ER was behind it all the way. The media had gotten a hold of the story, and the service grew.

When it came time for the eulogy, I stepped up to the lectern. I looked out over the crowd. Seated in the front row was Carl in his full military uniform, including his Medal of Honor. Next to him was Tom in his dress uniform with Banshee in his police vest. Anne was there along with Linda and many other women from The U. Many of the ER team members who were not even on duty when Jenny had been in the ER had made time to stop by.

"Thank you to everyone who took time to come out here and celebrate the life of Jenny Smithton. I only had a chance to spend a few minutes with her in the ER, but in that short time, I could see the strength she had despite all the challenges in her life. In the last few weeks, I have had an opportunity to meet many of her friends who were also going through difficult times with her. Every one of them stressed how Jenny was their rock, their foundation, that provided stability in a difficult situation. When many of them had lost hope, it was Jenny who gave them purpose again. When times were toughest, Jenny was strongest."

"Jenny deserved so much better than this life gave her. She was young and had years left to make her mark on the world. Although she is gone too soon, Jenny will continue to leave her mark on this world in a positive way. The Jenny Smithton Foundation will focus on improving the lives of young women who find themselves in such difficult situations. It will provide housing, education, legal help and protection for these women. It will provide job training and a chance to start over. It will give them the chance to have the life Jenny wanted for herself and for her friends. May you find the peace that eluded you in life. Godspeed and safe journeys, Jenny."

• • •

My final ER shift arrived quickly, and despite my protest, a going away party had been planned. The ER found any excuse for a pizza party, but I told them absolutely no gifts. By now, everyone knew about the reward, and hopefully, they realized there was pretty much nothing they could give me that I couldn't afford already.

The party proceeded as everyone tried to be polite while wolfing down pizza before going back to work. Tom showed up and stole the show. Actually, his new partner stole the show. "Everyone, I would like you to meet Shade."

The sixteen-week-old Belgian Malinois struggled to walk in his vest. "Shade is gonna be my new police dog, since Banshee retired. He starts training next week."

Which meant that this week, he was a puppy. He successfully begged for food from everyone, chewed on the furniture, and peed on the floor. Someone noted that if he was sober enough to pee on the floor, he was ready for discharge over the sound of laughter.

Tom called everyone to attention. "We are all gonna miss Doc, the ladies more than the men, but we can't let him go without one final gift. Jean."

Jean sauntered in with Banshee on a leash with a huge bow on his collar.

I looked at Tom in disbelief, tearing up. "I can't."

"You can, and you will. He's retired and needs a home, and he can't live with Shade. Screws up their training. And for some reason, he likes you, so he's yours."

I gave Tom a big hug and got some more of that dust in my eyes that makes them water so much. "Come here, boy," and Banshee came over to give me kisses.

"You know where we're going? We're going to Montana!"

Deb asked, "Why you going there?"

Jean replied, "Lots of single women in Montana."

Tom added. "And no fucking Ukrainian gangsters."

THE END

ACKNOWLEDGEMENTS

I had the privilege to train at Ben Taub Hospital during the 1990s. The long shifts were at times terrifying, but the lessons learned in the PICU, NICU, ER and floor still resonate with me. The story line of billing fraud at the hospital is completely fictitious. I have no knowledge of any financial misdeeds by anyone ever.

The brief discussion of medical economics is unfortunately not fictional. The staggering increase in health care costs over the last thirty years is not due to increased wages for health care workers, which have remained relatively static when adjusted for inflation. The increase has come from hospital administration and from profits to pharmaceutical and insurance companies. The system is not sustainable on its current path.

For those who know me, Doc carries some of my own characteristics, but he is not meant to be an autobiographical character, but rather an amalgam of the best characteristics of all BAFERDS. Unlike most workplaces, the ER requires a certain type of person to succeed. The unique environment of a large urban trauma center and the sacrifices people make each day at work are difficult to describe. Hopefully, you will never need a trauma team, but if you do, they will be there for you 24/7/365 with their hearts and hard earned skill sets to help you the best they can.

The medical cases sprinkled throughout the book offer only glimpses of problems the ER grapples with each day. They range from mundane to life threatening, with little or no warning of what will come next. Tragically, the violence displayed on these pages is an all too frequent occurrence.

It takes a lot of support to write a book. Thank you to Gregory Lee for his help in the review of this manuscript. His corrections are greatly appreciated. I am eternally grateful to my developmental editor, Jo

Lane. She took my ideas and helped my characters and plot grow to their current form. If you are in need of editorial services, Jo can be found on Reedsy. I send heartfelt gratitude to Cindy Bullard at Birch Literary for taking a chance on a first time writer and to the entire team at Black Rose Writing for bringing my book into the world.

Finally, thanks to my family for their support of another one of my crazy ideas. My new adventures would be impossible without you.

ABOUT THE AUTHOR

Gary Gerlacher is a pediatric emergency physician who trained and worked in multiple Texas emergency rooms before opening his own pediatric urgent care clinics. His thirty years in medicine have focused on expanding access to high quality care for all children, and his stories give a unique view of the inner workings of the emergency room. He has three adult children and currently resides in Dallas with his wife, Tamara, and two rescue dogs. To stay up to date on future books, visit GaryGerlacher.com.

NOTE FROM GARY GERLACHER

Word-of-mouth is crucial for any author to succeed. If you enjoyed *Last Patient of the Night*, please leave a review online—anywhere you are able. Even if it's just a sentence or two. It would make all the difference and would be very much appreciated.

Doc and Banshee continue their adventures in *Crimson Betrayal*, available in Spring, 2024.

Thanks!
Gary Gerlacher

We hope you enjoyed reading this title from:

BLACK ROSE
writing™

www.blackrosewriting.com

Subscribe to our mailing list – *The Rosevine* – and receive **FREE** books, daily deals, and stay current with news about upcoming releases and our hottest authors.
Scan the QR code below to sign up.

Already a subscriber? Please accept a sincere thank you for being a fan of Black Rose Writing authors.

View other Black Rose Writing titles at www.blackrosewriting.com/books and use promo code **PRINT** to receive a **20% discount** when purchasing.

Made in the USA
Coppell, TX
24 February 2024

29364671R10152